FROM THIS MOMENT

MELANIE HARLOW

MH PUBLISHING

*For Paul and Danielle, without whom I would not have
finished this book. Love you both.*

Cover Design: Letitia Hasser, Romantic Book Affairs

http://designs.romanticbookaffairs.com/

Cover Photography: Wander Aguiar Photography

http://wanderaguiar.com/

Editing: Nancy Smay, Evident Ink

http://www.evidentink.com/

Publicity: Social Butterfly PR

http://www.socialbutterflypr.net/

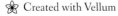 Created with Vellum

Your joy is your sorrow unmasked.

And the selfsame well from which your laughter rises was oftentimes filled with your tears.

And how else can it be?

The deeper that sorrow carves into your being, the more joy you can contain.

KHALIL GIBRAN

ONE

·

HANNAH

I THOUGHT HE WAS A GHOST.

The same one I'd seen a hundred times in the last eighteen months, doing all manner of everyday things. Driving the car behind me. Crossing the street in front of me. Jogging along the beach, sweat soaking one of his faded green Michigan State T-shirts that seemed to multiply in the wash.

And it never failed. Every time, *every single time*, my heart would beat a little faster. *I knew it! I knew he wasn't really dead!* They'd been wrong. I'd been right. He was still here.

Except he wasn't. Of course he wasn't.

"Hannah?"

But the voice was pitch perfect.

My breath caught as I experienced a euphoric millisecond of hope before I realized the man next to me in the produce section at Foley's, the one with my husband's face and voice and hands, was not an apparition at all, but his twin brother.

"Wes." I recovered, managing a smile I hoped would pass for glad, if not happy. But my insides trembled. I'd been dreading this moment ever since I'd heard he was moving back to take over his father's medical practice. Like Drew was supposed to. "Hey."

We hugged, and I had to rise up on tiptoe, just like when I used to hug Drew. His chest was hard and muscular, and his shirt was dark blue. Drew had a shirt almost exactly like it. *Don't breathe. Don't breathe. This has been a Good Day, and if he smells like Drew, it will slide the other way in a heartbeat.*

Pulling back, Wes crossed his arms and looked at me with Drew's gray-green eyes, unable to mask the sadness in them. "It's good to see you."

"You too," I lied, twisting my wedding ring around my finger. It was a diamond eternity band. *Eternity.* What a crock.

"How are you?"

"I'm—I'm fine." I wasn't fine, I'd never be fine again, but I'd learned it was the answer everyone wanted to hear. "How are you?"

"Okay. Still a little jet lagged."

I nodded. Wes had been in Africa working for Doctors Without Borders for the last several years. He'd come home for the funeral, but I'd basically been an automaton in those days. I don't know whether it was my body's defense mechanism or what, but I'd been so stunned, I'd barely felt a thing. It made no sense. A fatal heart attack at age thirty-four? But he was a doctor in perfect health! A man in the prime of his life! A father and husband and son and brother and friend!

He couldn't die—that was absurd. He had his entire life ahead of him.

And we had plans! We were going to have more children and plant a garden and take a trip to Europe. We had dinner reservations and his father's retirement and a three-year-old child to parent for the next fifteen years. And we were only halfway through the third season of Game of Thrones! He couldn't die *now*!

It took a week or so for the disbelief to subside into blind grief, and after that, I didn't get out of bed for weeks, except to vomit. I have no idea who I saw in that time. Thankfully, my mother had stayed on to take care of Abby, and by the time I emerged from the haze, Wes was gone again.

And I'd been glad.

Even now, the sight of him still made the edges of my vision go a little cloudy. Out of nowhere, a bolt of anger shot through me. *How dare you walk around with my husband's face and speak with his voice and look at me with those eyes that are so like his I want to cry?*

It was irrational and childish and unfair, but widowhood will do that to you—along with crushing all of your dreams and making the remainder of your life a Plan B you never imagined, didn't want, and couldn't escape.

"How's Abby?" he asked.

At my daughter's name, I softened. Took a deep breath. Abby was my reason for living. "Good. Can't wait to start kindergarten next week."

"Kindergarten. Wow." He smiled and shook his head. His eyes crinkled at the corners just like Drew's used to. "I can't wait to see her. Okay to come by sometime this week? I have a few little gifts for her from Africa."

No. Stay away from us. "Um, sure."

"Great. I'm staying with Mom and Dad while I look for a place, so I'm not far."

I nodded. My in-laws lived in a huge, custom-built home on the lake a few miles outside town. Still, it felt much too close.

"Hey, want to come to dinner at their house tonight? Bring Abby? I'm dying for a home-cooked meal, so Mom's making smothered pork chops. That's why I'm here. She forgot an ingredient and I offered to come pick it up."

"No, we can't," I said quickly. "I have plans." It wasn't a lie, although I would have lied before going to dinner over there tonight. Nothing against Lenore's cooking, but I wasn't ready to sit across the table from this ghost. And my mother-in-law stressed me out on a *good* day.

"Oh. Another time then." Wes glanced at my empty cart. "Well, I'll let you get back to shopping. It's really good to see you, Hannah."

I gave him a tight-lipped smile and moved toward the exit, abandoning my cart and hurrying out the door without purchasing anything. Adrenaline coursed through me. *Note to self, shop at different grocery store.*

Inside the safety of my car, I took a few deep breaths, my hands gripping the steering wheel tightly. *You're okay. You're okay.*

But I wasn't.

I pressed my lips together, waiting for my heart rate to return to normal. This would be hard, seeing him around town. I'd have to take precautions to avoid it. In my head, I made a list of all the places he'd be likely to go, living at his parents' house. Which stores, which post office, which barber shop. Which roads he'd take to go to work, which routes he'd be likely to jog, which restaurants and coffee shops and gas stations he might frequent. I'd stay away from all of them, and pray he stayed away from mine.

What little peace I'd made with my life was too fragile to risk.

ON MY WAY HOME, I picked up a pizza and small salad for dinner, since I hadn't bought any groceries. I also stopped at the liquor store, since tonight was my night to host the grief support group I was in. Wine with Widows, my mother liked to call it.

"Doesn't it get depressing?" she'd ask. "Week after week of talking about nothing but losing your husbands?"

"We talk about other things," I told her, although we really didn't. Every part of our day, every interaction we had, every emotion we felt, was colored by grief and loss and injustice. We weren't the same women we'd been before, and we felt like no one but us could understand that. Our old friends were painful reminders of our previous lives, and our new friends had no idea what we'd been through. I could be myself around them without worrying they'd judge me for the things I said or thought or did or felt.

Abby and her sitter were drawing on the sidewalk with chalk when I pulled into the driveway, and my heart lightened as soon as I saw her curly blond hair bent over her work. She was everything to me, and now I had to be everything for her. I blocked out the white picket fence that had sold Drew and I on this cottage-style house close to the lake, refused to look at the front porch where two big rocking chairs and one small one perched, ignored the giant rock at the foot of the driveway on which Drew had painted our address in thick white numbers, focusing solely on my daughter.

"Mommy!" She came running over to me as soon as I emerged from the garage. I scooped her up and she wrapped her arms and legs around me, burying her face in my neck. She always greeted my like this at the end of a work day, and it broke my heart to think it was because she'd been worried I might not come home. Her therapist assured me she felt safe and loved, which I supposed was all I could ask for, but could she ever really feel secure in a world where her daddy was here one moment and gone the next? Where he said *be right back*, dropped a kiss on her head, went out for a run, and never came back? How could she? How could anyone?

I paid the sitter, fed Abby, bathed her, read to her, and tucked her into bed. Every night, I answered a question or told her something about her daddy, in an effort to keep him alive in her memory. She'd been so young when he died. The injustice of it broke my heart—that she might forget the man who'd loved her so much, who'd cried when he held her for the first time, who'd never see all the milestones of her life. I'd grown up without a father too, and it crushed me that she would always have that same empty space in her life.

"What was Daddy like when he was five?" she asked me tonight.

"I'm not sure, sweetheart. I didn't know Daddy when he was five." *Why didn't I ask more questions about his childhood?*

"What did he look like?"

"We could ask Nana for a picture," I suggested.

"Okay," she said.

"What song do you want?"

"Lullaby of Birdland."

It was a tune I'd told her Drew had liked hearing me sing to her when she was in my belly, and she requested it often. I sang it to her, and kissed her sweet-smelling cheek. "Night."

"Night."

After she closed her eyes, I sat there a moment, stroking her damp hair back from her forehead. She looked more like Drew every day, although her hair was lighter and her skin more fair. No trace of my Italian ancestry at all, which my mother-in-law often pointed out. Not that she was openly rude, but I'd always had the impression she didn't think I was good enough for her son.

I thought about Wes, and what it would do to Abby to see him. Would it confuse her? There was a picture of Drew holding her as a baby on the nightstand, and I picked it up. *If only they weren't so identical.* But other than a few lines around his eyes and coloring deepened by the African sun, the man I'd seen at Foley's today looked exactly like the man in this photo.

Sighing, I set it back on the nightstand and went downstairs. I caught a glimpse of myself in the mirror hanging near the front door, and was taken aback at how pale I looked, especially for August—my olive complexion was sallow, my brown eyes dull, my hair a drab shade somewhere between tree bark and dog shit. I leaned closer and saw the gray that was beginning to grow in at my hairline. Yikes. For a second, I wondered what Wes had thought when he saw me. Certainly I must have borne little resemblance to the girl he'd first met.

Not that she existed anymore.

I frowned as I took in my appearance. I'd aged ten years in the last eighteen months. Sorrow had etched permanent lines on my forehead and dark circles beneath my eyes. I considered it a good day if I remembered to brush my hair before throwing it in a ponytail. I'd finally lost the ten extra pounds I'd carried around after Abby was born, but then I'd lost ten more and all my curves.

What did it matter? Who would ever care again whether I had curves or not?

In the kitchen, I ate some salad and picked at Abby's pizza crusts, then I did the dishes and straightened up the living room. At first, I'd wanted every rug, lamp, and stick of furniture to remain exactly as they were when Drew was alive, as if the entire house was some kind of memorial to him, or at least to the life we were living. Six months later, I'd moved all the furniture around in a vain attempt to feel in control of my life. I'd bought a new bed, repainted the kitchen walls, planted new shrubs in front of the house, and donated his car, his clothes, and his books. None of it alleviated my grief or my fear that *nothing* in life is actually within our control, and we're all just flying blind in a vast, empty space full of uncertainty. God laughs at man's plans and all that.

I wasn't always this pessimistic. Once upon a time, I had hopes and dreams, and life stretched out ahead of me, full of possibilities. After all, I had love, and love conquered all, didn't it? Love could solve any problem, heal any wound, move mountains, build bridges, tear down walls.

But it couldn't save my husband. It couldn't give my daughter back her father. And it couldn't fool me again.

Give yourself time, friends said. And I had. I was doing much better day to day. I liked my new job at Valentini Farms Bed and Breakfast, enjoyed the company of people I worked with, had good friends, and was Mommy to an adorable, remarkably well-adjusted little girl. But I no longer harbored any little-girl illusions of my own.

Some problems were insurmountable. Some rivers too wide.

Love didn't always win.

"I FUCKED THE TREE GUY," said Tess, a forty-year-old mother of three who'd lost her husband to a brain tumor ten months ago after a decade of marriage.

We all gaped at her. Everyone had only just sat down. I hadn't even poured the wine yet.

But Tess was not one to waste time. "I totally did it. He came back to grind the stump of the tree they took down last week, and he was out there all shirtless and hot and male, and I completely lost my mind. I don't even know his name."

"What happened?" I asked, filling everyone's glasses. There were four of us in the group. We ranged in age from twenty-eight to sixty-something, had different jobs and education levels and skin colors and interests, but we were connected by an experience that had radically reshaped all of our lives.

"I stared out the window the whole time he was out there working," she began. "Then before I knew it, I was putting on these stupid short shorts, spraying perfume on my neck, and wandering into the backyard asking if he wanted to come in for something cold to drink."

Perfume. Did I still own perfume? It was one of those things I never thought about anymore, along with bikini waxes and birth control.

"Where were the kids?" someone asked as I took a seat

next to Tess on the couch, tucking my bare feet beneath me.

"They're visiting their grandparents this week," she said, tucking her blond hair behind her ears. "I've been alone in the house for days for the first time since Chuck died."

The group murmured in sympathy. We knew how empty a house could feel. It could make you crazy.

"So then what happened?" Grace prompted. She was the youngest of our group and had lost her high school sweetheart to a roadside bomb in Afghanistan. She'd been pregnant with their baby boy at the time.

"He came into the house and I threw myself at him. We did it right there on the kitchen floor." Tess squeezed her eyes shut and shook her head. "It was over in three minutes."

"Was it...good?" Grace wondered.

"Yes." She blinked at us as her eyes filled. "It was fantastic."

My mouth fell open. I'd totally expected her to say no. How could sex with a complete stranger compare to the sex she'd had with her husband? She didn't even know this guy. But I didn't want Tess to feel bad. I took a sip of wine and made an effort to keep my face sympathetic as she went on.

"I was almost hoping it wouldn't be, you know? But it felt great. I felt...*alive*. For those three sweaty minutes, I didn't think about Chuck or the kids or grief or guilt or anything—I don't even think I thought about the tree guy! I just wanted something for myself, something that would remind me that I'm still here. That I can still *feel*. That I'm not dead. Because..." Her shoulders lifted. "Frankly, I'd started to wonder."

We all nodded. It was familiar to us, that numbness inside and out, that fear that you'd never taste anything again. But the idea of being intimate with another man turned my stomach. I couldn't imagine it. And who'd want me, anyway? A thirty-five-year-old bag-of-bones single mother in love with a dead man wasn't anyone's idea of sexy.

"But I feel horrible." She sniffed, touching at the inside corners of her eyes. "I feel ashamed and disloyal."

"You shouldn't." Anne, the oldest member of our group and surrogate mom to everyone, spoke firmly. "You know you shouldn't."

I murmured agreement, but secretly I was with Tess. I felt disloyal when I even *looked* at another man and found him attractive. I couldn't imagine the shame I'd feel if I acted on it.

"But Chuck's only been gone ten months. It's too soon, isn't it?" Tess asked.

"Says who?" Anne grabbed a tissue from the box on the coffee table and handed it to her. "The grief police?"

There was a collective groan. All of us had experienced it, well-meaning friends or family—or even complete strangers—telling us exactly how we should grieve and for how long, as if there was one correct way to do it and we were screwing it up. It was especially bad in a small town, where everyone loved to gossip.

"God, I fucking hate the grief police." Grace made a face. "If one more person tells me it's time for me to move on, I'm going to punch them."

"Or it's too soon to move on," Anne said.

"Or they know how I feel, because they're divorced and single too." Tess took a big gulp of wine. "I wish I had a nickel for every time someone said that to me."

"Or he would want you to be happy, and you're not getting any younger." I shook my head. "Do they think I don't know that? And why is it that they think he would want me to jump in bed with someone else? That's not going to make me happy."

"Nobody gets it." Grace shook her head. "My sister saw that I still had Mark's cell phone number in my phone over the weekend and blew up at me. Told me I was crazy and that I didn't want to get better."

Tess closed her eyes and took a deep breath. "Let's talk about something else. Hannah, how are you doing this week?"

I took a deep breath. "Drew's identical twin brother Wes is home from Africa. I saw him today."

Grace gasped. "Where?"

"Foley's." I swirled sauvignon blanc around in my glass, a rueful smile stretching my lips. "I thought he was a ghost."

"Fucking ghosts," Tess grumbled.

"Yeah, I could barely talk, and I escaped as fast as possible. I didn't even buy any groceries."

"I don't blame you," Grace said. "No one would blame you. That's a pretty huge trigger."

I sighed. "He wants to come by the house and see Abby. I'm sure he'll want to be part of her life."

"That means part of your life, too," Tess said. "Can you handle it?"

"I don't have much choice, do I? It would be cruel for me to keep him away from her. The whole reason I stayed here was so she could be close to her dad's family. I don't have family up here. But seeing him with her is going to be *so hard*."

Anne reached out and patted my arm. "Well, don't pressure yourself. If he's a good person, I'm sure he'll understand how difficult it is for you to see him."

"He's a good person." I found myself almost smiling, at a

memory. "I actually met him first. He introduced Drew and me."

"Really?" Tess cocked her head. "I didn't know that."

"Yeah. I had just gotten a job at this diner in Detroit and Wes came in all the time to study. He and Drew were finishing up medical school at Wayne State that year. I remember being really surprised at how different they were, because they were so identical."

"How were they different?" Grace asked.

"Well, for one thing, Drew hit on me right away—he was *such* a big talker—but Wes had never even flirted with me. I even thought he might not be into girls, but later I realized he was just really shy, especially compared to Drew, who was always the life of the party."

"Has Wes ever been married?" Tess wondered.

"No." I tried to think back. "Drew told me once he had kind of a serious girlfriend in college, but that was over well before I met them. And he didn't bring anyone to our wedding. I think he's just been really dedicated to his career all this time. I mean, in the four years Drew and I were married, I can count on one hand the number of times Wes was around. Drew always missed him so much."

"I bet. Twins are usually so close." Anne cocked her head. "Is there any chance talking to him might *help* you?"

I thought about it. "I don't know. I like Wes, but I'm scared, you know? I finally feel like I have a handle on things, and when I saw him today, I was so rattled. I nearly had a panic attack in my car."

"Then take your time," Anne said. "A good guy will respect your boundaries. Maybe he can see Abby at your in-laws' or something. Then, if and when *you're* ready to be around him, you can reach out."

I nodded, but I wasn't sure I'd ever be ready for that.

TWO

WES

SHE STILL GOT TO ME.

How many years had it been since I'd first seen her behind the counter of that diner? I'd walked in, she'd greeted me like an old friend, and I'd known without a doubt the most beautiful girl in the world had just smiled at me.

I'd been instantly drawn to her.

But I wasn't great at talking to girls. I could never find the right words. And what if I said the wrong ones and got rejected? Drew, on the other hand, had a golden tongue. He never had any trouble talking to girls. He never had any trouble talking to *anyone*. He could convince a teacher to give him a higher grade, persuade our parents to un-ground him, or coax a cheerleader right out of her skirt and into his bed in no time flat.

It never bothered me, though. When we were kids, he'd do all the talking for us. I liked it that way, because I was so shy. He was fiercely protective of me, as if he were four years older instead of four minutes. And if we got in trouble, he was quick to take the blame. He never wanted anyone to yell at me. In return, I gave him first choice of everything. The top bunk. The bigger cookie. The front seat. Sometimes I let him win a race, even though I was slightly faster. I passed the puck to him instead of taking the shot. I was quick to celebrate his victories and reluctant to draw attention to my own.

But we were inseparable. Beyond best friends. Beyond brothers, really. People used to joke that we could read each other's minds, but really I think it's just that we knew each other so well. I'd have done anything for him, and he'd have done anything for me—including step aside if I'd told him I was interested in Hannah.

And I was.

I went to that diner almost every day for a month. I liked everything about her. The way she made talking to her so easy. The way she teased me about studying on a Saturday night. The way she made every customer smile. The way she sang along to Sarah Vaughn and knew all the words. The way she served me extra big slices of pie so good I could have licked the plate.

Oh God, those pies. Apple and peach and pumpkin and pecan. Served heated with a scoop of vanilla ice cream on the side. She made the ice cream too, can you fucking beat that? She made the pie *and* the ice cream.

I only found out because I asked if I could buy a pie and bring it home for my mother's birthday. I'd never forget that night—the beginning of *them*.

Hannah had beamed. "Which pie?"

"Uh, the pecan one maybe?" From where I sat at the counter, I glanced over at the display case.

"The Salted Caramel Pecan? Sure, I can make one of those for you."

"*You* make them?"

Her cheeks colored and she dropped her eyes to her hands as she refilled my coffee cup, her lashes fanning over her cheeks. She had the longest, prettiest eyelashes I'd ever seen. "Yes. And the ice cream too."

"Are you serious?"

Her grin was wide and a little sheepish, but I could tell she was proud. "Yes. And the muffins and cinnamon rolls and cake pops."

"You should have your own bakery or something."

She set the cup down in front of me and shrugged. "I don't have much of a head for business. I just like the baking part. The creative part."

"Well, my mother is going to go crazy. She's from the South and claims you can't find a decent pecan pie north of the Mason Dixon line."

Hannah's smile faded fast. "She doesn't bake her own, does she? Because if she does, you can't bring my pie home. She'll be insulted."

"Really?"

She nodded solemnly, her eyes wide.

"Huh. Okay. I guess I won't then."

"Sorry. I'm just trying to protect you. My mother is that way about her meat sauce." She brightened. "But I'd be happy to bake something at your request any time. How was everything tonight?"

"Great." *I think you're beautiful.*

"How's the studying going?"

"Fine." *Go out with me.*

"You'll be done soon, huh?"

"A few more weeks." *So we don't have much time.*

"And then what?" She leaned on her elbows across the counter in front of me, and I tried not to stare at her mouth.

"Then residency. I'm heading to Texas." *And if I leave without kissing you, I'll always wonder*.

"Will you stay in Texas when you're done?"

"Probably not. I'd like to work for Doctors Without Borders."

"Wow." She straightened, picking up my plate and setting it down behind the counter, and sighed. "I really admire that. If I was smart enough to become a doctor like you, I'd do something like that."

"You're smart enough to do anything you want."

"You're sweet to say that, but I'm really not book smart. I had to work really hard to get B's in school, and I didn't do very well in college. I didn't even finish."

"But you're..." *Fuck, now what do I say?* My heart was thumping so hard. What I wanted to say was, *You're people smart. You make everyone who comes in here feel good just by talking to them. And you have a beautiful voice. And you make the best pies known to man. Fuck book smarts. You're amazing.*

But the words wouldn't come.

She was waiting for me to finish my sentence, and I swallowed. My throat was so dry. She was so beautiful. *Say something. Say anything.*

What happened next changed everything.

"Hannah, I—"

"There you are!" The bell over the door of the place jangled, and the energy in the room spiked. I knew instantly it meant Drew had walked in. He had a presence like that. "I knew I'd find you in here. Thought you wanted to come with us tonight."

I looked up at Hannah, and saw the surprise on her

face. "There are two of you?" She started to laugh. "Oh my God."

"Well, there's only one me." Drew's voice radiated confidence as he swooped in. "But that's probably all a little thing like you can handle."

I watched it happen.

Watched him charm her, say all the things I wanted to and couldn't. Watched her expression change from outrage at his cocky flirtation to blushing pleasure at being the object of his attention. Watched the chemistry between them spark and start to sizzle.

"What are you doing tomorrow night?" he asked her. "A bunch of us are going to the Wings game. Want to come?"

"I'd love to." She'd glanced at me. "Are you going too, Wes?"

I hesitated, debating the choice. I could say yes, and when Drew and I left tonight, I could tell him I had feelings for her, and he'd back off. On the other hand, if she really liked Drew, and the look on her face told me she did, it would be wrong to stand in the way. What girl would ever choose me over him, anyway? Plus, Drew's residency was here in Detroit. He'd be around here the next few years, and I'd be gone. What was the point? "Nah. I have to study."

"Come on, bro. Live a little. You've studied enough, you know this shit." He dismissed my notes on Clinical Pharmacology with a wave of his hand. "You deserve a break." To Hannah he said, "He's always been like this. Way too hard on himself. Tell him not to be a hermit crab for once."

She giggled. "Don't be a hermit crab for once, Wes."

I tried to smile. "You guys go."

"You sure?" Drew put a hand on my shoulder.

"Yeah." *But you better be fucking good to her.* More than once I'd had girls cry on my shoulder after Drew had moved on, but my loyalty had always been to him. This was the first time I was tempted to give him a warning—Hannah wasn't just any girl.

A week later, he said, "Dude, thanks for introducing me to Hannah. I'm really into her."

"No problem," I said.

And that was that.

It wasn't the first time—or the last—I gave something up for my brother's sake.

But it's the time I regret most.

"I RAN into Hannah at the store," I told my mother, unpacking the bag of groceries I'd bought. On the drive home, I'd decided that it wasn't Hannah herself who'd gotten to me; it was the visceral reminder of my brother. In Africa, I'd been able to throw myself into my work and disconnect from my grief. We'd been apart for so long, it was almost like I could pretend he was still alive, that he'd still be here when I got back. It had allowed me to cope. But seeing Hannah so visibly upset at the sight of me was a painful reminder that my brother was gone, and there was nothing I could do about it.

After the pain of missing my brother, I hated that the most. The helplessness. But a close third was the guilt I felt that he was gone and I was still here. He'd had a wife and daughter. It was hard not to lose myself to thoughts of *it should have been me*.

I braced myself on the counter and took a few deep breaths.

"Oh?" My mother was chopping vegetables and didn't look up as I turned around. "Did you invite her for dinner?"

"I did, but she said she had plans." I stuck some cheese in the fridge and a box of crackers in a cupboard.

"Plans? I wonder what kind of plans."

"She didn't say." I could practically see the wheels spinning beneath my mother's shellacked blond bob, which I was pretty sure had been in place since her sorority days at Tulane. Was there tension between her and Hannah? Drew had sometimes complained to me that our mother was hard on his wife despite everything Hannah did to please her. Both of us agreed it wouldn't have mattered who either of us brought home—*no one* was ever going to be good enough for her boys. Deep in my gut I felt a stab of loneliness for my brother. How was it possible we'd never have those conversations again? *I'll stick up for Hannah*, I promised him silently. That was something I could do to feel less helpless. To honor him.

"She's been working way too much, bless her heart. The early hours she keeps are ridiculous, and I think she has a babysitter for Abby going on five days a week. You'd think she'd want some family time at night." My mother never criticized anyone without blessing their heart. I think she felt like it smoothed the rough edges of whatever she was saying, but I could hear the disapproval in her tone.

"She's a single parent. She's got to work, doesn't she?"

"Oh, I don't know about that. I think they had decent money in the bank, and there was the insurance money, too."

"Well, then," I said, taking an apple from a bowl on the counter. "She must really like her job. What's she doing?"

"She makes breakfast over at Valentini Farms Bed and Breakfast."

I bit into the apple. "I didn't know the Valentinis had a bed and breakfast."

"The old Oliver place, right across from the farm. It's been open a year or so. Pete and his wife Georgia run it."

"Oh yeah?" Drew and I had grown up hanging out with the Valentini brothers, and we'd graduated with Pete. Hadn't seen him in years, though. "I'll have to check it out."

"I didn't see how they were going to turn that old mess of a house into anything," said my mother, "but it really is lovely. Jack's wife Margot did a lot of the decorating, I think. She looks like she has the best taste of anyone there. And I think she comes from money." She whispered this last part, as if someone else was in the room with us and might over-hear her saying something crass.

"So Jack remarried?" There was nothing my mother liked better than small town gossip, and I figured asking about everyone else in town would keep her off the subject of Hannah.

"Yes, last year. They just had a baby in April, a little boy. I sent a casserole—the chicken with the mushroom and sage. Everyone was so happy for him after losing his first wife. I wrote you about that, right? I think you were already in Africa. It was right about the time Abby was born."

"I remember hearing about it."

"Anyway, that man was a mess for years. No one thought he'd ever get over it. So how did Hannah look?" My mother wiped her hands on her apron and turned to face me. "She's lost way too much weight, but I can't get her to eat much of anything I make."

"She looked fine." She *had* looked a little pale to me, and definitely thinner, but I wouldn't mention that. And for God's sake, I was the spitting image of her dead husband. Who wouldn't go a little pale?

"I just hope she's feeding Abby better than she feeds herself."

"I'm sure Abby is fine. I can't wait to see her."

"Did y'all make plans to get together?" She went to the fridge and took out a stick of butter, eggs, and milk.

"No." I took another bite, weighing my next statement carefully. "I think it was hard for Hannah to see me. I don't want to push her."

"She can't keep you from Abby. You're her uncle."

"She's not, Mom. She said I could come by the house. I'm just saying I want to be sensitive to the fact that I'm probably a painful reminder of Drew for her. She looks at me and she sees him."

"Well, she'll have to get over that." She sniffed as she started whipping something in a large mixing bowl. "She's not the only one who misses him. She can't just shut us out."

"She's not shutting us out. Give her a break."

"I have," she said petulantly. "I've tried to help her. It doesn't seem like she wants my help. I offer to watch Abby at least once a week and she turns me down. Says her sitter is already booked."

"Are you giving her enough notice?"

She shrugged. "I don't know. A day or so, I suppose."

"Why don't you try giving her a week?"

Another sniff. "I don't always know when I'll be free a week in advance. But she needs someone to look in on her and Abby. She didn't even catch the warning signs with Drew."

"*Mom*. Drew's death was not her fault. It was no one's fault, you know that." My voice was sharp.

She didn't say anything, just kept whipping and whipping and whipping. I was amazed whatever was in the bowl didn't slop onto the counter.

Finishing the apple, I tossed the core in the trash. I was

beginning to realize why Hannah might have turned down the dinner invitation. "Well, if you'd like to go over and see Abby with me tomorrow or Friday, let me know. I'm going to take a run before dinner if there's time?"

"Yes. There's time." Suddenly she turned to me, her eyes wide with fear. "Be careful, Wes."

"I will." After Drew had his heart attack, I'd had all kinds of tests done, but there was no sign of the hypertrophic cardiomyopathy that had caused my brother's sudden death. I gave her a hug and she wrapped her arms around my waist. "You've got nothing to worry about, okay?"

"I miss him so much." Her voice was muffled against my chest.

My throat tightened. "Me too."

"Oh, Wes, it's so good to have you back home."

I hugged her, thinking there was at least one person in town who might disagree.

I RAN ALONG THE BEACH, waving at neighbors, smiling at dogs and kids, getting my feet wet where the lake encroached high upon the bank. After two miles, I paused to take stock of my body, making sure my heart rate wasn't too high, my chest felt loose and pain-free, and breathing wasn't too difficult. I'd brushed off my mother's concerns, but the truth was that hypertrophic cardiomyopathy was usually inherited, and our father had high blood pressure. Like many physicians, I'd tended to ignore my own health concerns over the years in favor of helping others, so a little extra vigilance when it came to monitoring my own health was warranted.

But I felt good, and my pulse was in the normal range. Rather than turn around and head back, however, I decided to take advantage of the empty strip of beach I was on and stretch a little. Looking out over the lake I'd grown up on, I caught the top of my right foot in my right hand and felt the pull in my quadriceps. After counting to twenty, I repeated it on the other side and then switched positions to stretch out my hamstrings.

Childhood memories skimmed across my mind like the rocks Drew and I used to skip across the calm surface of the lake. I remembered the day our dad had taught us to skip them, and how we'd both struggled at first. I'd caught on before Drew, but after seeing the crestfallen expression on his face after I'd successfully skipped three stones five times, I'd stopped doing it and instead helped him find flatter, smoother stones. Showed him exactly how I angled the rock —he kept trying to skip it completely flat, but that didn't give him enough friction—and flicked my wrist for just the right amount of spin. Once he got the hang of it, we had endless stone skipping contests every summer.

There were other competitions too—sand castles and rock throwing, and later, kayak races and waterskiing tricks. Drew loved showing off daring feats on the water, especially if there were girls on the boat. I wasn't bad, but I was too scared to make an ass of myself in front of girls to try anything really crazy.

Sometimes, after a day out on the water with friends, we'd have bonfires on the beach at night, sneaking beers and cigarettes and first kisses. I could still hear the crackling of the fire and the pounding of my heart as I leaned toward Cece Bowman, fueled by curiosity, two cans of Pabst Blue Ribbon, and a raging hard-on. She'd tasted like beer and bubble gum. Later we'd gone to my room—our parents must have been out—and made out on my bed, where I'd fumbled my way through removing her bathing suit top and feeling her up in clumsy disbelief. She'd put her hand in my shorts and I'd immediately come all over her fingers.

Shaking my head, I started jogging again, hoping that experience wasn't as terrible for her as I imagined it. Drew, who'd already had sex five times with two different girls by the summer we were seventeen, couldn't believe I hadn't even tried to go all the way. "How could I?" I'd asked him. "It was over too fast!"

"Yeah, you have to think about other things, or else that's what happens." We were in his room, me on the floor and Drew on the bed tossing a baseball in the air and catching it again right above his face.

"What kind of other things?"

"Whatever will distract you. Hockey or baseball stats usually work for me. Or I say the alphabet backward. Shit like that."

It wasn't until college that I had the opportunity (and the nerve) to try again, and I'm pretty sure I recited at *least* the Preamble to the Constitution before losing complete control.

I liked to think I'd come a long way since then.

I'd never had the kind of feelings for someone Drew and Hannah had shared, but I'd at least learned a thing or two about sex during the short-lived fuck flings I'd had in the last ten years. Those kinds of relationships suited me best— physical gratification with little to no talking, especially about feelings.

"Don't you want to get married? Have a family?" my mother would ask me any time I came home.

I'd shrug. "Maybe. If I find the right person."

"Leave him alone, Mom." Drew would always defend me. "It's his life, and he's doing important work."

"Having a family is important too," she'd insist. "And I know some nice girls who'd just love to meet a handsome doctor."

Drew and I would exchange an eye roll and then he'd change the subject. But I wouldn't have him around to defend me anymore. Or change the subject. Or commiserate about our mother's meddling.

Fuck. I miss you, Drew. I should have come home more often. I should know your daughter better. I should have reached out to Hannah sooner.

But I knew why I hadn't, and it didn't make me feel any better.

When I reached the stretch of sand in front of my parents' house, I slowed to a jog, then a walk, pacing the length of their beach as my heart rate slowed. Then I yanked off my shirt, ditched my shoes and socks, and waded into the lake. When I got deep enough, I dove beneath the surface of the water and stayed under for a long, long time.

THREE

HANNAH

ON FRIDAY AFTERNOON, while I was getting ready to leave work, I got a text from a strange number. My heart began to pound as soon as I read the first four words.

Hey Hannah, it's Wes.

Fuck. I'd been on edge the last day and a half, expecting him to turn up on my doorstep unannounced. My stomach started to churn as I read on.

I wanted to come by and see you and Abby. Does this evening work?

"Everything okay?" asked Georgia Valentini, one of the two chefs and owners of Valentini Farms B and B. She was technically my boss, but I considered her a friend as well. "All the color just drained from your face."

I looked up and blinked at her. Gave her the usual lie. "Fine."

"You sure?" She cocked her head as she tied an apron at the back of her waist.

"Yes. It's..." I felt dizzy and sweaty hot all of a sudden and had to close my eyes, take a few deep breaths.

"Hey." Georgia took my arm and led me over to a chair. "Sit down. I'll get you some water."

"Thanks." I lowered my head between my knees and waited for the uneasy feeling to pass, listening to the clink of ice cubes in a glass and the running faucet.

"Here." Georgia placed the glass on the table and took the chair opposite mine.

Grateful, I took a few sips of cold water. "Thanks. I had a little dizzy spell there."

"Have you eaten today? Did you have lunch?" Her eyes held concern.

I nodded, but I couldn't recall if I actually had.

"Probably not enough." She got up and went to the huge fridge, pulling the door open. "I'm getting you something."

I didn't have it in me to argue. Sleep hadn't come easy the last couple nights, and exhaustion was catching up with me. "Okay."

A moment later, she set a plate of chicken salad in front of me with two deviled eggs on the side. I wasn't hungry, but I dutifully took the fork she held out and poked at a grape in the salad. "Thanks."

She sat down opposite me again. "Want to tell me what's going on? You've been sort of tense and quiet the last couple days."

"Have I?" I frowned. "Sorry."

"Don't be sorry. You're entitled to be quiet sometimes. Everything okay?"

"You don't have time to deal with my issues. You need

to prep for dinner." It was Labor Day weekend, and we were fully booked with reservations.

"I have time. And Margot will be here shortly to help. Spill."

I took a breath. "It's Wes. He wants to come over later, and seeing him is really hard for me. I ran into him the other day, and it's got me all messed up."

Georgia nodded in understanding. Her husband Pete, who was the other owner and chef here, had grown up with Drew and Wes, and she'd met them both. "I bet."

"And the thing is, rationally, I know I should just face the fact that I have to get used to seeing him. It's not his fault he looks just like Drew or that being around him is a trigger for me."

"But fuck rationally."

I sighed. "Exactly."

"So what'll you do?"

"What can I do?"

"Tell him it's a bad night."

"Putting him off tonight only delays the inevitable, though. And it isn't fair to him. Or to Abby." I pushed some chicken salad around the plate.

"What if you dropped Abby off at your in-laws'? Then you wouldn't have to be around him."

I shook my head. "I thought about that yesterday, but I feel like I need to be there for Abby. At least in the beginning. I don't want her to be confused."

"So say yes. See how it goes. What's the worst that could happen?"

"Uh, I could have a seismic emotional meltdown in front of him?"

She shrugged. "At least he wouldn't want to come over anymore."

In spite of everything, I laughed a little. "Right."

"Listen." She scooted her chair in and put her hand on my forearm. "You don't have to do anything you're not ready to do, but you're stronger than you think. That much I know for sure."

I'm not, I felt like saying. *I'm just fooling you all. I'm pretending so you'll stop asking me how I'm doing all the time. I'm pretending in the hopes of fooling myself. I'm pretending because the alternative—the truth—is that I'm sad, scared, sick, worried, angry, guilty, lost, and alone. I'm so fucking alone I could scream.*

But I didn't say that.

"Thanks." I set down my fork. "I'll text him back."

Hi Wes. Yes, tonight is fine. Six o'clock will give me time to feed Abby dinner first.

Georgia patted my shoulder and started prepping for dinner, and I picked up the fork again and ate a few bites, tears dripping into my chicken salad.

WHEN I GOT HOME, I made spaghetti for dinner and sat at the table with Abby while she ate. I wasn't hungry enough to eat anything, despite what felt like an ever-widening pit in my stomach. Instead, I poured a glass of wine, hoping it would take the edge off my frazzled nerves.

"So you remember I told you about Daddy's twin brother, Uncle Wes?"

"The one that looks like him?" she asked as a blob of meat sauce fell off her fork and into her lap.

I got up to get a paper towel. "Yes. He's been in Africa

for a while, so we haven't seen him much, but he's home now."

"Does he live at Nana's?" She shoveled in a forkful of pasta.

"Yes," I said, wiping up what had spilled. "But he wants to come over here for a visit. Would that be okay?"

"Sure."

"It might be a little strange because he looks just like Daddy, but it's not him."

"Okay." She reached for her milk.

"And it's okay to feel sad about it."

After a few swallows, she set down the cup. "Okay. But does he have any kids he could bring?" Abby had recently learned what cousins were and was desperate to have some of her own.

"No, he doesn't have kids. Maybe he will someday, if he gets married."

"Oh." She dug into her spaghetti again, and I lifted my wine glass to my lips. I was tempted to keep talking about Drew and Wes, press further, tease out any ambivalence she might be trying to hide from me, but it appeared the only mixed feelings about Wes around here belonged to me.

She's five, reasoned a voice in my head. *She doesn't realize how difficult it might be.*

I'd keep a close eye on her while he was here. If the visit seemed too traumatic for her, I'd cut it short. "Do you have any other questions about him?"

She thought for a moment. "What time is he coming?"

"Six." I glanced at the clock on the wall. "In about half an hour."

"Maybe he'll want to get ice cream. Daddy liked to get ice cream after dinner."

I wasn't sure if she actually remembered that or if it was a memory manufactured after the fact based on stories I'd told her. It was one of my favorite memories, going to get ice cream after dinner on summer nights, and Abby asked me about it often. We'd walk into town, and he'd carry Abby on his shoulders. We always ordered the same thing—Moose Tracks in a waffle cone for Drew, pistachio in a cup for me, Birthday Cake in a sugar cone for Abby, which would drip from the bottom of the cone all down her shirt. God, we'd had everything in those days. *And I thought we'd have it forever.*

"Mommy?" Abby was looking at me. "Do you think he likes ice cream?"

My throat had gotten tight, and I swallowed hard. "Um, yes. At least, he used to. You can ask him."

She looked happy about that, and I peeked at the clock again before taking another sip of wine.

HE WAS A FEW MINUTES EARLY.

Abby had insisted on waiting for him outside, so I was sitting on the porch when he drove up, my stomach in knots. He parked a black Cadillac I recognized as his dad's in the street in front of the house, and waved at us through the passenger window. Abby, drawing on the sidewalk with chalk, waved back before scrambling up the walk to stand next to me. I rose to my feet, feeling a little dizzy and short of breath.

Wes got out of the car, and Abby took my hand. Together we watched him walk toward us, carrying a brown paper bag in one hand. He smiled at both of us, and it was so familiar I wanted to cry. To throw myself at him. To beg him to be someone else and give me my life back.

My knees felt weak.

"Hey," he called as he came up the walk. "How's it going?"

Abby looked up at me, and I knew I had to keep it together for her sake. "Good," I said, squeezing her hand. "Abby, do you remember Uncle Wes?"

She looked at him and shyly shook her head. But then, to my amazement, she let go of my hand and went right to him with open arms. He crouched down and hugged her, balanced on the balls of his feet. Over her shoulder, he looked at me and smiled in surprise. Then he closed his eyes a moment, and I knew he had to be thinking of Drew. A huge lump formed in my throat.

Abby was an affectionate, loving child, but I'd never seen her cling like that to someone she didn't know very well, especially a man. *I miss him too, baby.* I twisted my wedding band around on my finger.

Eventually she let go and he straightened up. "She's beautiful," he said to me.

"Thanks. She looks like her daddy." Abby came and stood next to me, and I tousled her hair.

"I see a lot of you in her too," he said, his eyes on her face, then mine. I'd forgotten how much more quietly he spoke than Drew.

I took a deep breath. "Would you like to come in?"

"Sure. Thank you."

I opened the screen door and let Abby go in first, then Wes held it open for me. Automatically, I went into the kitchen. When I'm nervous, I tend to fall back on what I know how to do—feed someone. Pour them some coffee. Offer a drink.

"Smells amazing in here," he commented, looking

around. "And it looks great, too. But were the walls a different color before?"

"Yes." I poured some more wine for myself. "Can I get you anything? A glass of wine? Some pasta? Are you hungry? Have you eaten?" *Whoa, Hannah. Whoa.*

"I'd love some pasta. It smells delicious."

"Nothing fancy, just some tomato basil sauce." I pulled the leftovers from the fridge, glad to have something to do.

"We growed the basil!" Abby climbed into her chair at the table. "And Mommy let me pick it."

"She did? I bet you're a great helper in the garden." He set his bag on the table and sat down next to Abby.

He chose Drew's chair. That's Drew's chair.

Squelching the urge to ask him to sit somewhere else, I stuck a bowl of pasta in the microwave. *Don't be ridiculous. Many people have sat in that chair since Drew died. And it's not his chair anymore, because he's gone.*

"We don't really have a garden," I said, trying to keep my tone natural. "Just some pots in the yard. But I'd like to plant one." *It's on my list of Things Drew And I Wanted To Do Together But Now I'll Have To Do Alone.* "Would you like a glass of wine?"

He glanced at the wineglass in my hand. "Sure, thanks."

I poured him a glass of pinot noir and prepared a salad for him while he shared the gifts he'd brought for Abby from Africa—a hand-made musical instrument, a stuffed elephant, a bright yellow dress, and a children's book about African animals. Abby loved it all and wanted to put the dress on right away.

"I hope it's the right size." He watched her run out of the kitchen with it, and a moment later I heard her feet on the stairs.

"I'm sure it's fine." I set the pasta and salad in front of

him, placed a napkin and fork on the table, and took the chair across from his.

"Wow. This looks great. Thank you."

"You're welcome."

He dug in, and I sipped my wine. For the first time since he'd arrived, I allowed myself to really look at him. He wore jeans and a white collared shirt that set off his golden skin, and his hair was closely cropped on the sides and back, just like Drew's had been, and a little longer on the top where brown curls traitorously beckoned my fingers. I wanted to touch it.

Would it feel like Drew's? Were his curls the same soft texture? Would they cling to my fingers as I ran a hand through them?

Jesus. Stop it. You can't touch his hair.

I looked out the window, lifted my glass to my lips.

"This is delicious, Hannah." He wound a huge mound of pasta around his fork. His wrists and forearms were nice and thick—a little thicker than Drew's, and the slight difference pleased me. If I could focus on the differences, I'd cope better.

"Thanks. I got the tomatoes from work. Everything we serve there is grown on their farm."

"That's right. My mom mentioned you've been working at Valentini Farms."

"At the new bed and breakfast, yes. Although we serve dinner now, too. But sometimes I work over at the farm if they need extra help with something."

"I'll have to check it out. I'd like to catch up with Pete. It's been a while. Sounds like they're doing really well with the new business."

I nodded. "They are. Summer has been really busy there. And it's completely booked this weekend."

"High season up here. Things will seem quiet next week." He set down his fork and picked up his wine. "So you're enjoying the job? I remember how good your baking was."

"Thanks."

"And everything is good with the house?"

"Yes. I've had a crash course in things like mortgages and taxes and insurance in the last year and a half. Your dad has helped me a lot."

"Good. I'm always happy to help you out, too. Don't ever hesitate to ask." He paused with his glass halfway to his mouth. Was his top lip a little fuller than Drew's? Maybe it was that he wore his scruff a little shorter than Drew had. "I feel bad that I haven't been here for you, Hannah."

"Don't. Really, don't." I met his eyes, and we exchanged a look that felt like a conversation. *I couldn't have handled your being here anyway. I can barely handle it now.*

But I feel guilty.

There's nothing you can do.

There must be. Tell me what it is. I'll do it.

"It fits!" Abby came bounding down the stairs and into the kitchen.

Glad for the intrusion, I focused on my daughter, who twirled happily in her new dress, which was ruched with elastic across the bodice and halter style, but the straps were hanging down. "Come here, let me tie it."

"I want Uncle Wes to do it." She stood next to his chair, presented her back and lifted her hair off her neck.

He looked at me, eyebrows raised, as if to ask permission.

I shrugged. "She's all yours, Uncle Wes."

He smiled back and set his glass down before reaching for the straps. His fingers looked big and masculine as they gently worked the straps into a bow. I almost laughed at how hard he appeared to be concentrating on the task.

"There," he said. "How did I do?"

"Good." She twirled around again.

"What do you say, Abby?" I prompted.

"Thank you." She beamed at him. "I love it."

"You're welcome." He picked up his fork again. "I'm so glad it fits."

"Can we go for ice cream now, Mommy?"

I looked at Wes. "She wants to walk into town for ice cream. It's no problem if you don't have time."

"Of course I have time."

"Abby, let Uncle Wes finish his dinner, and then we'll go, okay?"

"Okay. Can I go back outside?"

"You can go in the backyard. Not the front."

"Kay." She went out the back door, leaving us alone again.

"She's so cute, Hannah."

"Thanks."

"How is she doing with...everything?"

"Pretty well, I guess." I sighed, lifting my shoulders. "She was so young, you know? And sometimes I'm torn between hoping she remembers everything about him and how much he loved her, and other times I'm glad she probably doesn't. I don't want her to have the pain of missing him the way I do."

He nodded. "I get that."

"She doesn't talk about him a lot," I confessed. "At least not with me. Her therapist thinks it's probably because she thinks it will make me sad, not because she doesn't want to remember him."

"Makes sense."

"So each night at bedtime, she'll ask me something about him, or I'll tell her a story."

"That's a good idea." He picked up his wine. "I could tell her some, too, if you'd like."

"She'd love that. In fact, she just asked me last night what Drew looked like at her age. I told her maybe Nana had a picture at her house."

"Definitely. Albums full of them. And she loves looking through them. Why don't you bring Abby over tomorrow? Mom would love to see you both."

"I have to work," I said, glad for the excuse.

"All day?"

I hesitated. "Until two. She'll be here with her sitter."

"Bring her after that. We'll swim and have a cookout or something. I can show Abby how her dad and I grilled hot dogs over a bonfire at the beach. And made s'mores."

"She does like hot dogs and s'mores," I admitted.

"Good. Then it's settled." He finished eating and carried his dishes to the sink, and I followed with two empty wine glasses. For a moment, we stood shoulder to shoulder looking out the window into the yard, where Abby was sitting on a swing Drew had hung from a tree for her. We could hear her singing "Lullaby of Birdland" softly through the screen.

"She sings Sarah Vaughn," he said. "Just like you used to."

I looked up at him in surprise. "How do you know that?"

He shrugged. "My mom loves those old standards. I grew up hearing them."

"No, I meant how do you know that about me?"

He met my eyes. "You used to sing along to the music at the diner while you worked."

"Did I?" I laughed, a little self-conscious. "Sorry. You were probably trying to study."

He looked out the window again. "Don't be. I liked it. You had such a pretty voice. I never forgot it."

Something warm hummed beneath my skin at the compliment. Something I hadn't felt in a long, long time. Something just for me.

It was a nice feeling, and I held onto it, worried that any minute, Grief and Guilt would rear up and snatch it from me. But it lingered as we wandered into the yard to collect Abby. The sun was setting behind the trees, throwing dappled light onto the lawn and giving the air a golden quality so pretty I wondered if I was imagining it.

Abby jumped off the swing when she saw us. "Uncle Wes, will you carry me on your shoulders?"

Oh, God. The contentment I'd felt a moment ago vanished in an instant. My world was full of shadows again. "Abby, no."

"It's fine. I'd like to, actually." Wes picked her up and swung her onto his shoulders, and she laughed gleefully. "Point me in the right direction, okay?"

"Like I'm the princess and you're my ship!" she squealed. "Go that way!"

Abby pointed toward the street, and I followed them silently around the house to the sidewalk. Abby chattered the entire way into town, playing the princess game, and Wes played along, doing her bidding. I stayed quiet, arms crossed over my chest, worried about what was coming. *I knew it. I knew this would be confusing for her.*

At the ice cream place, it went exactly as I'd feared. When Wes ordered mint chocolate chip, Abby balked and tugged on his arm. "No, you have to have Moose Tracks in a waffle cone. And Mommy will have pistachio in a cup, and I will have Birthday Cake in a sugar cone."

"Abby," I scolded. "Let Uncle Wes order what he likes."

"No, it's okay." He patted her head. "I love Moose Tracks. I was having trouble deciding. Thanks, princess."

She grinned, satisfied.

My stomach was upset, but I ordered the pistachio ice cream anyway and protested when Wes insisted on paying. "You don't have to," I told him, pulling a twenty from my pocket. "You already brought gifts for her."

"I want to." He gently gripped my forearm, and we locked eyes. "Let me."

He's too close. He's touching me. "Okay," I said, mostly so he'd let go of my arm. "Thank you."

We walked back slowly, and I ate a few spoonfuls of ice cream without tasting it. Had this been a mistake? Was Abby going to confuse Wes with Drew from now on? Would they somehow merge in her mind? Did she plan on acting out every memory she had of Drew with his brother in order to feel like she had her daddy back again? I watched her slurp happily on her oversized scoop of Birthday Cake, skipping along between Wes and me. She certainly didn't look traumatized. Maybe I was overthinking things.

Although she ate it too quickly for it to drip down the front of her dress, ice cream was all over Abby's mouth and in her hair by the time we got home.

"You're a mess," I told her. "I should turn the hose on you."

"Yes!" She clapped her hands.

"How about a bath instead?" I asked, glancing up at the house. "And then we can—oh, our porch light is out."

"Do you have a bulb?" Wes asked. "I'll change it for you."

"You don't have to. I can reach it with the stepladder."

"It's no big deal, really. It will take me two minutes."

I hesitated. On one hand, I didn't want Wes to feel he had to step into the role of handyman around here. I was perfectly capable of changing the porch lightbulb. On the other, I'd likely put it on my endless list of things that needed to get done around the house and check it off sometime next year.

"Mommy, I have to go to the bathroom." Abby hopped from one foot to the other.

"Go on," said Wes, nodding toward the house. "I can wait."

"Okay. Thanks."

Inside the house Abby scurried up the stairs and Wes stood in the front hall, hands in his pockets. I tossed my half-eaten ice cream in the kitchen trash, slipped my sandals off and climbed onto the counter to reach the high cupboard where Drew had always stashed the light bulbs.

"Can I help you?" Wes called from the doorway.

"I can reach it, I think." Kneeling on the counter, I opened the cupboard door and peered in.

Wes came up behind me. "Let me help you."

"I guess I should move things to where I can reach them, but this is where he always kept light bulbs, so..." My voice trailed off. "That sounds stupid, doesn't it?"

"No," Wes said. "It doesn't at all." With his left hand, he pulled down a box with two big bulbs in it. "These?"

I nodded, sitting back on my bare heels. Then I embarrassed myself completely by bursting into tears. "Oh God, I'm sorry. It's just one of those things, you know? That he always did."

"You don't have to be sorry." He looked around, grabbed a tissue from the box nearby, and handed it to me.

"Thanks." I blew my nose and kept talking. I have no idea why. "Sometimes it's those small things that make me miss him more than the big things. I just picture him. Changing the porch light. Mowing the lawn. Moving a heavy piece of furniture. Stupid, mundane, everyday things that he should be here to do. But he isn't."

"I know."

I felt a hand on my back. A couple awkward pats. I frowned. Drew would have wrapped his right arm around my waist, buried his face in my neck, and swung me down before teasing me about being too short to reach the high cupboards. Fuck, I missed that kind of touch. Playful and tender and loving. I missed it so much that some secret place in me wanted Wes to do it—grab me and touch me that way. I wanted to do what Abby had done, bring a memory to life, pretend he was Drew, act like nothing had changed. *Let me feel his touch and his kiss and his body against mine just one more time. Let me feel like everything is okay. Let me forget I'm alone.*

"Sometimes I get mad at him for it," I whispered, clutching the tissue. "For leaving me alone to do everything —the trivial shit like this, and the huge stuff like parenting our daughter. I didn't want this. He left me. He left us."

"Hannah." His palm stilled on my back, warm and reassuring. I didn't deserve it. What kind of person gets mad at her dead husband?

"Isn't that horrible?" Another sob worked its way free from my chest. "That I feel anger at him for something he didn't choose? Go ahead, you can say it."

"It's not horrible. It's grief. Earlier today, Mom was digging at me about something and I thought, *Damn you,*

Drew, for leaving me alone to deal with Mom for the rest of my life. And then I felt like shit."

"Exactly. It makes no sense." I wiped my runny nose with the back of my wrist.

He handed me another tissue. "It never will."

Nodding, I closed my eyes against the tears. He rubbed my back again, and for a moment, *just for a moment*, I let myself pretend.

He's not gone. Everything is gonna be okay.

But then Wes took his hand off me, and I was alone again. Alone and snot-nosed and embarrassed. I got down from the counter, keeping my face to the floor. "Screwdriver is in here," I said, pulling open the junk drawer. My fingers were shaking. "I need to get Abby in the tub."

"No problem. I'll get this changed and head home."

"Thanks." I didn't even look at him as I left the room. I couldn't.

I BATHED ABBY, read her a story, sang her a song, and tucked her in.

"Everything okay?" I brushed her hair from her face. She'd been uncharacteristically quiet since we'd gotten home, and I was still worried about her.

"Yes." But she didn't sound sure.

"Want to ask me a question?"

"Yes." She looked up at me. "Are you sure he's not Daddy?"

The desperate hope in her eyes crushed my broken heart. "Yes, honey. I'm sure."

"He looks just like him." She glanced at the photo on her nightstand.

"I know. That's because they're identical twins. Remember, I told you it might be strange to see him."

"And he likes Moose Tracks, too. Just like Daddy. And he's a doctor just like Daddy."

"Lots of people like Moose Tracks. And lots of people are doctors. Uncle Wes is not your daddy. He's a different person."

She turned onto her side and hugged her new stuffed elephant close.

"Want me to sing another song?"

"No. I'm tired."

"Okay. Night, baby."

"Night."

I kissed her forehead and left the room, leaving the door open.

Downstairs, I noticed the porch light was on, the front door was closed, and Wes's car was gone.

Thank God. I'd had enough for one night. And I'd have to think up an excuse for tomorrow. Clearly, Abby needed some time to process the fact that Wes was not Drew and couldn't fill that role.

To be honest, so did I.

FOUR

WES

I ROLLED down the windows and took the long way home, needing some time and space to think before facing what would surely be an inquisition by my mother the moment I walked in the door.

She'd annoyed me earlier when she said she didn't want to go see Abby with me because she never felt comfortable in Hannah's house. She'd wanted them to come to *her* house. "Well, that's not what I suggested, Mom. I want to make this as comfortable as possible for them, and she accepted my offer to drop by. I don't want to switch things up on her."

"But six is dinnertime, and I'm making my gourmet mac and cheese for dinner. You love my mac and cheese."

"Save me some."

Except I'd eaten dinner at Hannah's house. I could just imagine how that was going to go over.

Propping my left elbow on the window, I rubbed my

index finger beneath my lower lip. *She still has the prettiest smile.*

But there was so much sadness in her eyes. She only really smiled when she looked at her daughter. Was she happy?

I frowned. *No, asshole. Of course she's not happy. She lost her husband, the person with whom she had a child and an entire life planned. You saw her nearly fall apart tonight just because she can't bring herself to put the lightbulbs on a shelf where she can reach them. There must be a hundred moments like that in a day.*

My heart ached for both of us. I couldn't get the memories of Drew out of my head, and she couldn't stop thinking about what should have been. I wanted to help her, but how? Did she even want me around? Tonight had seemed comfortable enough—maybe a little tense at the start, but I felt like she was able to smile and relax a bit. And I loved that she felt close enough to me to break down a little. To tell me what she was feeling. It felt like trust, and it had made me want to wrap my arms around her and hold her tight, tell her I missed him too, but everything would be okay.

But I hadn't. I couldn't. She wasn't mine to touch that way—she never had been.

And then right after that, something changed. She hadn't even looked at me when she said goodbye. Come to think of it, she hadn't even said goodbye. It was like she couldn't get away from me fast enough.

You shouldn't have touched her at all.

I shifted uncomfortably in my seat. Was that it? Had she been upset that I'd rubbed her back? I'd only done it to soothe her, to let her know she wasn't alone, to be there for her. And if I left it there a little too long, it was only because

I knew the power of human touch. Not only as a physician, but as a person who often felt that words failed him. Or maybe it was me who failed words. Either way, I'd only wanted to comfort her.

Are you sure? asked a voice in my head.

Frowning, I pulled into my parents' driveway and tried to convince myself that there was nothing untoward about my concern for Hannah. That was ridiculous, wasn't it? So many years had gone by since I'd harbored that stupid, one-sided crush. For God's sake, I'd been the best man at their wedding, and I'd been genuinely happy for Drew even as I continued to silently envy him and admire her. And maybe I still found her pretty, but I wasn't drawn to her any longer because of my feelings. We had a *connection*—we had both loved Drew more than anyone else in the entire world, and we felt his absence most deeply.

The front door to my parents' house had barely clicked shut behind me when I heard my mother's voice.

"Wes? Is that you? Come on in here," she called from the great room.

I slipped out of my shoes in the foyer—house rule as long as I could remember—and headed into the great room, where she was curled up on one end of the couch reading a magazine and my dad was on his recliner doing a crossword puzzle. The TV was on, tuned to the baseball game, but the sound was off. I leaned on the far arm of the couch and eyed the screen, looking for a score.

"Well? How'd it go?" My mother's tone was a little impatient.

"Great. Abby is adorable."

"Isn't she? Don't you think she looks just like Drew?"

"I think she got the best of both parents."

"Did she like her gifts?"

"Loved them. Put the dress on right away."

She clucked her tongue. "God love her, did she really?"

"Mmhm."

My mother set her magazine aside, got off the couch, and headed for the kitchen, her bare feet silent on the shiny wood floor. She pulled a big white casserole dish with a glass cover from the fridge. "Let me make you a plate."

"Don't bother, Mom. I ate at Hannah's."

"What?" She blinked at me like she must have misheard.

"I ate dinner at Hannah's." I braced myself for the icy wind about to blow through the house.

The casserole dish thunked on the granite counter. "Well...you didn't tell me you were going to eat there."

"I didn't know. But she offered, and I was hungry. I'm sorry." I tried to look as contrite as possible. "I'll eat the mac and cheese for lunch tomorrow."

Her chin jutted forward as she turned her back to me and slid the casserole back into the huge stainless fridge. "What did she make, pasta?"

I didn't miss the snide note. I wondered how Drew had managed this—his mother's obvious resentment of his wife. It was ridiculous, especially since Drew was gone. *No wonder Hannah seemed reluctant to come over tomorrow.* "Yes, pasta with tomato basil sauce. It was delicious."

She didn't say anything to that, just switched off the light in the kitchen and went back to her seat on the couch. "How'd the house look?" she asked, resettling on the couch. "Last time I was there it didn't look too clean. But she works so much, I don't know how she has time for housework, bless her heart."

"The house looked fine."

"What's a six-letter word for 'thinking only of oneself'?" my dad interjected.

M-o-t-h-e-r, I thought.

"Starts with a G," he added. It was hard to tell if he was interrupting on purpose because he heard what my mother was doing, or if he was oblivious to our conversation. My dad could be wily sometimes.

"Greedy?" my mother suggested.

"Aha!" He pointed a finger in the air and filled in the squares with his pencil. "That's gotta be it."

"So Mom, how about having a cookout tomorrow on the beach? I invited Abby and Hannah to come over in the afternoon."

"Did she say she'd come?"

"Yes. She works until two, but after that."

My mother's face brightened. "I could make sweet honey ribs. And salad with grilled peaches. Deviled eggs, and green goddess potato salad."

"Don't go to all that trouble. Really, I just wanted to cook some hot dogs and s'mores over a fire on the beach with Abby like Drew and I used to."

"Oh." She stiffened. "I guess if we're not invited…"

I took a breath and counted to three. "Everyone is invited. I just didn't want you to go to any trouble."

"Since when is feeding my family any trouble?"

"I like hot dogs and s'mores," my father put in without looking up from his crossword.

"There. See? We can just keep it casual."

My mother sniffed. "Fine. Casual. But that doesn't mean I can't make a few things on the side."

"That sounds great, Mom." A compromise. I'd take it. "Thanks."

"I also want to talk about your birthday dinner."

"My birthday isn't until October."

"I like planning ahead. And you haven't been around for your birthday in years. I want to make sure we celebrate it."

I understood that she needed something fun to focus on for my birthday. Otherwise, it would just be another day to mourn the loss of Drew. It would have been his birthday, too. It was still strange to me that I was older than he would ever be. He'd been older than me for thirty-five years. "We can do whatever you want, Mom."

She smiled. "So what are you up to the rest of the night?"

"I was thinking of giving Pete a call." I hadn't actually thought of it until right that minute, but despite the cathedral ceiling above me, the house was feeling a little stifling.

"Might as well." She sighed and picked up her magazine again. "Since you already had dinner."

I ignored that and wandered out through the sliding screen door onto the wooden deck that overlooked the lawn and, beyond it, the lake. Scrolling through my contacts, I checked to see if I still had a cell number for Pete. I did, so I shot him a quick text and he called me right away.

"Hello?"

"Hey! I heard you were back in town! Welcome home."

"Thanks."

"How are you? Is it good to be back?"

I thought about it. "Yes and no. Mostly yes, I guess."

"It's gotta be strange for you without Drew here."

Looking out over the lawn, I saw a thousand games of catch and Frisbee and capture the flag with my brother and our friends. Nights just like this at the end of summer, August heat still hanging on even though it was September, the breeze warm, the temperature of the lake finally perfect. "It is."

"Man, what a shock. I still can't get over it."

"Me neither."

"Hey, I'm on kid duty tonight because Georgia is working, but want to come over for a beer?"

I slapped at a mosquito on my leg. "Yeah. I'd like that. My mother is driving me fucking crazy. I really need to move out."

He laughed. "Come on over. Pull around the back of the inn and park in the drive. We live in an addition off the old part of the house."

"Okay. See you in ten."

"YOU'VE GOT A GREAT PLACE HERE," I told Pete after he'd shown me around. "Whoever did your addition did a really good job staying true to the style of the old house."

"Thanks. We like it." He pulled two beers from the fridge and took off the caps. "Let's go out back and sit on the deck. I can hear the monitor from there."

Outside, he lit a few citronella candles to keep the bugs at bay, and their wicks sizzled in the dark. We sat in a couple Adirondack chairs that needed a new coat of paint, our legs stretched out in front of us.

"Have you seen Hannah yet?" Pete asked. "She works for us here."

"I heard that." I took a slow pull on my beer, not entirely comfortable with the way my heart beat a little faster at the sound of her name. "Yeah, I saw her earlier tonight, actually. I stopped by the house."

"She's had it rough."

I nodded. "Yeah."

"But it worked out really well hiring her. I had no idea how good she was in the kitchen. When Georgia came to me and suggested it, I wasn't sure."

"I knew she was pretty good. Does she still bake pies?"

Pete moaned. "Oh God, the pies." He rubbed a hand over his stomach, which was slightly paunchy. "They kill me. But everything she makes is good."

We drank in silence for a moment before Pete spoke again. "So what about you? Your dad's retiring, I hear. You taking over the practice?"

"That's the plan."

"So you're sticking around, then."

"Yeah."

Pete laughed. "You don't sound too excited about it."

"Sorry." I took a long swallow before elaborating. "My mother is stressing me out."

"Moms are good at that. I love mine, but most days I'm pretty glad she's in Florida."

"Exactly. I think I'll like her better once I get my own place. I'm just feeling a little smothered. She was always easier to deal with when Drew was around."

"You should talk to my brother, Brad. He sells real estate, and I bet he could find you a great place pretty quickly. Lots of people sell this time of year here."

"That's a good idea. I'll do that. How are your brothers? I hear Jack is remarried and has a baby?"

"Yep. So he's exhausted, that's how he is." Pete laughed. "His wife is Margot, I'm not sure if you've met her. Their son James was born a few months ago. Brad's the same. Still single, has his daughter with him every other week."

"That's great." I tipped my beer back again. "I'm happy for you guys."

"Thanks."

We talked through another beer, getting caught up on family and friends and future plans. We laughed about the dumb things we did as kids and traded favorite memories involving Drew and all the dares he took.

"Oh, man, I thought for sure he'd break a leg when he jumped off that roof." Pete laughed. "And I can't believe he never got caught buying beer all those times."

"It's because there was always a female cashier," I said. "He could talk a woman into anything."

"Fuck yes, he could." Pete took another sip. "I was actually surprised he got married first. I thought for sure you would."

I raised the bottle to my lips. "Nah."

"Think you ever will?"

After a long swallow, I shrugged. "Not sure, Mom. I'll let you know."

He punched me on the shoulder. "Asshole."

I grinned before finishing off my beer. "I should get going. Hey, if you're not busy tomorrow, come by my parents' place. Hannah and Abby are coming over for a cookout. Bring your family. Invite Jack and his family, too."

"Shit, I'd love to, but we're so busy at the restaurant this weekend. I have to work tomorrow."

"Another time then. It would be fun to get everyone together."

"Definitely."

We stood up and he clapped me on the upper arm. "I'm glad you're back. Let's get you into a house so you don't lose your mind. And you should come by the inn for dinner sometime. Or even breakfast. Hannah makes waffles that will slay you."

"Oh yeah?" We collected our empty bottles and went back into the kitchen.

"Yes. BLT waffles, carrot cake waffles, ham and cheese waffles, apple and prosciutto waffles..." Pete groaned. "They're all amazing. She's so talented."

"I'll definitely come in."

We said goodbye and I drove home, my stomach growling at the thought of Hannah's waffles. It made me happy to know she was appreciated at her job, that she had friends to support her. She seemed strong in a lot of ways, but fragile too. Not that I knew her all that well—but I wanted to. She was family to me, and making sure she was okay made me feel closer to my brother. Like I was doing right by him. When I thought of it that way, my protective feelings for her made perfect sense. They were acceptable on every level.

Maybe I'd try the inn for breakfast in the morning.

I WOKE UP EARLY, barely after sunrise, and went for a run, then a swim. After a shower, I dressed in jeans and a clean shirt, frowning at my lack of wardrobe choices. During the last few years, I'd basically lived in MSF T-shirts. It stood for Medecins Sans Frontieres, which was how I thought of Doctors Without Borders. Not that I'd cared. I'd never been all that fashion conscious, but now that I was back in civilian life, I probably should get some nicer clothes. I'd have to ask my mother where to shop, then hope she wouldn't insist on coming with me. Maybe I could just order some things online.

Happy that neither of my parents was up yet, I drove to the inn, hoping it would be open for breakfast business. It wasn't even eight yet. As I approached the massive front porch of the old Victorian, I admired the beautiful restoration. I remembered the place as an abandoned, falling-down heap from my youth, its paint peeling, roof sagging, and windows boarded up. The transformation was miraculous. The house was painted a pale, sunny yellow, the shutters a deep green. The home's roof had been replaced, and the white pillars supporting the portico looked strong and smooth.

The massive wooden front door was open, but the screen door was shut. It looked original to the house, its wood painted red and embellished with fancy scrollwork. Someone had put a lot of thought—and money—into this.

I knocked lightly before entering the front hall, which was empty. To my right and left were large, airy rooms with high ceilings and beautiful wood floors, filled with tables set for two or four. Straight ahead, at the end of the hall, I could see a portion of the home's original dining room. I wandered into it and found a large antique table set for a meal with china and silverware and crystal for twelve guests.

A swinging door at the back of the room opened, and a beautiful blond woman appeared carrying a vase of roses. "Oh, hello," she said, surprise lifting her eyebrows. She set the vase at the center of the table. "I didn't realize anyone was up yet. Good morning."

"Good morning." Our eyes met, and recognition hit us both. This had to be Margot, Jack's wife, and I *had* met her, but it was at the funeral. I could tell by the look in her eye she was a bit disconcerted by my appearance for a moment —I'd have to get used to that—but her smile returned when she realized I wasn't an apparition. "Wes, right? I'm Margot Valentini."

I nodded and stepped forward, holding out one hand. "Of course."

She clasped my hand with both of hers. "So nice to see you. I ran into your mother last week in town and she was so excited about your homecoming. Welcome back."

"Thanks."

"Did you come for breakfast?"

"I did, but..." I rubbed the back of my neck nervously. "I guess I'm early."

She dismissed that with a graceful flip of her wrist. "No such thing. Let me get you a cup of coffee and tell Hannah you're here. Take any seat you like in here, or if you'd prefer, I can seat you at a table in the parlor or the music room."

"Thank you. In here is fine."

She smiled at me again before turning and heading back into what I assumed was the kitchen area. I chose a chair at one end of the table and sat down, looking around at the room's fireplace, antique sideboard, and an old Victrola tucked in one corner. A moment later, the door opened and Hannah appeared with a cup and saucer in one hand and a small white pitcher in the other. My chest did something funny when I saw her—a quick catch and release—but it was over so fast, I thought maybe I'd imagined it.

"Morning, Wes." Hannah set the cup and saucer down in front of me and the pitcher of cream nearby. Unlike Margot, she didn't make eye contact, and she didn't smile.

"Morning. I'm a little early, huh? I saw Pete last night and he was talking about the waffles here. I think I dreamt about them last night."

That earned me a little smile and a brief meeting of our

eyes. "It's okay. On Saturdays we serve breakfast starting at eight, and it's nearly that. People will start to wander down soon. Oh! Let me get the sugar." She was through the door again before I could tell her not to bother on my account. I drank my coffee black.

I picked up the cup and sipped, worried I'd made her uncomfortable by coming here. When she returned with the sugar bowl and a silver coffee pot, I decided to be direct about it. It was what Drew would have done. "Hannah, can you sit for a minute?"

She set the bowl and pot on the table and glanced at the kitchen door. "I really shouldn't."

"Just for a minute. Please."

She looked uncomfortable, but she pulled out the chair adjacent to mine and sort of perched on the edge of it. Immediately, she began fussing with her wedding ring, a delicate band of tiny diamonds on the fourth finger of her left hand. I'd noticed her doing that a couple times last night too, a nervous habit. I felt bad I made her feel that way.

"I know this isn't easy for you. Seeing me."

She swallowed, and her eyes flicked toward me. "No. It isn't."

"I understand. It's my fault. I shouldn't have waited so long to come home."

"No, I—"

I touched her forearm. "Let me say this. I couldn't say it last night because...I don't know. Because I was nervous. And you were nervous. And I didn't want to make things any more upsetting for you. But I feel sick that I stayed away so long. It was selfish—it was me not wanting to face life without my brother. Over there, it was easier to pretend I wouldn't have to." If it wasn't the whole truth, it was at least half of it. The half I could admit to, anyway.

"I get that, believe me."

"But I feel like I abandoned you and Abby and my parents. And I'm sorry. Things are going to be different from now on."

"Last night after you left, Abby asked me if I was sure you weren't Drew," Hannah blurted.

It felt like a punch in the stomach. "Oh, God. I'm sorry."

"Stop apologizing. None of this is your fault." She closed her eyes and shook her head. "I just don't want her to be confused. It's...it's confusing to see you. For her, I mean. I think we shouldn't come over today."

"But don't you think that's exactly why you *should* come over?"

"What do you mean?"

"The best way to clear up confusion would be to get to know me as her uncle, right? She needs to see me as myself, not as a substitute for Drew."

"Maybe," Hannah hedged.

"And I think talking about Drew would help, too. To clearly differentiate us in her mind. After all, we were pretty different in a lot of ways."

A little smile. "Yes."

I wrapped my hand around her wrist on the table. "Come today. Please. Bring Abby and we'll have fun and tell her about her dad when he was a kid and celebrate life. I need that." Until I voiced the sentiment to her, I hadn't even realized it was the truth.

She stared at my hand on her skin, but I didn't let go. "Okay. We'll come. Can I bring something?"

"Just you and Abby."

"Come on. Let me contribute. Potato salad?"

Remembering what I'd told my mother, I hesitated. But I didn't want to say no to Hannah. "Sure."

She'd seen my hesitation. "You don't like potato salad?"

"No, I do."

"Do you like curry? Drew hated it, but I have this recipe for curried potato salad that I really like."

"I love curry."

She smiled, looking genuinely happy for the first time this morning.

The door to the kitchen swung open and Georgia peeked out. Immediately I retracted my hand. "Hey, Wes. Heard you were here."

I stood up and we met halfway across the room, exchanging a hug. "Good to see you, Georgia."

She patted me on the back. "I'm so glad you came in."

"Me too." We let go and I glanced at Hannah, who had stood and was refilling my coffee cup. "I heard about the breakfast here and couldn't resist."

"Oh, you won't regret it. She's making champagne waffles this morning."

I cocked a brow at Hannah. "Champagne, huh?"

She blushed as she set the pitcher down. "They sound fancier than they are."

"Ready, Han?" Georgia asked. "Waffle irons getting hot. Want to mix up the batter?"

"Yes." Hannah gave me a smile before heading for the kitchen. "Hope you enjoy your breakfast."

"I know I will."

The table filled quickly—with guests, with locals hoping to get in for breakfast, with regulars who talked nonstop about how much they loved coming here since there was no menu. You got what was fresh and available, and that was that.

Pete hadn't lied, the waffles were akin to a religious experience. Light and fluffy, a little crunchy, a little soft, topped with real blackberries and cream. Several times I found myself closing my eyes just to savor the bite in my mouth. And it wasn't just the food—being home again felt good. Reconnecting with my roots felt good. Spending time with people from my past felt good. Until my mother called and asked me to please consider coming home and relieving the professional burden on my father, I hadn't really planned on coming back. But now I realized how much I'd needed this.

I kept glancing at the door to the kitchen, but Hannah never appeared again. Margot brought out the dining room meals alongside another server who worked the front rooms as well. But I couldn't stop thinking about her. I wanted today to be perfect, and I was going to do everything I could to make her and Abby feel comfortable, safe, and welcome. I owed it to my brother.

Didn't I?

FIVE

HANNAH

"SO HOW DID it go last night?" Georgia asked as we worked alongside each other in the inn's kitchen.

"Good, I guess." I poured waffle batter into the two irons on the counter and closed the lids. "But it was strange for Abby, I think. She asked me later if I was sure he wasn't her dad."

"Awww, that had to be hard."

"It was," I admitted. "It felt like telling her Drew was gone all over again."

"Do you think she understands?" Georgia went to the fridge and took out more eggs.

"Yes." I sighed. "But I think she also hoped for a different answer." I lifted the lids to check on the waffles, but they needed about thirty more seconds. "Wes thinks the best way to clear up any confusion is to spend more time with him."

"He's probably right." Georgia dropped a few eggs into

the frying pan and stirred her Hollandaise. "Don't you think?"

"He has me mostly convinced. We're supposed to go over to his mom's this afternoon and I tried to get out of it, for Abby's sake. But he says it would be better to come."

"I think he's right," Georgia said confidently. "You should go. It will be fun for Abby *and* for you. When's the last time you spent an afternoon at the beach?"

"I can't even remember." Carefully, I took the waffles from the irons, plated them, and added the blackberry compote and crème fraîche. Margot breezed in and scooped up both plates for serving.

"Two minutes on the eggs Benedict," Georgia told her.

Margot nodded and hustled back out the door.

"So what about you? Georgia asked, pouring sauce on top of the eggs. "Was seeing him as painful as you thought? Did you have a seismic emotional meltdown?"

"No. More like a mini emotional quake. But we handled it. Actually, it sort of helped to talk to him. I felt like he understood." *And then I pretended he was Drew while he rubbed my back.*

"See? This could be a healing relationship for both of you."

"Maybe."

Margot and the other servers swung into the kitchen again, and we got busy with new orders, which left us less time to talk. But what she'd said made sense—as did what Wes said. Maybe the best way to drive home that Wes was not Drew was to let him in, not shut him out. Maybe keeping him at a distance would only feed Abby's hopeful confusion. Maybe what we really needed was more time together, not less.

But just to make sure, I called Tess on my way home

from work. Of all the women in my widow support group, I felt the closest to her, maybe because our journeys were the most similar. We also shared a therapist, which was how both of us found the group, and we often called each other to agonize or celebrate a particularly difficult session.

Tess listened to my side of the story, murmuring sympathetically and assuring me my reactions were totally understandable.

"Even wanting to pretend he was Drew just to feel his arms around me?" I asked doubtfully.

"Totally. It would be understandable even if you didn't want to pretend he was Drew, and just wanted to feel a man's arms around you!" she cried. "My God, look what I did with the tree man. Sometimes you just want that. Not love, not a relationship, not a date, but arms. Chest. Shoulders. Skin. Stubble. Muscle. The smell of a man. The solidity of him. Remember how those things used to make us feel?"

Did I? "Vaguely."

"Well, it's okay to want them again. To want to feel that way again—taken care of. That's all you needed. It had nothing to do with him being Drew's brother."

I wasn't sure about that, but I went with it. "Right."

"And I think he's right about letting him into your lives," she went on. "It's like Exposure Therapy. Remember that shit?

"Ugh, yes. It was so hard." Exposure therapy involved us sort of deconstructing the event of our husbands' deaths, facing all of our fears and anxieties about it. It was excruciatingly painful, and I wasn't entirely sure it had worked for me, since I still had boatloads of anxiety, but after those sessions, I'd at least been able to get off the pills I'd been taking to cope.

"So I think this could be like that for you and Abby. Stare that fucker down. Look him in the eye and tell yourself, 'This is not my husband because my husband is gone. This is his brother and he is going to be part of our lives from now on.'"

"Okay. I'll try. Thanks, Tess."

"You're welcome. Of course, fuck if I really have any answers, I'm feeling my way just like you are."

"I know you are. How's the weekend going for you?" Weekends were always tough for widowed people. If we got invitations at all, we felt like the fifth wheel, the odd man out, the third person on a bicycle built for two. It's one of the reasons I liked my job—it kept me busy on weekends.

"It's okay. Kids will be back tomorrow, so I'm doing all the laundry and cleaning. Boring stuff."

"Want to come to the beach with us this afternoon? I'm sure it would be okay."

"No, no. I'm fine, really. I'm getting to the point where I can enjoy a little solitude again."

"Good. Call if you need anything."

"Same. Have fun today."

We hung up, and I took a quick detour to the grocery store to get the ingredients I'd need for the potato salad. I didn't want to show up empty-handed today, although sometimes with Lenore it was hard to tell if she was more put out when I brought something for the table or when I didn't. Inside the store, I filled a small hand-held basket with what I needed along with a bottle of wine, and got in one of the long lines to check out. Holiday weekends were always busy.

"Hannah? Is that you, dear?"

I turned and saw my mother-in-law behind me. "Oh hi,

Lenore." Dutifully, I left my place in line and went to kiss her cheek.

"Is Abby with you?" she asked, looking around.

"No, she's with the sitter. I just got off work, and I wanted to pick up a few things to bring to the house later."

Lenore clucked her tongue. "You don't have to bring a thing, dear! We're just so glad you and Abby are coming over."

"It's just a curried potato salad," I said, shrugging it off.

"My, that sounds exotic. I've never cared for curry myself."

I forced a smile. "No?"

"No, my family always preferred good old-fashioned American potato salad."

My fingers tightened around the handle of my basket. "I mentioned it to Wes this morning, and he said he liked curry."

"Yes, he told me about breakfast." She sighed dramatically. "Guess his mother's waffles aren't good enough for him anymore."

"I'm sure it's not that," I said. "Oh, I just remembered one more thing I need. I'll see you in a little while. About four?"

"Perfect, dear. See you then."

I made a beeline for the wine aisle and added another bottle to my basket. I had a feeling I might need it.

AT A FEW MINUTES TO FOUR, Abby and I knocked on the screen door of my in-laws' house. I'd never forget the first time Drew had brought me here—I'd been bug-eyed at how big and beautiful their place was. Expansive green lawn, gorgeous flower gardens, golden sandy beach, the view of the lake from almost every room in the house. The place had six bedrooms!

I'd grown up in a tiny, two-bedroom bungalow with a view of a Rite Aid parking lot, daughter of a single mother who worked her fingers to the bone at her family's tailoring business but still found time to put a home-cooked meal on the table every night. We hadn't had a lot, but it was a happy enough childhood. Although I'd never known my father (my mother said I was better off), she was part of a big Italian family and I had lots of cousins to play with at big, noisy, extended-family Sunday dinners. I wished Abby could experience something like that, but the Parks family was very different from what I was used to. We'd probably have linen napkins and crystal glassware on the beach for this cookout. Back when Drew was alive, we used to laugh about his mother's insistence on formality and her not-always-subtle digs at my humble upbringing. Dealing with her had been so much easier when he was there.

Wes came to the door and opened it with a warm smile on his face. His smile was slightly different than Drew's, I was beginning to notice. A little less crooked and rakish, a little more straightforward. "Hey, guys. So glad you're here." He held the door as we passed through, then reached for the bowl of potato salad I'd brought and the bag containing the bottles of wine. "Let me take those."

"Thanks." As soon as my hands were empty, I began twisting my ring around my finger.

"There she is!" Lenore came barreling around the corner and scooped Abby up, setting her on her hip, even though she was really too big for that. "I'm so happy to see you. And do you know what? I heard you wanted to see some pictures of your daddy when he was a boy and I've got just hundreds of them! Would you like to see them?"

"Yes," said Abby happily, her feet swinging. She also clutched the little stuffed elephant Wes had given her yesterday.

Lenore glanced at me. "Hello, dear."

"Hi, Lenore."

"Make yourself at home. There's lemonade and sweet tea if you'd like it, and I've set out some snacks on the island."

"Thank you."

She carried Abby off into the great room, sat on the couch with her, and opened a photo album on her lap, one of a stack of albums on the coffee table.

Wes appeared with both bottles of wine I'd brought in his hands. "Which one would you like?"

"The sauvignon blanc would be great." Thank God for Wes. I did not want sweet tea right now.

"You can look at the pictures with them if you want. I'll bring it out to you."

I glanced at Lenore and Abby, who seemed thoroughly engrossed in the album, and decided it was a moment best left to grandmother and granddaughter. If I went over there, Abby would likely have climbed onto my lap, and as satisfying as that might have been, I decided against it. "You know what? I think I'll let your mom spend a little time alone with Abby talking about Drew. I think it would be good for both of them."

Wes nodded. "I think you're right. How about the deck? Or we could head down to the beach?"

"Beach sounds wonderful." I followed him into the kitchen.

While Wes opened the wine, I perched on a bar stool at

the marble-topped island. "Where's your dad?" I asked. Dr. Parks was wonderful, and I had a soft spot for him. I liked to think he had one for me, too.

"He got a call from his answering service and made a house call."

"I love that he still does that. It's so old-fashioned."

Wes poured two glasses of pale amber wine. "It is. Although I'm kind of used to the idea that a physician should go where he's needed."

"So will you do that too?" I asked. "Make house calls?"

"Sure," he said, sliding a glass toward me. "That's one of the best parts about being a doctor in a semi-rural area. More flexibility to go where people need you."

"Drew didn't make house calls very often." I shrugged. "But I don't know if that's because he didn't want to or because your dad really liked doing it."

"I don't know either," he admitted.

We were silent, both of us taking a sip of wine.

"Do you ever feel guilty about those things?" Wes asked. "Like the things you didn't ask him that aren't really that important big picture, but things you wonder about?"

"All the time," I said. "For example, I'm not even sure what his favorite color was. Is that horrible?"

Wes cocked his head. "Was it blue?"

I threw my hands up. "I don't know. I don't think I ever asked. He had a lot of blue shirts, so maybe?"

"Maybe."

"What's yours?" I asked.

"I like blue. It reminds me of the lake."

Both of us glanced out the windows toward the water. "Did you miss it?"

"I did. Africa is beautiful, though."

I sighed and took another sip of wine. "I'd like to go there someday. I've never been anywhere."

Wes took another drink too, his brow furrowing. "What do you mean?"

"Well, I've never been anywhere *far*." I lifted my shoulders. "Drew and I never quite made it to Europe like we planned, and I didn't have the money growing up. The farthest I've been is probably Florida."

"Where would you go? If you could go anywhere."

"Hmmm. Maybe Italy? My mother is Italian and I really do love Italian food and culture. I think it would be cool to explore my roots. Or something." I laughed, a little embarrassed. "That sounds silly."

"No, it doesn't. Not at all. I've been having those same kinds of feelings lately. Maybe because I've been away from home for so long. And even though it was by choice, there's still something to be said for that feeling you get when you come back."

"Yeah. I get that."

A whoop of laughter made us both look toward the great room. Wes spoke softly. "This is so great for my mom. She loves Abby so much."

"I know." I stared into my wine. "I haven't been that good about making Abby...available to her. I don't know why."

Wes didn't reply, but his silence didn't feel at all judgmental. I remembered that about him. His silences, and the way they invited confidence.

"My therapist said I might be punishing her."

He tilted his head. "What do you mean? Punishing who?"

I took a deep breath and another gulp of wine. I'd never talked about this with anyone outside therapy, not even

Tess. "My therapist thinks that I might be unconsciously trying to punish Lenore by keeping Abby from her, because I never felt fully accepted by her when Drew was alive. It always seemed like we were in this, I don't know, *competition* for his affection. It sounds stupid and he always said I was crazy, but it was how I felt." I met his eyes. "Do you think I could be doing that?"

He didn't answer right away. He held my gaze, then dropped his to his wine, which he swirled in his glass. "I think," he said, "that you've suffered a lot. And that it's only natural to want to keep your daughter close to you."

I took another drink and let that sink in.

"We're not perfect, Hannah. And grief is overwhelming. It makes you feel helpless, like everything is out of control. Since time with Abby is something you *can* control, maybe you sort of cling to that as protection." He paused before going on. "I think it's why I threw myself into my work—along with being a distraction from grief, helping people made me feel more in control. Like I wasn't powerless against death."

"I hate that feeling," I said, shivering. "The fear that no matter what we do, death is just coming for us when it wants to and there's nothing we can do about it. Do you know I still hate the sound of my doorbell, because every time it rings I think it's the police coming to tell me someone else is dead?"

He nodded. "I have nightmares a lot. Where I'm trying to operate on someone's heart and I don't know how to do it. I can't save them. In the end, the person is always Drew."

"Oh God, I hate the nightmares," I said. "You wake up screaming and sweating and frantic, and then there's the moment of relief when you realize it was just a dream, except it's taken away from you the very next second because you look around and realize he's still gone. You're still alone."

"I wonder all the time if I could have saved him," Wes went on. "Like, if I hadn't been halfway across the world, maybe we'd have been running together. Maybe there would have been something I could have done." His beautiful, familiar eyes grew shiny. "But I wasn't here."

"Wes, don't." I touched his arm. His skin was warm beneath my palm. "Don't do that to yourself."

"I'm sorry." He backed away from me a little and shook his head. "I invited you over to have fun today and here we are talking about death."

"Hey, listen. I know better than anyone what a constant companion grief is. And she's a bitch, too. Just when you think you've gotten rid of her, she shows up again."

Wes laughed a little, rubbed the back of his neck. "Yeah."

"And we *are* going to have fun today." I sipped my wine. "Tons of fun. And then later..."

"We'll feel guilty about it," he finished.

"Exactly." Our eyes met. Something was exchanged between us—understanding, sympathy, regret—I don't know what it was. But it eased something within me. It was like we were both in on the cruel joke our feelings played on us. I smiled ruefully.

He put a hand on my shoulder. "You're not alone, Hannah. I promise."

Something happened when he touched me. Something floaty and quivery in my stomach I hadn't felt in years.

"Should we go down to the beach?" he asked, taking his hand off me.

But the feeling lingered. I wasn't sure I liked it. "Sure." With one more glance at Abby, who was totally swept up in her grandmother's stories and photos, I faked a smile at Wes. "Let's go."

He refilled our glasses, tucked the bottle of wine into a sleeve pulled from the freezer, and led the way across the lawn, past the seawall, and down the steps to the beach. Before I could stop myself, I realized I was staring at his butt as he walked ahead of me. It looked nice and round in his red bathing suit.

What on earth? Stop that.

It was warm and a little breezy on the beach, but the waves were gentle. They calmed my nerves.

"Want to go out in the canoe?" he asked.

"Okay." I ditched my flip-flops on the small, beach-level deck, and we set our wine glasses and the bottle on the deck's little round table. Wes was already barefoot. Together we dragged the forest green canoe from the tall beach grasses on the side of the deck down to the water's edge and tipped it over.

"Let me rinse it out a little," Wes said, frowning at the dirt and spider webs inside. "Want to grab the paddles? They should be in the shed."

"On it." I went to the small shed on the embankment, opened it up and grabbed the oars, which stood in one corner. On the shelves were life jackets and sand toys and deflated rafts that probably had holes in them, and scratched into the wooden door among other graffiti was WP + CB. Huh. I'd never noticed that before. Who was CB? I glanced over my shoulder at Wes, who'd taken off his T-shirt and tossed it onto the sand.

My stomach full-out flipped.

Quickly, I shut the door to the shed and brought the oars down to the canoe.

Wes stood up straight and stuck his hands on his hips.

He wore different sunglasses than Drew had worn, more of an aviator than a wayfarer. The body was similar, though Wes's arms seemed more muscular, especially through the shoulder. Other things were the same and caused a rippling low in my body—the soft maroon color of his nipples, the trim waist, the trail of hair leading from his belly button to beneath the low-slung waistband of his red swim trunks. In my head I heard Tess's voice. *Arms. Chest. Shoulders. Skin. Stubble. Muscle. The smell of a man. The solidity of him.*

"What's the law on drinking and canoeing?" he asked.

What's the law on staring at your brother-in-law's nipples? I wondered, swallowing hard. What was wrong with me?

"I think we're okay," I said, handing the oars to him. Our hands touched in the exchange. "Let me grab our glasses."

"Perfect. If you hold them, I'll take us out."

I retrieved the wine glasses from the table and walked carefully across the sand to the lake's edge, taking deep, slow breaths. A sweat had broken out across my back. I was wearing a swimsuit beneath my cover up, a modest tankini, but I didn't want to remove it. Wading ankle deep, I attempted to step into the canoe, but it wobbled beneath my foot.

"Whoa." Wes took me by the elbow and didn't let go until I was seated at one end, facing the other. "Okay?"

I nodded. Despite the heat, my arms had broken out in goose flesh.

"All right, here we go." As he rowed us away from shore, the breeze picked up, cooling my face and chest and back.

"Drew and I used to have canoe-tipping contests."

I snapped my chin down and skewered Wes with a look over the top of my sunglasses. "Don't even think about it."

He just grinned, the muscles in his arms and chest and

stomach flexing with every stroke of the oars through the water. Momentarily mesmerized, I allowed myself the pleasure of watching him. It was okay if we were both thinking about Drew, wasn't it?

In fact, it was only natural that I was intrigued by the sight of Wes's body. He was my husband's identical twin, for heaven's sake, and I missed his physical presence in my life. I missed looking at him naked. I missed feeling the weight of him above me. I missed the feeling of being aroused by him, of my body's responses to his touch, his kiss, his cock.

Deep in my body, the rusty mechanism of arousal creaked to life. My nipples peaked, my stomach hollowed, and something fluttered between my legs.

Oh, Jesus.

I sat up straighter, pressed my knees together, and closed my mouth, which I realized had fallen open. Hopefully I hadn't moaned or anything. After another sip of wine, I turned my head and studied a freighter off in the distance. My heart was beating way too fast.

It's only natural. It's only natural.

Wes stopped paddling and set the oars in the bottom of the canoe, their handles resting against the seat in the middle. "We'll have to bring Abby out here."

"Definitely." Did my voice sound normal? "She'll love it. Here, want this?" I held his wine glass toward him and he reached out to take it. His fingers brushed mine, and I pulled my hand back as if the touch had burned me.

"Thanks." He tipped the glass up then looked along the shore. "I'd like to find a place on the lake. Maybe not along *this* stretch of beach, though."

I caught his meaning and smiled. "A little too close to home?"

"Yeah. But I don't want to be too far away. I'd like to get a boat too."

"What kind of boat? Drew always talked about it, but we never quite settled on one."

"Not sure. Maybe just a little fishing boat, something to ski behind."

"That sounds fun. Drew loved to ski."

"We'll have to teach Abby."

I laughed. "*You*, not we. I managed to get up and stay up a few times, but I am not the expert."

"You can teach her to cook, I'll teach her to water ski."

"Deal." Separate activities seemed like a good idea.

"Breakfast was incredible."

"Thanks." I tucked a strand of hair that had escaped my ponytail behind my ear, but the wind blew it right back into my face. "I really like working there. I'm so glad Georgia suggested it to me."

"How long have you been there?"

"Since spring, when they got busy. I'm not sure what I'll do this winter when it slows down. I'm dreading it, actually. Abby will be in school full time, and it will just be me at home alone." This was something else I hadn't talked about with anyone, how worried I was that the gray skies and cold weather and silent hours would set me spiraling into depression. "I always thought I'd have another baby to take care of, but life saw things differently."

"You're still young, Hannah."

I shook my head. "I'm really not. And I feel even older than I am." *Please don't go Grief Police on me and tell me I'm being ridiculous*, I begged him silently. *This isn't the life I chose. It was handed to me and I'm doing the best I can.*

But he didn't say anything more, just sipped his wine and looked out at the horizon. I was grateful.

"What about you?" I asked. "Think maybe you'll get married now that you're back? Have a family? Abby won't have any siblings so she needs some cousins."

"That seems to be a popular topic of discussion around here," Wes said, shaking his head, "but I really have no idea."

"Small town. We like to know everyone's business." I smiled. "Hey, what about CB? I saw your initials carved with hers on the door of the shed. Maybe she's still around."

He groaned. "Is that still there? Jesus. That had to be twenty years ago."

Hugging my knees, I leaned forward. "First love?"

"Not even." He hesitated, as if he were trying to decide whether to confess something.

"Come on," I cajoled, carefully reaching out of the canoe, and splashing water toward him. "Tell me. I've been spilling my guts for an hour."

"First kiss."

I squealed. "And?"

He cringed. "It's too embarrassing."

"Wes, I had a completely humiliating breakdown in front of you last night. I got snot on my arm."

"This is worse."

"Get it out. You'll feel better."

"Let's just say it was a very awkward, very *fast* experience."

I gasped. "You lost your virginity to her?"

"No. Just my dignity."

Laughing, I tilted my head back and felt the sun on my face, the wind in my hair, and something like joy in my heart.

It had been a long time.

SIX

WES

IT WAS EXACTLY the kind of day I'd wanted—for Abby, for Hannah, for my parents, for myself. We took Abby out in the canoe, we built a sand castle complete with a moat and keep, we walked along the beach looking for fossils and sea glass. We talked. We laughed. We remembered Drew with funny stories and favorite memories. It was the first time since he'd died that we had all been together without being overwhelmed by sadness.

After dinner, I helped Abby find a stick to roast marsh-mallows. My mother tried to talk us into using metal skewers she'd brought down to the beach, but I insisted we had to do it the real way. We stood side by side holding our sticks with the marshmallows over the flames, watching them get warm and brown and bubbly. I like mine nearly charred, but I left my first one over the fire too long and it plopped into the ashes, which made Abby giggle uncon-trollably.

And Hannah—I hoped she felt as happy as she looked. She had a smile on her face all afternoon, and I saw no trace of the tension I'd sensed in her this morning. In complete contrast, she seemed relaxed and contented, joking with my father, tolerating my mother's criticisms-disguised-as-compliments ("My goodness, look how thin you are in that swimsuit! I can't hardly see your shadow!"), and giving me a grateful look when I went back for seconds of her potato salad and told my dad he had to try it. (He did, and enjoyed it, much to my mother's chagrin.) She'd even stopped playing with her wedding ring. Everything about the day was perfect.

There was only one problem.

My heart beat faster every time I looked at her. My stomach tightened every time she came near me. My breath hitched every time I caught the scent of her skin—a potent mix of Coppertone and waffles. I was nearly drunk on it by day's end.

I wasn't imagining my body's responses to her, and by the time the sun went down I was finally forced to admit it had nothing to do with how much we both loved or missed Drew, and everything to do with the fact that I was attracted to her, plain and simple. I always had been.

Other truths I'd buried threatened to surface.

She's part of the reason I stayed away.

I measure every woman I meet against her, and no one ever comes close.

What if? What if? What if?

I tried hard to ignore my feelings. Deny them. Convince myself there was nothing wrong with appreciating a beautiful woman.

Yeah, but you don't just want to appreciate her, do you?

asked my conscience, which seemed to have a direct line of communication with my dick. *You want to—*

Don't even think it.

I thought it.

I wanted to touch her. Kiss her. Know what it was like to be inside her. Feel her hands on my body. Hear her soft moans and loud cries and make her come over and over again.

You're an asshole.

God. I was an asshole. In no universe were these feelings about my brother's wife okay. They'd never been okay. But what could I do? Tell her to put her cover-up back on because the sight of her slender curves in a bathing suit was too tempting? Tell her to stop giggling at my stupid jokes and stories because the sound of her laughter was too sweet? Tell her to stop looking at me that way when I took off my shirt because I wasn't my brother no matter how much I looked like him? I wasn't an idiot. I knew it wasn't me she was seeing.

No matter how much I wished it was.

Look, you can't turn back time. You made your choice, and they made theirs. And you know what? If you had to do it all over again, you'd make the same decision. You'd step aside for him, you always did.

I frowned into the fire.

"Hey, you." Hannah nudged me with her bare foot. She and I were sitting next to each other in chairs by the dwindling bonfire while Abby played nearby in the sand. My parents had just gone up to the house. "Everything okay?"

I sat up straighter, took a drink of my scotch. I'd poured some over ice when it became clear my stupid feelings for her had not gone away, no matter how much time and distance I'd put between us. "Yeah. Fine."

"*Fine*, huh? I give that answer a lot too."

I braved a glance at her, and her expression was shrewd. Then she nudged me again with her foot. "I'm on to you, pal."

For fuck's sake, did she have to touch me? She was making things worse. "Sometimes I'm just quiet."

"I remember that about you." She tipped up her wine glass, and I couldn't take my eyes off the hollow at the base of her throat. "But actually, I think you've been very talkative today."

"Have I?"

"Yes. And you're an amazing listener. I appreciate it."

Not if you knew what I was thinking. "Any time."

A minute or two went by. The sun was sinking fast behind the trees, deepening the shadows on the beach. Abby began to sing softly, backed by the rhythmic shush of waves on the shore. "Can I tell you something?" Hannah asked.

"Of course."

"Lots of people have told me, 'You're not alone.' But I haven't felt that way until *you* said those words to me today."

I looked at her and vowed I would never violate the trust she placed in me. "I meant them."

She smiled at me as she stood up. "I better get Abby home and in the tub. But Wes, you were right about today. Thank you. I had such a good time."

"I'm glad."

Then she did something that shocked me—she reached out and slowly slid her fingers through my hair.

I couldn't speak. I wasn't even sure I could breathe.

She smiled. "You have sand in your hair." A moment

later, she was walking away from me. "Come on, Abs. Let's get the toys put away. Time to go home."

I was still sitting there in disbelief when I heard my mother's voice. I hadn't even seen her come down the steps and I was looking right at them.

"Hannah, dear," she called, making her way toward them, "I was thinking earlier, why doesn't Abby just stay the night here? I've got a room all set up for her, and she hardly ever uses it."

Hannah hesitated. "I have the sitter coming in the morning." Then she glanced at me. "But I guess I could give her the day off. Sure. She can stay."

Good girl. I felt proud of her for letting go of the reins a little.

"Perfect!" My mom clapped her hands together. "I'll keep her until you're done with work. You can just pick her up here."

"What about clothes for tomorrow?"

"Oh, I have plenty of things here. You know how I love to shop for her. I always wanted a little girl and ended up with two boys!"

"I can hear you, Mom." Oh good, I could still speak.

She turned to me and stuck her hands on her hips. "Now I'm not saying my boys weren't everything to me, but it is fun to have Abby to shop for. I'd shop for your kids too if you had some," she scolded.

"I was telling him earlier Abby needs some cousins." Hannah turned and gave me a wicked smile over her shoulder. "Make that happen already, why don't you?"

I grimaced and took another swallow of scotch. Just what I needed—Hannah and my mother united in their nagging at me to procreate.

"Abby," my mother said, "let's go up and you can take a bath in the big tub in my bathroom. Would you like that?"

"Yes." The little girl jumped to her feet, brushing sand off her hands and knees.

"And then you can put on your princess nightgown and I'll read you a story if you're not worn slap out."

"I'll get the toys put away down here. Do you need help getting her into the bath?" Hannah asked.

My mother dismissed that idea with a wave of her hand and headed for the steps, Abby in tow. "Not at all."

While Hannah texted her sitter, I started gathering up buckets and shovels and adding them to the big plastic laundry basket my mother used to keep them all corralled. Hannah joined me a couple minutes later, scooping up brightly-colored molds of fish and mermaids and castle walls. If she felt strange about what she'd done a few minutes ago, she didn't let on. Maybe I was making more of the gesture than was warranted. Maybe I'd even imagined it.

"Are you proud of me?" she asked.

"Yes."

She sighed dramatically. "I decided today after our chat that I should try harder with Lenore. I know she means well."

"Good. Get everything settled with your sitter?"

"Yes. All set. She's probably glad to have the day off. It's supposed to be beautiful again tomorrow, although it looks like it might rain tonight." She glanced at the sky.

"If you want to hang out on the beach after work when you come to get Abby, feel free." But I sort of hoped she wouldn't.

"Thanks. Maybe I will."

When the toys were all in the bin, I took a bucket out

again and headed for the lake to fill it up. "You can go up if you want. I'm just going to put out the fire."

But she didn't go up. She stood and watched as I doused the remains of the fire, her arms crossed over her chest. I wished I'd put my shirt back on. I felt her eyes on me through the smoke. They wandered over my shoulders and chest and stomach, but when they moved lower than that, she caught herself and looked down at her feet, her lower lip caught between her teeth.

Hannah, you're killing me. Don't look at me that way. You don't really mean it. When the smoke clears, I'm not who you want. I'm not him.

Neither of us spoke. The sky above us darkened unexpectedly, and thunder rolled softly in the distance.

You shouldn't be alone with her like this.

"Sounds like a storm. You should go up," I told her.

"I'll wait with you. I don't mind."

"Hannah." My voice was stern. "Go up."

A pause. "Okay. Goodnight."

Quickly, she gathered her things—bag, towel, flip flops—and disappeared up the steps.

I exhaled.

LATER, as I lay in bed feeling despicable and shitty, listening to a summer rain drum against the roof, I replayed the memory of her hand in my hair a thousand times. The slow drag of her fingers, the warmth in her eyes, the hushed voice. I thought about how she'd looked at me by the fire and the dangerous way it made me feel. I wish I knew what she'd been thinking.

She was thinking about her husband, jerkoff. Remember

him? Your brother? Maybe she was even pretending you were him.

That had to be it. I couldn't even blame her. But God, I wished things were different.

Rolling to my back, I put my hands behind my head and stared at the ceiling for a moment before closing my eyes.

There she was. Smiling and soft and sweet and reaching for me. *Me.* Finding ease in *my* kiss. Seeking pleasure in *my* body. Whispering *my* name in the dark.

My cock started to stiffen, and I suppressed the urge to take it in my hand.

How many nights had I refused to let that fantasy take root in my mind because it was so wrong? A hundred? A thousand? *It's still wrong. Nothing has changed. She doesn't belong to you. She never has, and she never will.*

I had to get over this. But how? Avoid seeing her? That wouldn't work. Earlier today I'd campaigned to see each other more often, and now she agreed with me.

Maybe it would go away on its own. Maybe I simply had to get used to being around her again, desensitize myself to her charms. Maybe spending time with her would be sort of like allergy shots. Immunotherapy for the heart.

And other parts of my body that like to come alive around her.

Groaning, I rolled onto my side, punched my pillow a few times, and went to sleep.

SEVEN

HANNAH

AFTER SAYING good goodnight to Abby, I left my in-laws' house and called Tess on my way home.

"How was it?" she asked by way of greeting.

"Fine." I smiled, even though she couldn't see it. "It was fine, and I'm not even lying."

She laughed. "Good."

"Actually, you know what? It was better than fine. I had the best day I've had in months. I felt...happy. I think everyone did."

"That's great, Hannah."

"I won't say it isn't hard to deal with the fact that Wes looks exactly like the dead man I'm in love with, and there may have been some covert staring and borderline-inappropriate touching of his hair—"

"What?" She coughed. "You just made me choke on my wine."

Wincing a little, I tried to explain myself. "I just really

loved Drew's hair. And Wes wears his the same way. I've been dying to run my fingers through it. Like a comfort thing, I guess. Finally I just reached out and did it. It was almost involuntary, I swear to God."

"Did anyone see?"

"No. Only Abby was on the beach with us at that point, and she wasn't looking."

"What did he do?"

"Nothing. I think he was kind of stunned, but I also think he gets it. He gets *me*, you know? It's almost eerie how well he understands my feelings."

"Really?"

"Yes."

"I'm so happy for you. You're even giving me hope. Maybe they aren't all lying when they say, 'It gets easier.'"

I laughed sympathetically. "Maybe they aren't. That's what it felt like today, anyway."

"That's all that matters."

"YOU LOOK PRETTY TODAY," Georgia told me at work the next morning. "I mean, you're pretty every day, but you look especially glowy this morning."

"Thanks." I tied an apron around me and began gathering ingredients for spinach, ricotta, and bacon crepes. "Must be the sun I got yesterday. Or maybe the good night's sleep."

"A good night's sleep." Margot shook her head wistfully as she poured herself a cup of coffee. Beneath her blue eyes were the puffy bags worn by all new moms. "I remember those. Tell me I'll have one again someday."

"You will," I said. "In about eighteen years. The only

reason I managed to grab eight straight hours last night was because Abby slept at her grandparents' house. Most nights she wakes me up at least once for something or other."

"Did you guys have fun yesterday?" Georgia asked.

"We did. I'm so glad we went." In fact, all I could think about was getting back there today. I'd brought my beach bag with me to work, figuring I might as well take Wes up on his invitation to hang out at the beach a little this afternoon.

The morning passed quickly since we were so busy, and the crepes were especially popular. Because I thought Wes might like to try them, I made an extra batch up after the last order from the dining room had been filled and put them in a container for him. Just after two, I said goodbye to Georgia and Margot and hurried out the door.

Despite the rain the night before, the weather today was hot and sunny, only a few puffy white clouds in the sky. I opened the sunroof on my Honda, tuned into a satellite radio station playing old standards and sang along as I drove, windows down, breeze rushing through my hair. It was the closest to happy I'd felt in a long time.

Wes answered my knock, smiling broadly when he saw me. "Hey, you. Come on in. How was work?"

"Good. Busy." I went inside and held out the container. "I brought you something."

"You did? What?"

"Spinach, ricotta, and bacon crepes. They were really popular today, and I thought you might like them."

His eyes lit up. "My mouth is watering. Can I taste them?"

I laughed. "Yes! They're yours. You don't have to eat them now, but—"

"I'm eating them now." He'd grabbed them and was

already on his way into the kitchen. "This is perfect. I just came up to get something to eat."

"Where is everybody?" I followed him, glancing around the quiet house.

"They're all down on the beach. My mom got Abby a little fishing pole and my dad is showing her how to use it." He took a fork from a drawer, set the container on the marble-topped island, and pried off the top. "Damn, that looks good. Wait, I should warm it up, right?"

"Here, I'll do it." I stuck the container in the microwave and nuked it for twenty seconds before setting it in front of him again. "There you go. *Bon appetit.*"

He dug in, moaning as he chewed the first bite.

I smiled. "You like them?"

"Are you kidding? God, between your cooking and my mother's, I'm going to gain ten pounds in a month."

"I doubt that."

"Have you eaten? Share this with me." Without waiting for me to answer, he grabbed another fork from the drawer and stuck it in my hand.

Normally I wouldn't have, but I'd skipped lunch, and I was feeling unusually hungry. "Thanks."

We ate standing next to each other at the island, and he told me about how much fun he had reading Abby a story, eating the breakfast she helped make this morning (chocolate chip pancakes with bananas), and looking through the old photo albums with her. "She loved the ones of Drew and me from kindergarten. She's so excited to go."

I nodded, then shoved the thought aside as I rinsed my fork and put it in the dishwasher. I'd deal with the kindergarten thing eventually, but not today. "I'm just going to throw my suit on," I said, grabbing my bag and heading for the first floor bathroom, which Lenore called the "powder room."

"Okay. Want me to wait for you?"

"No, that's okay. You can go down."

Since the suit I'd worn yesterday was dirty, I'd brought a different one today. A two-piece. It was still modest by any standards, sort of a retro style with a high-waist bottom and a halter-style top that covered my chest completely. I did a quick assessment in the mirror, turning side to side. I wished I filled out my suit a little better, but I agreed with Georgia that a little sun on my face did wonders. I smoothed my ponytail, noticing the ends were pretty scraggly. I couldn't even remember my last trip to the salon. *Definitely time for a trim.* Leaning closer to my reflection, I inspected a couple lines around my eyes I hadn't noticed before and rubbed my lips together, wishing I'd brought along a lipstick.

What the hell are you doing? Why would you need lipstick at the beach?

As if I'd been caught misbehaving, I straightened up, snapped off the light, and hurried down to the beach. Why did I suddenly care about my appearance? And why did I feel guilty about it? Wouldn't it be a positive sign if I put a little more effort into looking nice?

Not if it's because of Wes.

Fuck. Was it? I stopped halfway down the steps. My eyes went first to Abby, who was standing ankle-deep in the water next to Dr. Parks, and then to Wes, who was dragging the canoe toward the lake's edge. He'd taken his shirt off. My insides tightened, and I touched my stomach.

Just keep looking at him, I reminded myself. *The more you do it, the less effect his appearance will have on you.*

Except...I kind of liked the effect. How long had it been

since I'd felt the long, slow pull of desire? Since I'd considered my body something other than a vessel for my emotions? Since I'd felt like a *woman* and not simply a widow?

A long fucking time.

And even though it was wrong of me to want to hold on to it for a little longer, given who was inspiring the feeling, I did. God help me, I did.

He looked up and saw me. "Hey, Abby and I were just going to go for a ride. Want to join us?" he called.

"Definitely!" I jogged the rest of the way down the steps. "Let me just get some sunscreen on."

Dr. Parks greeted me with a wave. "Hi, honey."

"Hi, Doc."

"Mommy!" Abby came running over and threw her arms around my legs.

"Hi, baby! I missed you! Did you have a good time?" I ruffled her damp hair.

"Yes! Nana and I made pancakes, and Papa is teaching me to fish."

"Fun!" She went back into the water, and I walked over to where Lenore was sitting under a big red umbrella. "Hi, Lenore."

"Hello, dear." Lenore looked at my swimsuit a little too long. "Make sure you put some sunscreen on that tummy. Are you sure you shouldn't wear a shirt over that suit? I don't want you to get burned."

"I'll be fine." Pulling a tube of lotion from my bag, I rubbed some SPF 30 all over my face and chest.

"Only 30? Are you going to wear a hat, too? Oh, but then I guess you've got that olive complexion." She clucked her tongue. "I always had to be so careful because I was so fair. Had that peaches n' cream skin, just like Abby does.

Abby," she called out. "Come over here and let Nana put a little more sunscreen on you! I tried to get her to wear a hat today since she had so much sun yesterday, but she's got quite a little stubborn streak, doesn't she? Just like her daddy."

Abby did have a stubborn streak, but I didn't particularly feel like agreeing with Lenore on anything at the moment, so I stayed silent. Part of me wanted to put more sunscreen on Abby myself, but I let that go too, focusing instead on spraying my own arms and legs and stomach.

"Here, let me get your back."

I turned around, and Wes was standing there. "Um. Okay." Handing him the can, I presented my back to him, hoping my face wasn't flushed bright red. *What the hell? It's not like he's going to give you a massage. It's fucking sunscreen.*

Still.

Wes sprayed my upper and lower back, and I'd have sworn you could hear my skin sizzle. "Want to lift up your hair and I'll get your neck?"

I held my ponytail on top of my head while he sprayed my neck and shoulders.

"I smell cake. Is that your hair or the sunscreen?" He laughed. "Or do I just want dessert?"

My heart was pounding. "My shampoo, maybe?"

He came closer and sniffed my head. "Yeah, that's it. Smells good."

Next thing I knew, I felt his fingertips brushing down one shoulder blade. Too quickly to be called a caress, but too slowly to be ruled an accident.

I dropped my arms and turned around, but his expression gave nothing away. He smiled as he handed me back the can of sunscreen. I bent down and stuck it back in my bag, taking an extra moment to process what had just happened.

He touched me. And I liked it.

It made me feel pretty. And admired. And flattered. Things I hadn't felt in forever. Things I'd never thought I'd feel again.

"If you're hungry, I'd be happy to make you a plate, Wes." Lenore finished rubbing lotion onto Abby's scrunched-up face and recapped the tube. "It will just take a minute."

"No thanks, Mom."

"But you didn't eat lunch yet, did you?"

"Actually, I did. Hannah brought something from the inn. It was delicious."

"You didn't tell me that." Lenore sounded injured.

"Sorry, Mom. I'm a guy. We tend to eat and move on to the next thing. Ready to go, Abby?" he asked.

"Yes! Mommy, will you come too?" Abby's voice yanked me out of my daze.

"Sure I will." I stood up. My skin was still tingling from his touch.

"What was it?" Lenore asked.

Wes looked at me. "Uh…"

I smiled at his guilty expression. "Bacon, ricotta, and spinach crepes."

He snapped his fingers. "That's it. Sorry, couldn't think. But they were amazing. Thanks for bringing them."

"You're welcome. I'm glad you liked them." I began walking toward the canoe before Lenore could say anything else that would dull the pleasant hum beneath my skin.

TWO HOURS WENT BY, and I didn't want to leave. Then three. Four.

Lenore and Doc had gone up to the house to get ready for a cocktail party friends of theirs were throwing, so Wes and Abby and I had the beach to ourselves most of the afternoon. We did all the things we'd done yesterday, but it felt more intimate today with only the three of us. We swam and played in the sand and walked along the shore, swinging Abby between us by the arms. *This is what it would be like if Drew were here*, some part of my brain kept reminding me. *This is what we'd have.*

It was hard to keep myself from running away with the fantasy, especially with the memory of his fingers on my skin. But other than that one incident, he never touched me again. He talked and laughed and teased me sometimes, but it was nothing that could be construed as flirting. It almost reminded me of when I'd first met him—I'd thought he was so cute and smart and sweet, and I'd hoped he'd ask me out, but when weeks went by and he didn't so much as ask for my last name, let alone my number, I'd given up. And then Drew came on like a hurricane—just as good-looking, just as smart, but with all the confidence and swagger his brother lacked. Swept me right off my feet.

"Do you remember the day Drew and I met?" I asked. We were sitting next to each other on towels in the sand watching Abby play with her toy fishing rod in shallow water.

Wes laughed a little and glanced at me. "Yeah. I do."

"What's funny?"

"Nothing. I just..." He draped his arms over his knees. Stared straight ahead. "I think about that day a lot, actually."

"You do?" That surprised me. "Why?"

He was quiet a minute. "It was an important day, wasn't it? Lives were changed forever."

"But we didn't know that then."

Another pause. "I think I knew."

I looked at him, but he kept his eyes on Abby. When he didn't offer anything further—not that I knew what I wanted him to say, just *something*—I went on. "I was thinking about that day just now."

"Oh yeah?"

"Yeah." I hugged my knees to my chest and wiggled my toes in the sand. "I couldn't believe how different you two were."

He smiled slightly.

"You were always such a gentleman, and he was so obnoxious. I couldn't believe some of the things he said."

"Yeah. But it worked for him." Wes looked at me. "He got everything he wanted."

"You think so?"

"I know it."

Tears blurred my eyes, and my throat tightened. What the hell? I'd been having such a good day, and suddenly my emotions were all over the place. What came out of my mouth next shocked me. "Drew cheated on me."

Wes froze. "What?"

"Once. When Abby was a baby and things were tough at home. She wasn't a good eater or sleeper and things were difficult. I wasn't paying attention to him." The words gushed out like blood from a wound.

Wes opened and closed his mouth several times, then focused on Abby again, clearly at a loss for words. His hands had closed into fists.

"You don't have to say anything." A tear slipped from one eye, and I wiped it from my cheek. "He told me afterward. He felt so bad about it. He cried. I'd never seen him cry before. But I was so hurt and angry. Because he'd promised me, you know? He'd promised me." I looked at Wes, watched his Adam's apple bob as he swallowed. "I've never told this to anyone before. I don't even know why I'm telling you now."

Wes's lips were pressed together in a thin line, but he still didn't respond.

"I think it's that...I forgave him, but I'm still angry about it. And there's nowhere for that anger to go now. How can I be mad that he cheated on me in the face of what happened? What's one transgression, for which he was truly, deeply sorry, compared to all the wonderful things he was? He didn't deserve to die."

"Of course he didn't."

I sniffed, wiping another tear from my cheek. "But what kind of person am I to hold on to anger like that? I couldn't even bring myself to tell my therapist, because it felt so disloyal to speak ill of him."

"Fuck, Hannah. You're human. He hurt you."

"Yes."

"He shouldn't have done that." Wes's voice was low and hard.

"No, but it was just one mistake. He was so much more than that. You know he was. But no one else does. They might...judge him."

"Of course I know it. But he wasn't perfect. And we don't have to pretend that he was just because we loved him and he's gone now."

I took a few deep breaths, letting that sink in. "You're right. I know you're right. I guess it's just one more thing that feels...I don't know. *Unresolved.* But there's nothing I can do about it."

A few minutes passed before he spoke again. "I'm sorry he did that to you."

"You don't need to apologize for him."

"It's not for him. It's for me."

"Thanks." I couldn't resist leaning his way and tipping my head to his shoulder, the way I used to do with Drew. "I'm sorry I just unloaded that on you. It wasn't fair."

"It's okay." A moment later, he went on. "I'm here for you. I always will be."

I wished he would put an arm around me, but he didn't, and I decided I'd imagined his earlier touch. It couldn't have been Wes. It was something Drew would have done—he was casually affectionate like that—so my mind, knowing how desperately I missed his touch, had played a trick on me.

Just another ghost.

I HAD trouble sleeping that night, dreading the sunrise that would officially make it the day before Abby started kindergarten. All I could think of was how Drew would miss it. Just like he'd missed her first day of preschool. Just like he'd missed her first wiggly tooth. Just like he'd miss every conference and concert and school play. Her Prom. Her graduation. Her wedding. It would be me alone through it all, watching her grow up until finally she left me, too. What would I do then? Who would I be? How would I survive when she no longer needed me?

I was bleary-eyed and silent the next morning at work. Georgia would have forced me to talk about it, which probably would have resulted in a meltdown right there in the kitchen, but thankfully, it was Pete working the Labor Day breakfast shift. If he noticed something was off with me, he didn't mention it.

After work, I tried to combat the feeling of impending doom by taking Abby to the park, helping her pack up all her new school supplies in the pink and purple backpack she'd picked out, and letting her help me make Italian meatloaf for dinner. It was my mother's recipe, and made me a little lonesome for her. I thought of calling her, but she'd ask me how I was doing, and I didn't feel like I could answer that question without breaking down.

After dinner, Abby asked if we could walk into town for ice cream.

"Sure," I said, not particularly eager to start the bedtime routine.

"Let's call Uncle Wes."

An alarm bell pinged in my head. I wasn't sure I could handle seeing Wes tonight. "Oh, honey, let's not bother him."

"But I told him we'd call him next time we got ice cream," she wailed. "We have to."

I thought about pretending to call him and saying he didn't answer, but felt too guilty. *This is not just about you.*

He picked up quickly. "Hello?"

Maybe there would be a day when the familiar sound of his voice—so like Drew's—didn't throw me, but that day wasn't today. "Hey, Wes. Abby and I are about to walk into town for some ice cream and wondered if you'd like to come along." *Say no. Say no. Say no.*

"I'd love to. Give me ten minutes?"

"Of course."

We hung up, and I told Abby to use the bathroom. While she did, I went upstairs into my bathroom and dug around in my makeup bag. Dabbed some concealer on the circles under my eyes. But it didn't do enough to erase the anxiety or exhaustion from my face, so I added a little blush and mascara. Ran a brush through my hair. When I was putting my makeup bag back in the drawer, I noticed a bottle of perfume in there. I took it out and sprayed my throat.

But the scent, Drew's favorite, was both a painful reminder of happier days and an accusation—*why are you putting on perfume for another man?*—and a few choked sobs wrenched free from my chest.

Stop it. Get yourself together. You have Abby to think about. And Wes is on his way over. Do you want either one of them to see you like this?

A few deep breaths later, I'd wrested control of myself back from my feelings. The damage to my face wasn't too terrible, and I repaired the eye makeup best I could, figuring a pair of sunglasses would hide the worst of it.

Abby and I waited for Wes outside, and my heart beat erratically when he pulled up and got out of the car. It kept up its uneven rhythm as we walked into town, and I tried to tame it by keeping my eyes on the sidewalk.

"Everything okay, Hannah?" Wes asked when we were halfway there.

I nodded. If I opened my mouth to speak, I knew I'd cry.

It didn't help that Abby insisted on being carried on his shoulders again, and he was all too happy to do it. I envied both of them their carefree smiles, the brightness of their faces, the excitement in their voices as they talked about what flavors they'd get. I wanted to feel that way, too. As we walked, I spun my ring around my finger.

When we got to the shop, I said I didn't want anything, but Wes bought me a cup of pistachio anyway. "You need this," he said as he handed it to me. "Ice cream makes everything better. It's a medical fact."

I managed a smile. "Thanks."

I ate a few bites on the walk home, but couldn't taste it.

"Mommy, can I play on the swings for a little bit?" Abby asked as we walked up the driveway. "Uncle Wes said he'd give me an underdog."

"Five minutes, okay? We have to get you in the tub soon."

"Okay." She grabbed his hand and led him around the house into the yard.

I went inside, tossed my ice cream in the sink, and threw away the cup. Through the window, I watched as Wes pushed Abby on the swing, ducking beneath it as he ran forward and she squealed with delight.

My legs wobbled. It was all so perfect—the sunset and the ice cream and the swing and the first school night of the year and my daughter and this man, this beautiful, kind, smart, sweet, sexy, adoring man here making her laugh. Why couldn't I feel it? Why wasn't I a part of it?

Make me laugh too, I begged silently. *Make me smile. Make me feel things again like you did yesterday. Take this pain away. Take this loneliness. Take this suffering. I'm so tired of being alone.*

For a moment, I let myself fantasize—not that Wes was Drew, but that Wes was my husband and Abby's father. That it was Wes who'd asked me out all those years ago. That it was Wes who'd swept me off my feet, married me, shared my bed every single night.

It was Wes whose hands would undress me later, whose mouth would roam over my bare skin, whose body would move over mine until we were shuddering and clinging and crying out in the dark together—

Together. Together. Together.

My heart began to pound. I could hardly stand still. My hands were trembling. When they came inside and Abby asked if Wes could read her a story after her bath, I hid them behind my back and nodded yes without thinking.

"I have a quick phone call to make," he said, looking at me a little strangely. "I'll be out on the porch. Give me a shout when you're ready."

Upstairs, I put Abby through the motions of her bedtime routine, unable to think about anything other than the fantasy I'd concocted at the kitchen window.

I knew it was wrong.

But I wanted it. I wanted it so badly.

When Abby had brushed her teeth and I'd combed out her hair, she put on her pajamas and got in bed. "Send Uncle Wes up, okay?"

"Okay. I'll come in and say goodnight when he's done."

"Okay."

Out on the porch, Wes was just ending his call. "Thanks so much, Brad. I'll see you tomorrow at six. Yep. Bye." He tucked his phone in his pocket.

"She's ready for you." I stared at his face and imagined my lips moving along the scruff on his jaw, my hands sliding into his hair.

"Thanks. Should I just go up?"

"Sure. Her room is on the left at the top of the stairs."

"Okay. You alright?" Two lines appeared between his brows.

"Fine."

He didn't believe me, I could tell, but he went up the stairs, and I went into the kitchen to make a cup of tea. While it steeped, I sat at the table, my leg jittering nervously. *Stop it. Just stop it. Sex with your brother-in-law is not a good cure for loneliness.*

No matter how hot he was. Or how sweet to your daughter. Or how well he understood you.

Or how badly you suddenly wanted it.

Good God, was I losing my mind?

I sipped my tea and stared at my hands on the cup. Listened to the tick of the clock. Prayed he'd leave quickly once he came down.

About five minutes later, I heard his feet on the stairs. I bolted up from my chair, setting the cup down so hard, tea spilled onto the table. I left it.

We met on the landing, nearly bumping chests. He stepped aside. "She's all yours."

"Okay. Thanks for reading to her." *Say goodnight, Hannah.* But I said nothing, just hurried up the steps to Abby's room.

I sat on her bed and switched off her lamp. "How was the story?"

"Good." She hugged her elephant.

"Want to ask me a question?"

"I already asked Uncle Wes a question."

"What did you ask him?"

"If he could walk to school with us tomorrow."

"What did he say?"

"He said he wasn't sure he could. He's going to see."

"Okay."

"Sing me a song. The one about the trembling trees."

I sang to her, and she was asleep by the time I finished. I kissed her forehead and left her room, wondering if Wes was waiting for me downstairs or not. I hoped he wasn't.

Liar.

I walked down the steps slowly, my hand on the bannister. When I reached the bottom, I glanced out the screen door. His car was still there, and he wasn't in the living room. Taking a deep breath, I walked down the hall into the kitchen.

He was leaning back against the counter. "Hey."

"Hey." I twisted my ring.

"I wanted to make sure you were okay. You seemed a little upset earlier."

"I'm fine."

"*Fine*?" One brow cocked up. It was fucking sexy and adorable. "I'm on to you, pal."

"I don't know what to say. I guess I'm just...not feeling like myself tonight."

"What are you feeling?" he asked quietly.

"Like I wish things were different right now." I shrugged helplessly, giving in to it. "For us. Do you ever wish that things were different?"

He didn't even hesitate. "All the fucking time."

It was all I needed to hear. I threw myself at him, crushing my lips to his and wrapping my arms around his neck. He embraced me immediately, his arms warm and strong around my back, his mouth slanting over mine. He tasted like chocolate and desire. *Yes*, I thought. *Yes, yes, yes. This is the answer.*

I reached for his belt.

EIGHT

WES

THIS COULDN'T BE REAL.

I didn't care.

Even if it was a dream, it was the best damn dream I'd ever had. She wanted me. She *wanted* me. One second she was standing across from me, looking at me like a frightened little bird, and the next she was crashing into me, her lips seeking mine.

I didn't even think—I just pulled her closer and kissed her back like I'd always wanted to. It was almost like a moment out of time, a moment that was supposed to happen long ago, but didn't, and was happening now instead, as if the relentless arrow of time had unexpectedly looped back on itself to explore another possibility.

A terrifying, transcendent possibility.

How far could we let this go?

She reached for my belt.

"Hannah."

"Let me. Please."

I felt her breath on my lips as her fingers fumbled with my belt.

Oh God, this was so fucked up. I wanted to do the right thing, but I was having trouble remembering what that was. I groaned as she slipped the button of my jeans through its hole and lowered my zipper.

"Hannah." I grabbed her wrists, looked her right in the eye. The kitchen was bright enough that I could see her perfectly. She was breathless and wild-eyed and so fucking beautiful. But this wasn't right—I could see it in her face. She was in pain. Desperately lonely and longing for some-one...but how could I be sure it was me? What if she was missing Drew right now and I was just a close enough second? What if I disappointed her? What if Drew had some sort of magic dick or she expected me to know all his moves? Even worse, what if we did this tonight and she regretted it tomorrow? She wasn't in her right frame of mind right now.

And she trusted me.

"You don't want to do this," I said.

"Fuck you. Yes, I do." She struggled against me, but I had her arms captured at her sides. Tears of frustration glassed her eyes. "You don't know how I feel."

"I know you're lonely. I know you miss Drew. I know that you're angry, maybe even at Drew for cheating on you, and this feels like a way to get back at him."

"Right now, I'm angry at *you*." She gave me a look that threatened to singe my skin. "Let me go."

I waited another few seconds until she stopped strug-gling, and then released her wrists. Immediately she slapped me, a bare palm right across the cheek. Not that hard, not that painful, but still, it stung. I grimaced, closing my eyes for a second. "Goddammit, Hannah. I'm doing the right thing."

"Fuck you!" she cried, loud enough to wake Abby. "Fuck you and everyone else for telling me how I feel or what to feel or when I can feel it." She pointed directly at my chest, where my heart was cracking in two. "If you didn't want me, you should have just said so." With tears spilling over, she turned and ran out of the room, and I heard her feet pounding up the stairs a few seconds later.

Exhaling, I ran a hand over my jaw and stood there for a moment, mad as fuck. Hadn't I done the right thing? Hadn't I saved us both from the wretched fallout of what would certainly have been a terrible mistake? Did she know how easily I could have let it happen, how fast I could have torn off her clothes, thrown her down, and fucked her right there on the kitchen floor? Or on the table? Or standing right here with her legs wrapped around me, my hands gripping her ass as I drove into her again and again and again?

Fuck. I adjusted myself and zipped up my pants, but my dick stubbornly refused to surrender.

So now what? Did I just leave? Let her think I didn't want her? Let her believe she'd imagined the closeness between us? I'd felt it too, all damn day. I'd practically had to sit on my hands all afternoon to keep from touching her again after I lost my senses and ran my fingers down her back. But I hadn't been able to resist.

And then when she'd asked me tonight if I ever wished things were different for us, I answered honestly before I even had time to consider the consequences of the truth. Instead, I'd given her the invitation, hadn't I? I'd essentially admitted to feeling something for her, knowing how vulnerable and lonely she was. Knowing how conflicted she'd been feeling earlier today about Drew.

Knowing that when she looked at me, she felt something stir inside her—even if it wasn't for *me*. I'd taken advantage of that.

This was all my fucking fault.

Sighing, I made sure the back door was locked, turned off the light in the kitchen and made my way through the hall toward the front door. At the landing of the staircase, I paused and listened to the wrenching sound of muffled sobs. My heart couldn't take it. I had one foot on the bottom step before my head took over and forced me out the front door, pulling it tightly shut behind me and double checking it was locked. It was.

I needed to protect her, even if it was from myself.

Especially if it was from myself.

I'D TOLD Abby I'd see about walking her to school in the morning, but under the circumstances felt that would be a bad idea. Instead, after a sleepless night spent berating myself and worrying about Hannah, I decided I'd leave Abby a note instead. I could drop it off on my morning run.

I dressed quickly and went downstairs to the kitchen. The sun was just rising over the lake, a yellow-orange ball setting fire to the clouds around it and turning the horizon pink. I ripped off a sheet of paper from the notepad my mom used for grocery and to-do lists and snagged a pen from her desk.

Dear Abby,

I'm sorry I can't be there to walk you to school today, but I wanted to wish you good luck! I know you will have a great first day and I

will be excited to hear all about it. Take a picture for me!

Love,

Uncle Wes

P.S. Don't drink the water from the fountain on the playground. It tastes terrible.

I found an envelope in my mom's desk drawer too, and was just sliding the note inside it when she appeared in the kitchen in a flowery robe and slippers. She still had her hair pinned and her hairnet on, and I laughed, like Drew and I always had at her morning appearance. She looked like something from a 1950s sitcom. The memory sent an ache of longing for my brother through me.

"Wesley Parks, what are you doing up at this hour? And stop that laughing, I'm your mother." Mildly miffed, she went to the coffee pot and began filling it with water.

"Sorry, Mom. Good morning." I went over and kissed the cheek she offered. "I'm going to take a run. What are you doing up this early?"

She clucked her tongue. "I couldn't sleep. No idea why. Probably the full moon or something."

It was that kind of night, I thought.

"Want some breakfast? I could make you some eggs."

"No thanks. I'll get something when I'm back. I don't eat before a run."

"Okay, dear. What's that?" She gestured to the envelope in my hand.

"Nothing. Just a little note for Abby on her first day of school."

She beamed. "How sweet. You've really taken to her, huh?"

I shrugged. "Who wouldn't take to her?"

"I think it's sweet. You're just so good with kids. Not all men are. You'd be such a great dad."

I saw where this had the potential to go and cut it off at the pass. "We'll see. I'm off." I gave her a wave and slipped out the back door, setting out at a light jog to warm up.

Hannah's house was probably about three miles from my parents', and I covered the distance in about twenty-five minutes. Her mailbox was at the foot of the driveway, but I was worried Abby wouldn't see it before school if I put it in there. Instead, I quietly went up on the porch, opened the screen door, and tucked the envelope into the frame of the wooden door. Once it was secure, I stood there for a moment thinking about Hannah and the night before, feeling guilty and sad. I should have just gone home after reading the story to Abby. Hannah was entitled to feel upset sometimes, and she didn't need me poking around in her head thinking I could solve her every problem or take away her sadness just because she'd confided in me.

And what a jerk I was, stopping that kiss and then telling her how she felt, like I was some sort of fucking mind-reader superhero, saving us both with my inhuman strength and stalwart moral rectitude. As if I hadn't been thinking about kissing her all day. As if I hadn't touched her back that way. As if I hadn't wanted her even more than she wanted me.

I'm sorry, Hannah.

Suddenly the door opened, and there she was.

"Hey," she said. "I thought I heard something."

Her hair was wet but uncombed, like she'd just gotten out of the shower, and she wore a fluffy white bathrobe tied tightly at the waist. I could smell her shampoo, the one that always made me hungry. She looked beautiful, but her eyes were puffy. I felt horrible.

"I brought a letter for Abby."

"You did?"

I bent down to retrieve the envelope, which had fallen to the porch floor when she opened the door. "Just a little good-luck wish for her first day. She'd asked me if I could walk her, but I wasn't sure if you..." I stared at her lips and wanted to kiss them so badly I could have punched a hole through the front wall of the house. "Hannah, I'm sorry. About last night."

"I'm sorry, too." Her eyes closed. "And also mortified."

"Don't be."

A low, sarcastic laugh escaped her. "Really? After throwing myself at you? Telling you to fuck off? *Hitting* you?"

"I deserved it." *You have no idea how much I deserved it.*

"For what?" Her eyes widened. "Being my friend? Listening to me drone on about my feelings? Tolerating my mood swings and meltdowns and making me feel understood? Being so sweet with Abby?"

No. For wanting you the way I do. The way I always have. But I couldn't say that, of course. "For being a condescending dickhead. For putting words in your mouth. For assuming I knew how you felt."

"But you did." Her eyes filled. "You did, at least partly. I spent the entire night asking myself why I did what I did, and the truth is..." She shrugged. "I *am* lonely. I *do* miss Drew. I *do* feel some unresolved anger at him about the cheating, and it's entirely possible I went after you to get back at him. Or because you look like him. Or because I haven't had sex in forever and you're a safe opportunity. Or because I see the way you make Abby happy, and I want to feel that, too."

Jesus, why didn't she just pull out a knife and stab me?
"Hannah—"

"It could be all of those things," she went on, "or none of them. Maybe I just lost my mind. But either way, what I did was wrong and totally unfair to you and way, way out of line. You were right to stop it."

"You weren't unfair to me."

She held up a hand. "Please don't. I don't want you to feel like you have to soothe me or heal me or try to fix what's broken, Wes. I am not your responsibility. I had a bad day, I made a mistake, and you stopped me from taking it too far. I'm grateful."

I wanted to argue. I wanted to tell her that kiss wasn't a mistake; it was everything I'd always dreamed about. I wanted to take her in my arms right now and soothe her, heal her, fix what was broken.

But she didn't want me. She never really had.

After a painful silence, she sighed and looked down at the envelope in her hand. "I'll give Abby the letter. But Wes, I think maybe you should stay away for a little while. As much as I enjoy being with you, I think all the time we've been spending together is confusing me. Making me feel things that aren't real."

It is real. I feel it too.

But I nodded. What choice did I have? I had to respect Hannah's wishes, not to mention general rules of propriety, which dictated that it would not be okay to go after my late brother's wife.

No matter how much I wanted to.

"Okay. Thanks. Tell her I'm sorry I couldn't walk with her today."

"I will."

I let the screen door close, reluctant to leave but unable

to think of a reason to stay. "Well, have a good day. And... call if you need anything." *A lightbulb changed, an ice cream cone, an orgasm...*

She nodded. "I will."

But I knew she wouldn't.

I ran home, irritated with myself, with Hannah, with the entire situation. I was especially irritated with Drew, for swooping in and stealing Hannah's heart before I could work up the nerve to ask her out, for cheating on his beautiful, loving wife just because he wasn't getting enough sleep or attention, and for dying and leaving me to deal with all this shit. Hannah wasn't the only one with unresolved feelings.

Because I was mad, I pushed my body to the limit, running harder and faster than I was used to. By the time I reached home, my clothes were drenched with sweat and I could hardly breathe. My muscles were screaming, my head hurt, and my heart was pumping way too hard. But I ran all the way down to the beach before slowing down to check my pulse.

Once my feet were on the sand, I paced back and forth along the shore, fingertips on my throat. When I was sure I wasn't about to die, I allowed myself to mutter a string of curse words that would make a sailor blush. Why was everything so fucked up? Why did I have these feelings for a woman who was so out of reach? What was I supposed to do with them?

And why, *why*, had I stopped her last night? What if I'd blown the only chance I'd ever have to *be* with her that way? To feel her body on mine? To give her the kind of pleasure that only a lover could give? What the fuck did I care what her reasons were for doing it? We were two grown adults, weren't we? It wouldn't have hurt anyone!

I wanted to go back and do it all over. Everything. From the very beginning.

I wanted to make her mine.

I'd marry her and have children with her and walk them to school on the first day. I'd buy her a house and reach things on the high shelf and let her sleep in on Saturday mornings while I made the coffee and cooked *her* breakfast.

I could have made her happy, too.

But instead, I'd stepped aside—again.

I THOUGHT about her constantly over the next few days. On Tuesday night while I looked at houses for sale. On Wednesday morning as I ran on the beach before work. On Thursday evening as I drove home in my newly purchased SUV. I imagined what it would be like to go pick her and Abby up and take them to dinner or a movie or maybe an apple orchard. We'd pick apples and eat donuts and drink cider, and then we could bring the apples home and Hannah could make applesauce or, better yet, an apple pie.

I had a thousand questions for Abby. How was the first day of kindergarten? Did she like her teacher? Had she made new friends? Did she wonder why I hadn't come to walk her home yet? Late Tuesday morning I'd gotten a text from Hannah with an adorable photo of a grinning Abby wearing a little blue jumper, her new backpack, and a huge smile. Her hair was caught up in two pigtails, and she held the little elephant I'd given her underneath one arm. The message was sent to me, my mom, my dad, and another number I didn't recognize, which was probably her mother's. It said, **All set for the first day of school.**

But that was it—no other details and no follow up message later in the day letting us know how it had gone, unless she'd messaged someone separately. On Friday morning, I'd said casually to my mother, "Have you heard from Hannah?"

She seemed surprised I'd asked, pausing with her coffee cup halfway to her mouth. "No. Why?"

"Just wondering how the first week of school is going for Abby."

"Me too, but I don't like to meddle too much."

Since when? I thought.

Work was a welcome distraction, and compared to the challenges I'd faced in Africa, my father's family practice was fairly easy. We saw patients together so he could introduce me, and I saw a few patients on my own. There was a little bit of everything, and all ages, from babies with croup to kids with rashes to seniors with pain in their joints. Nothing serious or severe enough to really take my mind off Hannah, but if I hadn't had the work, I'd have driven myself crazy.

On Saturday afternoon, I was so restless I drove to the mall, even though I hate the mall, and picked up a few news shirts. While I was shopping, I got a text from Pete asking if I wanted to meet up for a beer around seven, and I answered yes. The last thing I wanted to do was sit around the house with my parents, listening to them bicker while I moped about Hannah.

When I got home, my mother was making dinner and Abby was coloring at the kitchen table. Trying not to be disappointed that Hannah had been here and I'd missed her, I tugged gently on one of Abby's pigtails before sitting down across from her. "Hey, kiddo. How was school this week?"

"Good," she said, concentrating hard on staying inside the lines.

"Like your teacher?"

"Yes. She's really nice."

"Good. Nice teachers are the best."

"Hungry, Wes?" My mom asked hopefully.

"Yep."

"Perfect. Dinner is in ten minutes."

I ate with Abby and my parents before running upstairs to clean up a little, then dodged my mother's questions about where I was going and with whom and drove into town.

When I got to the place we'd agreed on, Pete was already seated at the bar with his brother Jack, whom I hadn't seen since I'd been back. He greeted me with a firm handshake. "How's it going? Been a while."

"It has." I clapped Pete on the shoulder and sat down on the other side of him.

"Margot is home with the baby tonight, so I asked Pete if I could tag along," Jack said. "Hope it's okay."

"He needed to get out of the house," Pete added. "Even Margot said so."

"I needed to get out of mine too." I shook my head. "Living with your parents at this age is not fun."

"I heard Brad showed you a few houses." Jack tipped up his beer. "How'd it go?"

"There was one I liked a lot, but they're asking too much for the work it would need. Brad wants to show me a few others before I make an offer, but I don't want to wait too long." I ordered a local craft beer and drank half of it in a few long gulps the moment it was handed to me.

Pete laughed. "Rough week?"

"Sort of."

"Your mom? Or something else?"

I drank again, hoping a little alcohol would take the edge off my feelings for Hannah. "It's a little of everything."

They didn't push and I didn't elaborate, and like guys do, we just drank and made bad jokes and shot the shit about sports and old times, and how it sucked to get old and we couldn't believe we were still here in this town and going on forty.

"At least you guys have it all figured out," I said, well into my fourth local craft beer and enjoying a nice local craft buzz. "Wives, kids, houses, your own businesses. I feel like a loser in comparison."

They exchanged an amused glance. "Uh, I'm not sure what the fuck you're talking about, *Doctor* Parks." Pete shook his head. "Nobody's got it all figured out."

"Especially not me," Jack agreed. "I can't even tell you how many times I've fucked up my life. I'm sitting here because of sheer luck. And a woman who wouldn't take no for an answer."

That interested me. "What do you mean?"

Pete snorted. "Jack thought he should play hard to get. Margot kicked his ass."

I laughed. "Really?"

"No." Jack gave his brother the evil eye. "But I did try to warn her off. I didn't think there was any way a woman like her—who looked like that and came from old money—would be happy with me. I was a farmer, for fuck's sake. An Army vet with a shitty emotional history and a bad attitude. I didn't want anything to do with her."

"He was a total dick," Pete confirmed.

"So what happened?" I asked.

"She refused to give up on me." Jack shook his head, like he still couldn't believe it. "She just had it in her head that we were supposed to be together and nothing I did or said would convince her otherwise."

"But he wanted her, too," Pete added. "He just wouldn't admit it."

"So how did she finally convince you?" I wondered.

"She left. Packed up all her shit and went home. Left me here to brood alone forever, and it didn't take long for me to realize that was a stupid choice."

I nodded, imagining the elegant blond Margot throwing old-fashioned suitcases into her car and taking off down the highway, while Jack stood there frowning by the side of the road. It actually seemed kind of comical.

I was probably drunk.

"Fuck, you guys. I need to call it a night. I can't drink like I used to." I got off my stool, and the floor didn't seem as *floorish* as it should have. It wobbled a little.

They both groaned their agreement, although neither of them had drunk as much as I had.

"Can I hitch a ride home with one of you?" I asked. "I'm sorry, I know it's out of your way, but I shouldn't drive."

"Of course," Jack said. "We drove together, and it's no problem. I'd much rather go out of our way than risk it."

I climbed into the back of Pete's car, feeling sort of like this was high school again, and we were going out looking for girls, beer, and trouble. All three had been easy to find with Drew around. I glanced at the empty seat next to me, then quickly looked out the window.

At my parents' house, Pete pulled up to the front door. "Man, I haven't been here in years. You guys had some pretty cool parties on the beach back in the day."

"We did." I nodded. "We should do it again. You can bring your wives and kids." *I'll invite my sister-in-law, the one I'm secretly in love with, and she can bring her daughter, the one I wish was mine.*

"Sounds good."

I thanked them for the ride and got out, giving them a wave once I'd let myself in the front door.

But I didn't feel like being there.

The great room was dark, which meant my parents had already gone up to bed, so it wasn't that I'd have to deal with them, but I was too agitated to sit still, let alone sleep. I turned around and walked out again, locking the door behind me.

I knew where I was going, but I didn't admit it right away.

I walked leisurely, careful to stay on the highway shoulder, breathing deeply, letting the cool night air and the miles of road ahead of me sober me up. I told myself I was just getting a little fresh air and exercise in order to tire myself out, kill the buzz, quiet my mind. When I turned into Hannah's neighborhood, I had to face the truth. I wanted to see her. I needed to see her.

I needed more than that—I needed her to understand why I'd stopped her that night, that it wasn't because I didn't want her. I wanted her more than anything.

All I needed was a second chance to prove it.

NINE

HANNAH

THIS WEEK it was my turn to stun everyone at Wine with Widows.

"I threw myself at Wes," I told them. We were sitting around Tess's kitchen table, and she nearly spilled the zinfandel she was pouring.

"What?" She straightened up. "What do you mean, you *threw yourself* at him?"

"Picture one of the dragons from Game of Thrones swooping down on someone, breathing fire, wings outstretched. That was basically me." I shuddered at the memory of flying across the kitchen at him.

"When?" Grace asked.

"Monday night. He had the good sense to stop things before they went too far—before they went anywhere, really. But it was totally embarrassing. Worse than the time I cried in my fajitas at Applebee's."

"What made you do it?" Anne's eyes were wide.

"I've been asking myself that question for two days, and I think the answer is a complicated mix of I had a Bad Day, I was feeling extra lonely, I missed my old life, and Wes was there, looking exactly like my dead husband. I think I threw myself at a ghost." I could still remember staring out the window at Wes pushing Abby on the swing, desperately wishing things were different so I could feel happy again. The only hitch in my theory was that I wasn't thinking about Drew when I did what I did—I was thinking about Wes.

But I didn't want to dwell on that. As long as my friends saw my explanation as plausible, I'd stick with it. Anything else was too uncomfortable to deal with. Too sticky a mess.

Tess finished pouring and handed me a glass of wine. "You poor thing."

"At least he was a gentleman about it," Grace offered. "A lot of guys probably would have just done it."

"Yeah." Somehow that didn't make me feel any better. For two days, I'd been obsessing over that first minute where he'd kissed me back. It had felt so good to be held that way. Touched that way. Wanted that way. Not just by any man, but by *him*. It was awful of me.

"So then what happened?" Tess asked.

"Um, then it got worse." I winced. "After he pushed me away, I threw this massive tantrum. I screamed at him. I told him to fuck off. I slapped his face."

"Oh my *God*." She put a hand on her chest. "What did he do?"

"Nothing. Kept his cool and went home, like a gentleman would."

"Have you seen him since?" Anne asked.

"Only once. He came over the next morning, which was

yesterday, with a little note for Abby for her first day of school. I apologized profusely, and he accepted."

"Well, there you go. Don't beat yourself up about it, Hannah." Tess rubbed my shoulder. "Sounds like he understands."

"He does. That's the crazy thing, you guys." I shook my head. "Wes *gets* me. Talking to him is so easy. I find myself telling him things I haven't told anyone."

"Really?" Tess was looking at me differently now.

"Yes. It's almost eerie how safe I feel with him, given that he's only been back for a week."

"I think it's sweet," Grace said. "You have a connection. You trust each other."

"Yeah, but it's—it's messing with me a little," I admitted, shifting in my chair. "So I asked him to stay away for a while, and he agreed."

Anne and Tess exchanged a look. "What do you mean?" asked Anne.

"I mean, being around him was starting to make me feel things that aren't real." I launched into the extended version of my theory. "I look at him and see Drew, so my body reacts. Add to that how well we get along and how good he is with Abby, and it's no wonder I get confused, right? I'm obviously looking at him as a substitute for Drew."

Everyone was silent a minute.

"Are you sure you don't have some feelings for Wes?" Tess asked gently. "Feelings that exist outside your grief over Drew?"

"Positive," I said. "It was just my mind playing tricks on me."

But it was a lie.

The truth was, as the days went by, I couldn't get Wes out of my head. It was like that kiss had flipped a switch in me. For the first time since Drew died, *another man* was at the forefront of my thoughts. Not only another man, but his *brother*. And he wasn't just hanging around in my thoughts —he was *doing things*. With his hands. And his mouth. And his cock. Things I hadn't done in a year and a half. Things I'd never done. Things that made me blush. Things that made me feel swoony and hot. Things that made me want to reach between my legs at night to relieve the tension—but I didn't.

It was too wrong, I told myself. Too misguided. Too shameful. Guilt weighed heavily on me. What kind of woman got herself off while thinking about her dead husband's brother? Denying myself almost became a sort of punishment. And I truly deserved it—not only for what I had done or what I couldn't stop thinking about doing, but for letting my guard down. For making myself susceptible to rejection. For opening myself up to feel things, when I should have known better.

I didn't want *feelings*—not for any man, but especially not for Wes. No matter what it took, I had to shut them down.

The only thing that made it a little easier was knowing the feelings were one-sided. Wes stayed away like I'd asked. No texts, no calls, no drop-in visits. *He doesn't miss you*, I told myself. *He isn't thinking about you. He doesn't want you.* It hurt, but I could handle it.

Pain, I was used to. Pain was familiar. Pain was safe.

Saturday after work, Lenore called and asked if Abby could sleep over, and I'd been tempted to say no, since I didn't want to risk running into Wes when I dropped her off, but Abby was standing next to me with her hands clasped under her chin, chanting, "please, please, please," so I ended up saying yes. On the way over, I'd prayed he wouldn't be there, and I'd thanked my lucky stars on the way home because I'd been in and out of the house in five minutes and no one had even mentioned him.

Later, I fixed myself some dinner and tried to watch a movie, but my mind kept wandering. Where had he been this afternoon? Was he home tonight? Maybe he had a date. It was Saturday night, after all. That's what attractive single people did on Saturday nights. People who still believed in the fairy tale. People who were *desired*. I felt sorry for myself, sitting at home in sweatpants eating a chicken pot pie in front of the television. I gave up on the movie and the pot pie and went up to bed early.

I had just finished brushing my teeth when I heard the knock.

Panicking, I rushed into my bedroom and looked at my phone. No missed calls. If there was a problem with Abby, Lenore would have called me, right?

The pounding repeated, four sharp knocks.

My pulse began to race. Should I answer it? What if it was a crazy person? A burglar? A murderer?

Really, Hannah. Would he knock?

I went to my window and looked out at the street, but there was no car in my driveway or at the curb. Whoever it was must have walked. A neighbor locked out? A wrong address?

I made my way down the steps on tiptoe with my bottom lip caught between my teeth. At the front door I hesitated, but before I could ask *who's there*, I had my answer.

"Hannah, it's Wes."

"Wes?" I opened the door and there he was. Could he hear my heart pounding? "What are you doing here?"

"I had to see you. Can I come in?"

My gut instinct was to say no, slam the door, and hide in the closet. But I willed myself to have strength. I couldn't hide in the closet every time Wes was around. He was family. "Okay."

He entered the house and I shut the door behind him. We stood facing each other in the hall, and I was torn between turning on the light so I could see his face and keeping my ugly sweatpants and silly T-shirt a secret in the dark. The shirt was thin and pink and said OK BUT FIRST PANCAKES above a picture of a stack of them. I wasn't wearing a bra and my nipples were hard. I crossed my arms over my chest.

He wasn't talking. Why wasn't he talking?

"I didn't ring the bell," he finally said.

"What?"

"The doorbell. You said you hate the sound of it because it makes you scared something bad has happened. I didn't want you to be scared."

"Oh. Thank you." I waited for him to go on, to explain what he was doing here not ringing the bell at ten o'clock at night, but for a moment he just stood there, his hands clenching and unclenching at his sides. I started to worry. Did good news ever arrive late at night? "Wes. What is it?"

"I want to tell you something. I'm just...searching for the right words."

"The right words for what?"

He moved toward me and took me by the shoulders. His eyes searched mine in the dark. Hungrily, desperately. At that moment, he looked nothing like Drew. "The other night, you thought I stopped that kiss because I didn't want you. But I do."

"What?" I felt the floor drop.

"I *do* want you, Hannah. I can't stop thinking about you."

The edges of my vision clouded. Was this real? "You can't?"

"No. And I'm sorry. I know I'm making things worse for you right now. I know I said stopping was the right thing. I know you called it a mistake and asked me to stay away. And God knows I've been drinking tonight and probably shouldn't have come here to make a fucking fool of myself. But goddammit, Hannah." He tipped his forehead to mine, his hands clenching tight around my upper arms. "Goddammit, I want another chance. Just one."

My heart was doing something scary inside my chest. My breaths were short and fast. My stomach was cartwheeling out of control. All I could think was *he wants me, he wants me, he wants me*. Enough to walk here in the dark. Enough to ask for another chance. Enough to admit he'd made a mistake and couldn't stop thinking about me. All my walls fell. "Wes. Kiss me."

He put his lips on mine, and my body flooded with warmth. His mouth opened, his head tilting as his hands slid up my shoulders to frame my face. His tongue stroked mine, igniting a fire deep inside me, and I moved closer, slipping my hands around his taut waist. He kissed his way down my throat, his breath coming faster, his hands reaching beneath my shirt. His breath was velvet against my skin.

"Oh, God." I let my head fall back as his lips and tongue traced a path across my neck. It was like feeling the sun on your skin after a long, cold winter. "That feels so good."

He lifted my shirt, and I raised my arms as it disappeared over my head. "Jesus," he whispered. "You're so beautiful."

Impatient, I reached for his shirt, tugging it from his jeans. He helped me, whipping it off with his white under-shirt inside it. Both of us moaned as our bare chests came together. His was hard and warm and muscular, and I pressed myself against it as tightly as I could, kissing him like I'd never stop, like the night would never end, like he and I would go on forever.

His hands moved over me like wildfire, greedy and uncontrollable, setting every inch of my skin ablaze. In my hair, down my back, on my breasts, which ached for his touch. He shoved my pants and underwear down my legs, and I stepped free. Immediately he grabbed my ass and pulled me against him, but I was too short to feel his hard length where I wanted it. Where I needed it.

Frustrated, I fumbled with his belt until it was undone, unbuttoned and unzipped his jeans, and shoved my hand down the front of his pants. I wrapped my hand around his cock and fisted it tight. It was so *hot*. I'd forgotten how hot a man's erection was, how it felt to have that hard heat sliding through my fingers or between my lips or against my clit. Sensual memories I'd thought lost to me came rushing back, awakening nerve endings in my body I'd neglected and let wither. Now they were alive, screaming with hunger and demanding to be fed.

Looping my arms around his neck, I jumped up, wrap-ping my legs around him. He groaned and slid his hands beneath my thighs as I rubbed my clit along his shaft. I was wet and needy and brazen, writhing against him, plunging my tongue into his mouth, clutching fistfuls of his hair. He slid two fingers inside me, and I gasped. "Yes," I whispered against his lips. "*Yes*." And then, since I'd never felt so desperate for anyone and I'd checked my shame at the door, I decided to go on, to say things I'd never even said to Drew.

"I want you to fuck me, Wes. Hard. Now." It felt good to take control that way, to tell someone what I wanted and know it would be delivered.

Without a word, he put my back against the wall, kept me hoisted with one arm, and reached between us with the other hand, positioning himself between my legs. We both groaned as the smooth head of his cock slid inside me. He rocked in and out a few times, easing me open for him, giving me a chance to get reacquainted with the exquisite stretch and surrender. But I was impatient. "All of you," I panted. "I want all of you."

He gave me what I wanted with one deep, hard thrust. I cried out as he growled and gripped me tight, keeping me impaled on his body, his cock buried inside me. Sharp twinges ricocheted through me as he began to move, and I closed my eyes, teeth clenched against the pain.

But I liked it—I liked its depth and its strength and its intensity. It meant this was real, I was here, I was alive. *I can still feel.* He began to move faster, and I was out of my mind with the rapture of it, with the pleasure and pain, the heat and friction.

Our bodies moved together with ease and familiarity, as if they'd known this climb before and remembered the way. But there was newness too—the shocking thought that this was Wes's mouth on my skin, Wes's hands on my ass, Wes's cock driving inside me. I said his name over and over again, my lips barely brushing his.

"God, Hannah." He slowed for a moment, circling his hips, making my body arch in supplication. "It's so fucking good."

"Don't stop." Over his shoulder I caught our reflection in the mirror, and I nearly exploded at the sight of his naked back, my clutching hands, my wanton, half-lidded eyes and open mouth. Was it really me? Was that possible? I watched the mouth stretch into a lazy, erotic smile. Watched the hands slide into his hair. Watched the head tilt as I put my lips to his ear. "Make me come, Wes. I want to come for you."

He groaned, and I felt him throb once inside me. "Fuck. I don't want to come too—"

"Do it. Now. I want to feel it." It would be the final untethering from the anchor of grief and loneliness, this shared release, pulsing with vitality, the ultimate victory over death. "I need it. I need it." He resumed his earlier rhythm, moving faster and faster, taking me right to the edge while I begged him to come with me.

"Christ, Hannah." His voice broke. "You're killing me."

And you're bringing me back to life.

With a passionate cry, my body erupted, the orgasm emanating from the center of me and reverberating throughout my limbs in glorious, rhythmic waves. Wes came almost immediately after I did, as if the first clutch of my body around his had burst the dam.

He pressed his face into my neck, his groan vibrating against my skin, his cock surging again and again inside me. I wrapped my arms around his head and held him close like he was mine, like I was his, like we were in love and love would keep us safe.

But it wouldn't. Love was never safe.

I started to panic. *My heart. My heart. It's beating too fast.* Something was hurting me. My chest was way too tight.

A cold sweat broke out on my back. My body began to tremble.

Wes picked up his head, breathing hard. "Are you okay?"

I couldn't breathe. I couldn't breathe. Was he choking me?

He set me down gently and extricated himself from my body. "Hannah, you're shaking. I'm sorry. I'm so sorry. I don't know what came over me."

His voice was coming from far away. It was freezing in here. I was going to freeze to death, and he was going to let me. Maybe he was even going to kill me. My hands were already going numb. I shivered uncontrollably, gasping for air. My heart was beating out of control. I fidgeted, but I couldn't get away. My feet were like blocks of ice.

"I can't—I can't—"

Wes recognized what was happening, and the doctor in him took over. "Okay honey, it's okay. Breathe with me. In for four, out for four." He talked calmly, his hands brushing my hair back from my face. He inhaled and exhaled with me, long, deep breaths that eased the anxiety inside me. He took one of my hands and pressed his fingertips to the inside of my wrists. "Good girl. You're okay. Everything is gonna be okay."

I'm not sure how many minutes the panic attack lasted, but eventually my heart rate slowed. I regained feeling in my hands and feet. My senses returned. I registered the loud tick of the kitchen clock. The lingering scent of chicken pot pie. The broadness of his shoulders. The slow trickle of warmth from my body.

I found my voice. "Uh, I need a minute."

"I'm not leaving you."

"Okay, but I..." I glanced down at my naked thighs.

He realized what I meant. "Oh, God, Hannah. I'm *such* an asshole. I didn't even think."

My capacity for stringing rational thoughts together was working hard to keep up. We'd had unprotected sex. Were we okay? After a quick calculation, I thought we were. My cycle was really reliable, and I was due for a period in the next day or so. "It's fine. I didn't think either, but the timing is—it's fine. Just give me a minute."

"Of course."

I slipped past him, scooping up my underwear and T-shirt from the floor, and slowly moving up the steps. My mind was reeling. What had I done?

Lots of things. Here are the highlights: You had insanely good but unprotected sex with your brother-in-law in your front hall, followed by a panic attack when you realized you're falling for him. And by the way, you're still wearing your wedding band.

A fresh wave of dizziness hit me at the top of the stairs, and for a moment I feared I'd embarrass myself further by tumbling backward down. I placed a hand on the wall to steady myself and took a few more deep breaths. When the feeling subsided, I went into the bathroom and cleaned up. I could feel my emotions working themselves up inside me, gathering strength like a hurricane. Shock and guilt and shame and fear and confusion.

How had I let this happen? Was I crazy? Was I so desperate to feel desired that I'd actually lost my mind?

I looked at myself in my bathroom mirror. Flushed cheeks. Puffed-up lips. Some slight abrasions where his scruff had rubbed against my jaw. Tousled hair. Trembling hands. Finally, I met my eyes. If I couldn't look myself in the eye after what we'd done, how could I look Wes in the eye? Or Abby? Or Lenore?

Fuck. Don't think about Lenore.

If she ever found out what we'd done…

The thought terrified me, and I tried to talk myself out of the terror with reason.

She won't. It was a one-time thing, a moment of insanity born out of confusion and grief. A desperate attempt to latch on to something life-affirming in the wake of so much sorrow. You're lonely, that's all. Both of you.

Except I hadn't felt lonely in his arms. Not at all. For the first time in eighteen months, I'd felt safe. Strong. Protected. I'd felt connected to him, like I wasn't just a lost soul swimming through space alone. I'd felt loved again.

But feelings lied. Because I wasn't really safe or strong or protected, was I? Just because something felt real didn't mean it was. Look at the way I'd just been convinced I was going to die in the hallway downstairs. Our perceptions of things were faulty. Our senses deceived us.

He didn't love me. And I didn't want to love him. But I saw how easily it could happen if we weren't careful.

We can't. We can't let this happen. I can't let this happen.

Fighting off tears, I went back downstairs, where I found Wes standing in the hall with the light on. He'd pulled his shirt on and done up his pants, and the look on his face was worried. "Hey. You okay?"

"Yeah."

"Can I just look at you real quick?"

"Sure."

He checked each eye and took my pulse again, and listened to me breathe for a moment. I felt small and child-like next to him, and I wished I didn't like the feeling of being fussed over by him so much. As a single parent, it was always me doing the fussing.

"Do you have panic attacks very often?" he asked.

"Not anymore."

He frowned and stepped back from me. "I'm sorry, Hannah. This was all my fault."

I crossed my arms over my chest. "We both know that's not true. I wanted this just as badly as you did tonight. Don't make me a victim."

He swallowed and nodded.

"But that doesn't make it right."

"No," he agreed. "It doesn't."

"We need to forget this happened, Wes. And we can't do it again."

"But—"

"No! It's wrong. I feel like I've dishonored Drew's memory, and it's the only thing I have left. Look, we were lonely, okay? We were lonely and we miss him and we just wanted to feel close to each other, so we could feel close to him." I said it firmly, as if I believed it.

"This wasn't about Drew for me," he said quietly.

My heart squeezed. "Well, it was for me," I lied.

He came closer to me, nearly chest to chest. His eyes pinned mine. "I don't believe you."

I was scared he was going to kiss me and I wouldn't have the strength to resist, but he didn't.

Five seconds later, he was gone.

I shut the door behind him and leaned back against it, exhaling in relief. I was safe.

But relief was short-lived. Once I crawled into bed and pulled the covers over my shoulders, the house seemed more empty than it had ever been, and I sobbed into my pillow.

He was so good and sweet and beautiful. And maybe he really did want me.

But I couldn't fall for him. I just couldn't. For so many reasons. Because he was Drew's brother. Because it would be too confusing for Abby. Because no one would accept us.

And because life had taught me no matter what you did,

no matter how hard you tried, happily ever after was only an illusion. A beautiful distraction from the tragedy that was love, that was life.

There was no eternity.

Everything came to an end.

TEN

HANNAH

I WAS a red-eyed zombie at work the next morning, where again I was glad it was Pete sharing my shift and not Georgia since I felt like a scarlet letter was branded on my forehead. The one thing I felt unadulterated joy about was that I got my period this afternoon. *Thank God*, I thought. Could I blame PMS for any of this craziness?

For once, I was glad it was Lenore who answered my knock when I went to get Abby. But when she invited me in for iced tea, I hesitated. I couldn't handle seeing Wes. Not yet.

"If you're too busy for tea, maybe another time."

"No, no. I'm not too busy. I just... I was just thinking." *About banging your son. No, the other one.* I tried to shove the image out of my mind. "I'd like to come in for tea, thank you." The last thing I wanted was to give Lenore any ammunition against me when things seemed to be going better between us. And Wes and I couldn't avoid each other forever.

Abby was in the great room playing Barbies on the coffee table. "Hi, Mommy!"

"Hi, sweetie." I went over and gave her a quick hug. "Did you have a good night?"

"Mmhm. And we made the pancakes again this morning!"

"We did," Lenore said. "And she's such a big help to her Nana in the kitchen!"

"Good girl." I ruffled her hair and followed Lenore into the kitchen, where she took a pitcher of homemade sweet tea from the fridge and poured us both a glass.

"How's business at the inn?" she asked, sticking the pitcher back in the fridge.

"Good." I took a seat at the island, glancing at the corner where Wes and I had shared crepes last weekend. It seemed like a lifetime ago.

"Hannah?" Lenore was looking at me quizzically, and I realized she'd asked me a question.

"I'm sorry. I got distracted. What did you say?"

"I wondered if you'll take some time off now that summer is over." She began pulling things from the pantry and fridge—flour, garlic powder, salt and pepper, eggs.

"Probably not until closer to November. I think they'll need me up until then."

"Who takes Abby to school in the mornings?"

I'd already answered this question a hundred times. "I did this week, since it was her first, and I went into work a little later, but my sitter will take her from now on when I work. Then I'm off in time to pick her up, take her to her afternoon activities, do her reading and math homework."

"Homework!" Lenore squawked, cracking an egg into a bowl. "Who gives homework in kindergarten?"

I shrugged and sipped the sugary tea. "I think all schools give at least some. It's not too much. I think it's good for her to start learning the routine now."

"That's ridiculous." Lenore sniffed and dumped another egg into the bowl. "Kids her age don't need homework or scheduled activities. They need fresh air and play time and good meals and sleep, that's all."

I took another drink rather than reply. No sense arguing with Lenore. "Is Doc at work today?"

"He and Wes went to the hospital for rounds this morning, and then he was taking Wes to get his car. Apparently the boy had a few too many beers last night in town and one of the Valentinis had to drive him home. Honestly." She clucked her tongue as she beat the eggs with a little water. "You'd think he'd know better. But I suppose he deserves a good time, he's worked so hard and been through so much. I'm really hoping he'll settle here, get married, have a family. Otherwise, I'm a little worried he'll get antsy and take off again."

I tried to imagine how I would feel when Wes began dating someone, and was surprised by the vicious punch of jealousy in my gut. I had no right to feel jealous of anyone he chose to date.

But the thought of his hands on another woman's body made me want to vomit.

"I should go," I said, quickly dumping the rest of my tea in the sink. Maybe I couldn't avoid him forever, but I could avoid him today. In my current emotional state, it seemed wise.

I was about to make my way into the great room to collect Abby when the side door opened and Wes stepped into the kitchen. We locked eyes. My stomach filled with butterflies. I couldn't breathe.

But it wasn't the panic attack of last night. It was an airy, exhilarating feeling, a balloon of joy inside me at the mere sight of him. *I wanted to see him*, I realized. *Of course I did.*

"Hey," he said, dropping his keys on the counter. "How are you?"

Miserable.

"Fine," I said, a little too loudly. I ran a hand over the hastily-done braid at the back of my head. He looked perfect in gray dress pants and a white button-down with the sleeves cuffed, and I felt totally unkempt with my messy hair and work jeans and flour-dusted red T-shirt. *Not to mention my puffy eyes and sleep-deprived complexion.* "How are you?"

"Fine." His eyes told me differently.

Don't look at me that way, Wes. It makes me weak.

I broke the stare and mumbled something about getting Abby home, then left the kitchen on wobbly legs. Lenore invited us to come back for fried chicken later, but I made some excuse as to why we couldn't, and Wes didn't try to argue. Taking Abby by the hand, I slipped out the front door without looking back. *Keep moving. Just keep moving.*

I buckled Abby in, shut the door, got in the driver's seat, buckled myself in, and burst into tears.

"What's wrong, Mommy?" asked Abby from the back seat.

Good God. Where would I even start?

"Nothing, baby. Just having a bad day." I pulled myself together and started the engine, meeting her eyes in the rearview so she wouldn't be scared. "Tell me about your sleepover."

When we got home, I sent Abby outside to play and called Tess.

"Hey. I need to talk. Got a minute?"

"Sure. What's up?"

"I slept with Wes last night."

At first, silence. Then, "Define slept."

"We had sex."

She gasped. "Where?"

"My front hallway. Abby was at his mother's. And afterward I had a massive panic attack."

"Oh my God. Wait, I have to go into the laundry room so the kids can't hear me." A moment later, I heard a door shut. "Okay, tell me everything."

While I watched my innocent little daughter sing to herself and play on the swings, I filled Tess in on what I'd done. "I feel horrible about it."

"You do?"

"*Yes*," I said loudly, because wasn't it obvious? "Wes is Drew's *brother*."

"That's true," she said gently, "but Drew is gone, Hannah. He's not coming back."

"I know." I squeezed my eyes shut, and voiced the more complicated, more shameful feeling. "But I also feel horrible because I liked it. And I can't stop thinking about it. And I wish we could do it again." There. I'd said it out loud.

"Was it that good?"

"It was amazing, Tess. He made me feel..." I closed my eyes as chills swept down my arms and legs. "Like a different person. But somehow still myself, only *more* myself. Like I'd recaptured something. It was effortless and liberating."

"I know exactly what you mean."

"But it's so *wrong*."

"Hannah. I fucked the tree man, remember? A complete stranger."

"That still doesn't seem as wrong as what I did. Or why I did it."

"Why'd you do it?"

"Because I wanted him. *Him*, not Drew."

"I suspected as much the other night when you were talking about him. Your face changes. You light up. You have feelings for him Hannah, and it's okay."

I cringed. That wasn't what I wanted to hear. "No. It isn't."

"What about him?" she challenged. "How does he feel?"

"He says it's not about Drew for him. And then I lied and told him it *was* for me."

"Why? You didn't do anything wrong. You guys are two consenting adults who feel a connection to each other."

"But I feel like I dishonored Drew's memory," I said, resting my forehead on my fingertips.

"A memory can't keep you warm at night."

I squeezed my eyes shut against the seductive thought of Wes keeping me warm on cold winter nights. "I don't want this, Tess. I don't."

"Don't want what?"

"These feelings for him. I have to get rid of them somehow."

"How the hell are you going to do that? You can't put feelings out like a bonfire."

"No, but I can stay away from him until they die out on their own." I remembered sitting in the grocery store parking lot, making that same plan. *I should have stuck to it.*

"And if they don't?"

Straightening up, I turned around and looked for Abby out the window again. "They have to."

"There's nothing wrong with moving on, Hannah. It's healthy."

"I don't want to move on," I said stubbornly. "Not with Wes, not with any man."

"It just seems a shame if both of you—"

"*No.* It's pointless to even think about."

She stayed silent.

I sighed. "Thanks for listening, Tess. I had to get it off my chest, and this is just too personal to share with the group."

"Of course. I hope it made you feel better."

"It did," I lied.

The truth was, the more I thought about it, the worse I felt. Because as days of avoiding Wes stretched into weeks and my feelings for him didn't subside, I grew more and more terrified that they never would. I tried everything I could to distract myself—I cleaned the house top to bottom, I baked a zillion pies, I dug out my old sewing machine and tackled the long-ignored pile of clothing that needed mending.

But nothing worked. I thought of him constantly, missed him terribly. And I couldn't hide from him forever— Abby's sixth birthday dinner at Lenore and Doc's house was scheduled for the last Saturday in September, and there was no getting out of it.

I'd have to face him and act like I was okay, like what we'd done hadn't wrecked me, like I still believed the lie I'd told him that night—that it had been about Drew for me.

I don't believe you, he'd said.

Did he now? Did he think because I'd stayed away from him for two weeks I'd meant what I'd said? Was he hurt by that? I hated the thought that I'd caused him pain, but I was trying to protect us both.

Pain was necessary.

THE SATURDAY of Abby's birthday dinner was a sunny, cloudless day that didn't match my dark, foreboding mood at all. I couldn't shake the feeling that something bad was going to happen. Maybe I'd have a meltdown at the dinner table and cry into my chicken and dumplings. Maybe Wes would be so mad he wouldn't even talk to me and dinner would be a tense, silent affair. Maybe Lenore would somehow find new ways to cut away at my self-worth and I'd finally snap and flip a table.

That last one was actually kind of a satisfying thought.

We weren't too busy at work, and Georgia and I actually found time to sit down and have a cup of coffee during late morning.

"Everything okay?" She lifted her cup to her lips with both hands.

"Yeah," I said, but then my shoulders slumped. "No."

She smiled. "Want to talk about it?"

Did I? While I was thinking about it, Margot came into the kitchen.

"Whew," she said, taking a cup down and pouring coffee into it. "All gone. Kind of nice to have a slow day now and then."

I nodded, but the slow traffic made me kind of sad, too. It meant they wouldn't need me as much, and the start of the cold, lonely season I was dreading.

"Can I join you guys?" Margot asked.

"Of course," I said.

She sat down and flipped her long blond braid over her shoulder. "Actually, Hannah, I've been wanting to talk to you about something."

"Oh?"

"Yes. Georgia and I have been talking about a Valentini Inn cookbook for a while, a series of them actually, and we think you'd be the perfect person to start with. Maybe a breakfast edition?"

I found myself perking up a little at the thought of a creative project. "I'd love that. I mean, I don't know anything about putting a book together, but I can supply the recipes."

"That's all we need," said Georgia. "Well, that and photos, but we're going to hire someone for that."

"And I know someone who can take care of the design and layout for us." Margot inhaled the aroma of her coffee before sipping it. "But I'd like you to work with her. And I'd also like you to start posting some recipes on our website."

"I'd love to. Thanks for asking me."

"It's good to see you smiling," said Georgia. "You've been a little down lately."

I sighed and picked up my coffee, hoping a little caffeine buzz would lift my mood. "Yeah."

"It's the time of year, maybe," Margot suggested. "It's going to get chilly soon, and before you know it, winter is here."

"But I love autumn," I said, setting my cup down. "It's not that."

Both women looked at me with a mix of curiosity and concern. "We're here if you need to talk," said Margot. "No pressure, but sometimes it helps."

"I'm just...scared about something," I said carefully. I wasn't planning to blurt the whole ugly truth, but maybe they were right—maybe talking about it would give me strength.

"What are you scared of?" Georgia asked.

"I'm scared of what I feel...about someone."

They looked at each other. "You have feelings for someone?" Margot beamed. "Hannah, that's wonderful."

"No, it isn't." My eyes filled. "You wouldn't say that if you knew who it was. Or if you knew what I'd been through."

Margot put her hand on my arm. "I'm sorry. You're right. I'm sure this *is* scary for you. I don't mean to be insensitive."

"You're not insensitive." I put my elbows on the table and rubbed my temples, taking a few deep breaths to stave off tears. "I'm just a mess. I'm sorry."

"Is it...is it Wes?" asked Georgia hesitantly.

I closed my eyes and nodded, waiting for them to respond, half-hoping they'd go off about how inappropriate and morally wrong and just plain icky it was to have feelings for your late husband's brother. "Go on. Tell me I'm a terrible person."

"Oh honey, you're not." Margot shook her head. "We'd never think that, no matter who you had feelings for." She paused. "Unless it was Jack. Then I might have an issue."

I nearly smiled.

"You're not terrible," Georgia seconded. "You're human. And it's easy to see why you might develop feelings for Wes. He's Drew's brother. They were a lot alike in some ways. And they were identical."

"But they were really different too," I said. "I've only really just gotten to know Wes since he's been home. We've talked a lot, and he's such a great listener. A much better listener than Drew, actually. Drew loved to talk and tell jokes and be the center of attention. Wes is more quiet, more serious, maybe more intense."

"I can see that," Georgia said. "Drew was a life-of-the-party kind of guy, always fun, always spontaneous. But maybe that isn't what you're looking for this time around. Maybe at this point in your life, and after all you've been through, you'd appreciate a quieter life, one with fewer surprises."

"But I wasn't looking for anything," I insisted. "That's the problem. I don't want another time around. I just want to live on my own and be a good mother to Abby."

"Finding love again doesn't mean you won't be a good mother to Abby," Margot said.

"But she's confused about Wes as it is. She already asked me if I was sure he wasn't her father. And what about the way people will talk? This is a small town. Can you imagine the gossip that will spread?"

Georgia shrugged. "Gossip is gossip. And yes, it's a juicy story. People would be fascinated by it for a while and then they'd move on to something else."

"And you can't live your life in fear of what other people think," Margot added. "That was a lesson I had to learn too, and trust me when I tell you you'll be much happier if you can get over that."

"I don't know if I can," I admitted. "I'm not as strong as you."

"You are." Margot leaned forward in her chair. "And you deserve to be happy, Hannah. Don't you think Drew would want that for you?"

"Drew would want to protect me," I said stubbornly. "He'd want me to be safe, and you can't be safe when you give your heart away."

They looked at each other again. "What does Wes say?" Georgia asked. "Does he even know how you feel?"

"No. Two weeks ago, we...I... Things got physical between us," I blurted. My cheeks burned. "And it was amazing. But when it was over, I had a panic attack because I realized it wasn't *just* physical."

"I'm sure Wes understood," said Margot.

"He did, but then I—I lied to him. I blamed what we'd done on being lonely and missing Drew. But it wasn't true, and he knew it. Because he knows me." A tear slipped down my cheek. "He said, 'I don't believe you.' And then he left."

"And you haven't seen him since?" Margot asked, her voice rising.

I shook my head slowly. "But I will tonight. It's Abby's birthday dinner at Lenore and Doc's house. He'll be there, and I'm dreading it."

"Oh my God. No wonder you've been so tense today." Georgia's eyes were wide. "I don't blame you."

"I'm sorry to unload this on you guys," I said, getting up to grab a tissue. "You're probably sorry you asked what was wrong."

"Not at all," Georgia said. "I just wish there was something we could do to help you. It's all so sad."

"It is sad," I agreed, "but in the long run, I'm making the right decision."

"Are you sure?" asked Margot.

I sat down again and blew my nose. "Yes," I answered.

"Because I don't think you are," she went on. "If you were sure, you wouldn't feel so torn about this. And I can see on your face that you're torn."

"No, I'm not," I said, but my voice lacked the punch I aimed for.

"Yes, you are. And I don't blame you." Her voice softened. "You've got Abby to consider, and your situation is complicated by the fact that he's your brother-in-law. But Hannah." She put her hand on my arm again. "Don't let fear hold you back. You'll regret it."

"But what if—"

"You'll never be able to guard against all the what-ifs, Hannah," said Georgia. "No one can."

"Talk to him," Margot said. "Just trust me. Talk to him."

I sighed. "I'll think about it."

And I did—I thought about it in the shower, as I dressed for dinner, while I loaded the wrapped presents into the car, and on the short drive to the house.

But no matter how convincing or reassuring Georgia and Margot had been this afternoon, I couldn't help feeling like I was right on the edge of some huge, frightening abyss, and one misstep would send me careening into darkness. I didn't want to make a mistake. Wasn't it better just to stay where I was? Take no step at all, even if it meant being lonely for the rest of my life?

As I pulled into the driveway at Lenore and Doc's, I made up my mind. Maybe I *was* letting fear hold me back, and maybe I'd regret it later, but then again, maybe I wouldn't. Maybe I'd be glad someday that I hadn't taken the risk.

I couldn't guard against *all* the what-ifs in life, but dammit, I could guard myself from this one.

ELEVEN

WES

"HAND ME THE EGGS, will you, dear?" my mother asked.

"The what?" I was standing in front of the open fridge, but I'd completely zoned out. Happened to me all the time these days. I'd open a drawer, walk into a room, start a sentence, but then I'd see something or hear something or even smell something that would remind me of Hannah, and my body and mind simply froze, paralyzed by thoughts of her. I'd suddenly have no clue what I was looking for or trying to say.

"The *eggs*, dear." Her tone was slightly exasperated. "I've asked you three times."

"Oh. Sorry." I pulled out the egg carton and set it on the counter where she was mixing up cake batter for Abby's sixth birthday dinner tonight. It would be the first time Hannah and I saw each other in two weeks.

"What's got you so addled these days?" she asked,

eyeing me as I went back to the fridge, opened it up, and focused on taking out some lunchmeat for a sandwich.

"Nothing." I pulled out turkey, lettuce, tomato, and mayonnaise, wishing she'd stop fucking asking me that question.

"Are you getting enough sleep? You're working pretty long hours."

"I'm fine, Mom." The long hours were by choice, an attempt to distract myself from longing for Hannah, but it hadn't worked. The memory of that night at her house assaulted me approximately every half a second. On my early morning jogs. While I was in the shower. As I drove to work. During my lunch break. Even when I was immersed in caring for patients, she was always there at the back of my mind, a spectral presence with messy hair and bare feet and soft lips and warm skin, kissing me, touching me, inviting me inside her. And the things she'd said—every time I remembered hearing those words in her sweet, breathless voice, heat rose in my body and I'd have to loosen my tie.

I want you to fuck me.

I want all of you.

I want to come for you.

Come with me.

I want to feel it.

Jesus Christ, I had gone off like a rocket. And not a small rocket either. One of those deep space rockets. A fucking NASA-level rocket. A mission to Mars. I still couldn't believe I'd done it. Sometimes I wondered what the hell was in those beers I'd drunk. Other times I supposed it had nothing to do with my blood alcohol level and everything to do with the fact that I'd wanted her for way too long. Even a gentleman runs out of patience sometimes.

But I was beginning to think I wasn't much of a gentleman anyway.

"When will you hear back from Brad?" my mother asked.

"He said in the next day or so," I said, realizing I'd been standing there dumbstruck in front of the toaster with two slices of bread in my hand. I stuck them in. "By Monday for sure."

I'd made an offer on a house just north of town. It wasn't perfect, needed new flooring and paint and a kitchen remodel, but it was a good size, right on the lake, and nicely secluded. Best of all, it was not walking distance from my parents' house, at least not for them. And I needed some projects to keep me busy anyway.

"You know, there's no rush to move out." She cracked the eggs into the bowl and tossed the shells into the sink. "If that house isn't what you want, you can stay here as long as you want."

"I know, Mom. Thanks." What I *wanted* was something I couldn't have. Didn't really matter where I lived.

That said, I needed some fucking privacy. My mother had even taken to coming into my room while I was at work and collecting my dirty laundry, putting it through the wash, and returning it to my drawers, all folded up in neat little piles. She packed my dad a lunch every day and insisted on packing me one too. She fussed over me constantly, worried I was exercising too hard, working too much, and had no social life whatsoever. I tolerated it because I loved her and knew she loved me, but damn, she could be overbearing.

When my sandwich was done, I sat at the island to eat it and listened to her babble over the whir of the electric mixer, but I mostly tuned her out and thought about Hannah.

I'd gone over our conversation that night a thousand times. Had I been wrong? Had she been telling the truth when she said it had been about Drew for her? I racked my brain, searching for any clue I might have missed in her behavior, in her voice, in her eyes. But I couldn't find one. She'd wanted me. She'd said my name. She'd held onto me so tight, like she never wanted to let go.

Or was that wishful thinking? Maybe she had been thinking of Drew the whole time. Maybe the panic attack had stemmed from the realization of what she'd done, from the guilt and shame of dishonoring his memory. Maybe she really had given in just because she was lonely and I was a safe opportunity, like she'd said before.

Good old Wes. A safe opportunity fuck. But nothing more.

AFTER A LONG RUN on the beach that afternoon, I took a shower, got dressed, and poured myself some scotch. It had been a beautiful late summer day, and the temperature was still in the upper sixties at five o'clock. I took my drink out onto the deck and stood looking out at the lake, which always had a calming effect on my nerves. The house I'd offered on didn't have a deck, but I planned to remedy that if the purchase went through. I wanted bigger windows on the east side too, but that might have to wait a while.

Behind me, I heard the sliding door rumble open and shut. I thought maybe it was my dad joining me with a stiff drink of his own (away from my mother's watchful eyes), so I was surprised when I heard Hannah's voice.

"Hi."

I turned, and my heart beat faster at the sight of her. "Hi."

She wandered to my side, a glass of white wine in her hand. "Want company?"

"Sure." I brought my glass to my lips, but it was Hannah I drank in. Her hair swung loose around her shoulders tonight. She didn't often wear it down, and I saw now how summer had dusted the brown with gold. My stomach muscles tightened—she was still the prettiest woman I'd ever seen. Her shoulders were on display in the top she wore, and I was dying to press my lips to one of them. She had *perfect* shoulders. Why hadn't I kissed them when I had the chance?

"How've you been?" she asked. She was nervous, I could tell.

"Fine," I said, using our code word for not fine at all. "You?"

She turned to face the lake. Took a sip of wine. "Fine."

Conversation in the kitchen drifted through the screen, and I selfishly hoped no one would come out here. I wanted her to myself just a few minutes more. "Been busy?"

"Not really. I hear you offered on a house."

"Yes. It needs some work, but it's a nice place."

"When will you know?"

"Soon. Monday at the latest."

"Fingers crossed for you."

"Thanks."

Silence descended upon us, bringing with it a crushing disappointment. This was it. Or, rather, that was that. What we'd had was all we ever would, and it was pointless—no, *idiotic* to feel like I'd lost something. She'd never been mine to lose.

Suddenly I was angry. Why was I still carrying this torch for her? What was the fucking point? I swirled my scotch around in my glass and tossed the rest of it down my throat.

Then she spoke, and my life changed course.

"I lied to you."

"What?"

"That night. You said it wasn't about Drew for you, and I said it was for me." Finally she faced me. Her terrified eyes were shiny. "But I lied."

"Hannah." I took her by the arm.

"Oh God, Wes," she whispered, struggling not to cry. "I shouldn't have said anything. That wasn't the plan. But seeing you is just—I miss you."

"I miss you, too." I swallowed hard. "And I still want you."

"Don't." She took a step back and pulled her arm from my grasp. "Don't say things like that."

"It's the truth. No, it's a *fraction* of the truth."

She shook her head. "It doesn't matter."

"How we feel doesn't matter?"

"It can't." She refused to meet my eyes, looking frantically around the deck. "There are too many complications."

Suddenly Abby came running out onto the deck. "Mommy!" She threw her arms around Hannah's thighs. "Nana says I can open my gifts before dinner if you say it's okay. Is it?"

Hannah looked down at her daughter and pulled herself together with a delicate sniff. "How about, 'Hi, Uncle Wes?'"

The little girl looked up at me sheepishly. "Hi, Uncle Wes."

"Hi, princess." I patted her head and hoped my voice sounded normal. "Happy birthday."

"Thank you. So can I, Mommy? Please?"

"Don't you want to wait until we have cake and ice cream?"

"No."

My mother emerged from the house. "Abby, darling, you need to close the door so Nana doesn't get flies in the house." She slid it shut behind her.

"Sorry, Nana," Abby said.

"Ooh, what a nice night," my mother said as she approached us. "Abby, what did Mommy say?" But she wasn't looking at Abby. Her curious eyes were darting back and forth between Hannah and me.

I put a little more distance between us and prayed she wouldn't pick up on the tension.

"It's fine," Hannah said.

"Yay!" Abby let go of her mother and raced back inside, leaving the door open, of course.

My mother sighed and followed her into the house, pausing to look back at us. "Coming, you two?"

In a minute, I wanted to say. I needed more time to convince Hannah that our feelings mattered, that we deserved a chance, that I could make her happy. But she was already escaping me, following Abby into the house.

Not that I blamed her—her daughter came first, and I understood that she always would. And I wanted to watch her open gifts too; I'd gotten her a snow cone machine like Drew and I'd had when we were kids.

He should be here, I thought as I went inside. *He should be here to watch his daughter open birthday gifts and walk to get ice cream and keep his wife from being lonely. It should be him and not me, and I know it.*

But he wasn't here. I was. And if the situation were reversed, if I were gone, and he were alive and had these feelings for the wife I'd left behind, wouldn't he do everything he could to be with her? He'd never stepped aside in his life. That had always been my talent.

But things could change. People could change.

And I wasn't about to let her go again without a fight.

DINNER WAS TORTURE. I could hardly finish my plate, and I barely said a word. Twice during the meal my mother asked me if I was all right. Hannah was seated directly across from me, and both times, she and I exchanged a look before I assured my mother I was fine.

After cake and ice cream, I helped my mother with the dishes while my dad and Hannah began putting together the huge dollhouse my parents had given Abby.

"What were you and Hannah talking about on the deck?" my mother asked, handing me a platter to be dried.

"The house, mostly."

"Oh? It looked like a very intense conversation."

"It wasn't," I lied, and changed the subject.

When the dishes were done, I told my mom I needed some air and went down to the beach. Dropping onto the sand, I draped my arms over my knees and looked out at the water. *Am I wrong? What would you have done, Drew? If you were me, and you loved Hannah too, what would you have done?*

I closed my eyes, and when I opened them again, my brother was sitting beside me.

"Dude," he said. "You know the answer."

"Do I?"

"Of course you do. You knew me better than anyone. If I wanted something, I went after it."

"True." For a moment, I said nothing, watching the waves as I considered my next statement. "How could you ever have wanted someone else?"

He was silent.

"How could you do that to her?"

"I don't know. I fucked up. Everyone makes mistakes."

I knew that, but it didn't help. "You had *everything*, Drew. Everything."

"Maybe I didn't deserve it."

I frowned, unwilling to go that far.

"But you do, Wes. You'll be good to her."

"I would," I whispered.

"But you can't fuck this up. It's *Hannah* we're talking about. And Abby too."

"Abby." My heart swelled.

"They need you. And I trust you to love them both the way they deserve to be loved, Wes—enough for both of us. Can you do that?"

I swallowed hard. "Yes."

"Good. Because there's no one else on earth I trust more."

"Are you sure I haven't...broken some sacred bond between us?"

"I'm sure. Now get out of your head. And get Hannah out of hers, too. Life is short, brother. Go live it."

"I will. I want to."

"And for fuck's sake, get out of Mom and Dad's house already. What are you, twelve?"

"I'm going, I'm going."

"Good. I'll be around, but only when you need me."

"Thank you." I looked at the empty sand next to me. "For everything."

By the time I went back up to the house, Hannah was gone, my dad was sitting in his chair with a crossword puzzle, and my mother was following Abby up the stairs.

"I get to stay here again!" Abby shouted. "Can we make snow cones in the morning?"

"Sure," I told her, watching them disappear at the top of the stairs. When they were out of sight, I grabbed my keys from the kitchen counter. I'd waited ten years to do this.

It was now or never.

"I'm gonna go for a drive," I told my dad. "Maybe meet Pete for a beer."

He didn't even look up. "What's a synonym for gossamer? Eleven letters, starts with a T-R-A and ends with a T."

I thought for a second. "Transparent?"

He nodded. "That's it."

HANNAH'S HOUSE was dark and silent as I strode up the front walk to the porch, my heart pounding frantically. Before I could even knock, the door opened.

My breath stopped.

She wore a little white slip of a nightgown that seemed to glow in the moonlight. Her hair hung in soft waves I wanted to bury my face in.

"Wes," she said, her eyes begging me. "Please."

"Can I come in?"

"No."

"Why not?"

Her lower lip trembled. "Because. I don't trust myself to be alone with you."

"Please, Hannah. I have to talk to you."

"No, Wes. There can't be anything between us."

"There's already something between us."

She didn't deny it. "Even if there is, we can't act on it. And the more we agonize over it, the worse it will feel."

"Nothing will ever feel worse to me than walking away from you without telling you how I feel. I did it once before, and it was the biggest mistake of my life."

Her face registered shock. "What do you mean?"

"I mean that I've always wanted you. From the moment I saw you, only I was too chicken shit to do anything about it. I didn't know what to say or how to say it. I just knew you were the most perfect girl I'd ever met, and I would have done anything to be with you."

She closed her eyes in agony. "Wes. My God."

"I lost my chance with you then, and maybe I deserved to, for being too scared to speak up and tell you how I felt. Maybe I deserved to watch you fall in love with my brother instead of me. But maybe it just wasn't our time then. Maybe it's our time *now*."

Her eyes opened slowly. They were wet with tears.

"Tell me you feel nothing for me, Hannah, and I'll go. Tell me you could never be happy with me. Tell me I could never be what you want."

"I can't." Her voice quivered.

She hadn't invited me in, but that didn't stop me from crossing the threshold and taking her face in my hands. "Then let me love you, the way I've always wanted to."

A tear slipped down one cheek. "People will talk. People will say it's wrong."

"Fuck people. This is between you and me."

"I'm scared." Her voice was soft and plaintive.

"I know you are. But there's nothing to be scared of, I promise."

"There is," she insisted, but her body swayed toward mine.

"Say the word," I whispered, rubbing a thumb over her soft, full lips. "Say you want me, and I'm yours."

The three seconds she took to answer me were the longest of my life. "I want you, Wes. I want you to love me."

I wasted no time.

Kicking the door closed behind me, I scooped her up in my arms and carried her up the stairs, her white nightgown luminous in the dark.

Inside her bedroom, I set her on her feet, lifted the nightgown from her body, and stripped off the panties she wore beneath it. Then I picked her up again and lay her on the bed. Both of us were breathing hard.

"Wait," she said as I whipped my shirt over my head. "The lamp on my nightstand. Turn it on." She propped herself up on her elbows. "I want to see you."

I switched on the lamp, and the room brightened a little. My eyes devoured her sun-kissed limbs, her pale breasts, the hunger in her dark, glittering eyes. I undressed quickly, and she bit her bottom lip as she watched. When I was naked in front of her—*naked in front of Hannah, Jesus Christ*—she sat up and moved to the edge of the bed.

"Come here." She grabbed my hips and pulled me toward her, opening her knees so that I stood between them. Then she looked up at me with hooded eyes. "I want to taste you."

Next thing I knew, she had my cock in her hands and her mouth was descending on it, inch by inch. I groaned as her tongue stroked over the crown in slow, rhythmic circles.

She sucked as she took me in deeper, keeping one hand wrapped tightly around the base. The other one moved around my hip to grab my ass and pull me in deeper.

Oh, fuck.

I gathered her hair in my hands and watched as my cock disappeared into her hot, tight mouth again and again. She made little murmuring noises that weakened the muscles in my legs and strengthened my grip in her hair. When she looked up at me and saw me watching her, she slowed down. Slid her lips slowly up my shaft and over the head, pulling me from her mouth completely and pressing a kiss on the tip. Then she dipped her head to one side and ran her tongue from the base all the way up to the crown, smiling at the sound I made, which was something between a moan of agony and a moan of pleasure. She repeated the long, slow stroke up my hard length on the other side, and then again right in the center, before taking me into her mouth again, all the way to the back of her throat. Goose-bumps blanketed my lower body, and I knew I'd better stop her before I lost control.

"Hannah." I pulled back, springing free from her lips with a little pop. "You need to stop."

"Why?" She looked up at me with shiny lips.

"Because it's my turn." Letting go of her hair, I reached under her arms and moved her backward onto the bed, then gently pushed her shoulders down so she lay on her back. I knelt between her thighs, looking down at her. "Christ, you're beautiful."

She smiled, and it stirred a memory in me. Falling forward onto my hands, I kissed her lips, delighting at the eager sweep of her tongue against mine, the way she arched her back to get closer to me, the fingers she threaded through my hair. It was unbelievable. *She wants me. She wants me to love her.* Something in me opened up, and words I'd kept dammed for years began to flow.

"Do you know," I said, moving my lips down her sweet-smelling neck, "how much I love your smile?" I kissed her shoulder, her collarbone, the hollow at the base of her throat. "It was the first thing I noticed about you. The way you could light up a room."

"Was it?"

"Mmhm." I moved lower, planting a row of kisses straight down her sternum, stopping to rub my lips back and forth between her breasts. "Then it was those huge, dark eyes, surrounded by the longest, prettiest eyelashes I'd ever seen." When I picked up my head, I saw how her nipples had stiffened into little rosy peaks. I circled one with the tip of my tongue, and she arched even more.

"And your voice." I moved to the other one, although she made a little noise of frustration that I hadn't given her what she wanted. "I'd listen to you sing and talk and laugh, and imagine what it would be like to hear you speak to me softly in the dark."

"Just like this," she said, her voice breathless and dulcet, just a little bit rusty with need.

"Just like this." I closed my lips over one breast, and she moaned, her hands tight on my head, holding my mouth to her body. I sucked hard and bit lightly, and she gasped and bucked beneath me. When I brought my mouth to the other, I moved one hand between her legs, slid my fingers easily inside her.

But it wasn't enough. Slowly I dragged my mouth down her body until my head was right between her thighs. "Sometimes I imagined what you'd taste like." I pushed her legs farther apart and kissed one soft, smooth inner thigh, then the other. "But I shouldn't tell you that."

"Tell me," she begged.

"I imagined you'd taste like the vanilla ice cream you used to make." I licked my way up the center of her pussy, and her entire body shuddered. I circled her clit with my tongue, and she cried out. I sucked it gently into my mouth, and she lifted her hips, pushing closer. "Hmm, I was wrong."

She went still. "What?"

I licked her again. "You're sweeter." And again. "Warmer." And again. "More addictive."

She laughed, but it melted into something more plaintive and impatient as I devoured her even more greedily than I had in my fantasies.

"Oh God, I'm gonna come," she whimpered, her hands clawing at the sheets, her hips rocking beneath my mouth. "It's too good, too good, don't stop..."

Was she fucking kidding? I was never going to stop trying to consume her this way, desperate to get my fill, as if I had to make up for lost time. *Never*, I vowed as she cried out, her clit throbbing against my tongue, the rest of her body going still.

I kept going until she sat up and pushed me away, then reached under my arms and tried to yank me on top of her. "Please," she begged.

She didn't need to beg—I was desperate for her. It had only been two weeks, but this felt so different, almost like we'd never done it before. Last time was all about gratifying a physical need, finally answering the question, *What would it be like to be with you?* This was something else entirely—a beginning. A fresh start.

I moved up her body and she hooked her legs around mine. My heart raced as I looked down at her. "Hannah. We should be careful this time."

She made a small, frustrated sound. "You're right. We should. But I don't have anything, do you?"

I shook my head. *Fuck!* "I wasn't thinking of this on my way over. I wasn't even sure you'd let me in."

"I wasn't going to." She brought her hands to the sides of my face. "Did you mean all the things you said downstairs?"

"Of course I did." Braced on my elbows above her shoulders, I rocked my hips over hers, sliding my cock along her slick, wet heat.

She closed her eyes. "That feels so good."

It did feel good, but the body wants what it wants, and soon the skin-to-skin friction wasn't enough.

"Just do it," she said breathlessly. "I need you inside me again, Wes. Even it it's only for a minute. We'll be fine. We were fine the last time."

"Just for a minute," I whispered as I reached down and slipped the tip of my cock inside her. "I won't come inside you."

"Okay." She turned her head to the side as I pushed all the way in. "Yes," she breathed. "Right there. God, it's so deep."

I was completely buried inside her, and the expression on her face was one of torment. "Am I hurting you?"

"Yes." She looked up at me. "But I love it. It's a beautiful kind of pain."

I brushed her hair back from her forehead, the fierce urge to protect her clutching at my heart. "I don't want to hurt you."

"You aren't. You're making me feel alive again, Wes." She moved beneath me, her body undulating in a way that had me hanging onto control with the barest of thread. She picked up her head and whispered in my ear. "Don't leave me."

Her words were as arousing as her body, and I had to move, had to claim her for my own. I watched pain turn to pleasure on her face, filling me with an intoxicating sense of power and possession.

Finally, she was mine.

I took her arms and put them over her head, pinning her wrists to the mattress. "Come for me," I demanded, fucking her deep and hard with tight little thrusts. "Now that you're mine, come for me."

"Yes!" she cried out, her eyes locked on mine. She tried to get her arms loose, but I held her fast.

"I want you to come, Hannah. Now. *Now!*" I ordered, terrified she wouldn't come before I had to pull out, which was in about five more seconds. But she did—I recognized the high-pitched, wavering cry that echoed the pulse inside her, watched the flush overtake her face, and felt her body contracting around mine. She was so fucking beautiful, and she was mine. It was my name she had whispered in the dark, my body bringing her to this state of divine madness, my love she had asked for. I'd never forget the sound of her voice saying those words.

I want you to love me.

I want you to love me.

I want you to love me.

Oh, fuck.

I yanked myself out of her body without a second to spare and fisted my cock, leaning back on my knees and fucking my hand until I came in hot, rhythmic bursts all over my chest.

When it was over, I realized Hannah had been watching me.

"Wow." She was propped up on her elbows, her eyes wide.

I grimaced as my heart continued to race. "I'm sorry. That wasn't exactly a romantic ending."

"It was to me," she said. "Because you put me first."

"I'll always put you first."

She smiled, although it almost looked a little sad to me.

"You don't believe me?"

Her eyes fell. "Sometimes I have a hard time with words like *always*."

Of course she did. My heart felt heavy. "Maybe I can change your mind about them."

She looked up again, her smile a little more hopeful. "Maybe you can."

TWELVE

HANNAH

"FAVORITE MEAL." I was lying across the bed on my stomach, arms folded beneath my head. Next to me, Wes lay on his side, head propped on one hand. With the other, he traced a line down my spine, from the base of my neck all the way to my tailbone, over and over again. We'd been talking for hours about everything and nothing, fascinated by every word that came out of each other's mouths.

"Hmm. I'm not sure I have one." He watched his fingertips glide over each vertebra, from the arc of my ribcage to the ravine of my lower back. His eyes were full of wonder, like I had the most amazing spine he'd ever seen in all his life, personal and professional.

"Come on, I want to make it for you."

"Anything you cook, I will devour. And then, I will devour the cook." He leaned down and bit my shoulder.

I laughed. How long had it been since I'd *laughed* in bed? A wave of affection and gratitude washed over me.

Thank God he hadn't given up on me. "Were you scared tonight? Coming here, I mean. Were you scared I'd say no?"

"Hell yes, I was scared. I had no idea what I could say that would convince you to give me a chance."

"You did a good job."

"Yeah?" One eyebrow cocked up.

"Yeah. And...and it was all true? What you said?"

He laughed. "You keep asking me that. I'm a terrible liar, Hannah. I promise, those things were all true."

"You keep a good secret."

"I had to." He started another path down my back. "So what made you say yes?"

"Hmmm. Good question. Well, I liked what you said, obviously. But I also liked the way you said it. Somehow I knew you meant it."

He kissed my shoulder this time. "I did."

"And the way you looked at me. I liked that too. No one has ever looked at me that way before," I told him.

"What way?" He seemed surprised.

"Like nothing else mattered. Like everything in your life had been leading up to that moment, and what I said would make all the difference in the world to you." Even Drew's proposal hadn't felt so intense or dramatic, but maybe that was because Drew had been entirely sure I'd say yes.

He nodded slowly. "A fair assessment."

"And it was sweet the way you said 'let me love you,' as if you were asking for permission."

"I'd have loved you anyway, you know." He focused on his fingertips, stroking down my spine again.

Chills swept over my skin. When he talked like that, his voice low and sweet, it was so easy to believe we had a chance. "I don't want you to go."

"I don't want to leave." He exhaled. "But I have to. And it's late. You have to work in the morning."

I tried not to be sad about reality intruding on the secret little happiness cocoon we'd created tonight, but it was hard. While he was here, it was easy to shut out the world. Once he was gone, I'd have to be alone with my thoughts. Who knew what that would be like? "Just a little while longer, okay?"

He smiled. "You know I can't say no to you."

I flipped onto my back and looked up at him. "Tell me we'll be okay."

"We'll be okay." He said the words, but I could see in his eyes, he wasn't sure exactly how. How could he be? There was Abby to consider. His parents. My family. Our professional lives. Our reputations. It was easy to say we didn't have to care what people thought, but the reality was, we did.

But not right now.

"Wes. Kiss me."

He brought his lips to mine, a sweet, gentle kiss that was meant to be reassuring, but doubt had begun creeping into my mind. How were we going to do this? When were we ever going to see each other? I twined my arms around his neck and pulled him closer, deepening the kiss, frantic to get as much of him as I could. What if tonight was all we ever had? More than anything, I hated not knowing that I was doing something for the last time. He sensed the urgency in my body.

"Hey," he said softly, running his hand over my hip. "It's okay, sweetheart. This isn't goodbye."

"What if it is?" I searched his eyes. "What if you walk out the door tonight and..." But I couldn't bring myself to say what I was really afraid of. *What if loving me is bad luck? What if something happens to you? What if fate is against us?* "And you decide this is too difficult? I don't even know when I'll see you again." I'd begun to sound a little desperate in a bad way, and I hated myself for it—this was only our second "date," after all—but I was out of practice at calibrating my emotions.

"Hannah. Listen to me." Wes's eyes looked darker than usual. "I didn't come over here and confess ten-years' worth of pent-up feelings about you just to get you into bed. And I'm not going to give up on us just because our situation is difficult."

"What if you decide *I'm* too difficult?"

His brow furrowed. "Are you fucking serious?"

"Yes! I'm not that girl at the diner anymore, Wes. She was young and fun and carefree. Her whole life ahead of her, every door open. I'm thirty-fucking-five. I have a child. I'm moody and sensitive and carrying a fuckload of emotional baggage. I get anxious about everything. I have panic attacks. I cry easily. I don't have any boobs, and your mother doesn't like me."

He put two fingertips over my lips. "Shh. I know you're not that girl in the diner anymore. I'm not that guy, either, the one that let you get away. I know who you are, Hannah. And you still have a life ahead of you. I know it's not the one you planned, but it's still a life. I want to be part of it."

"But—"

He kept his fingers on my mouth. "And don't even get me started on your body. I think it's pretty clear I adore every inch of you."

"But—"

"And it's my *mother* who's difficult."

I pulled his hand down. "I'm still scared."

"I know you're scared. I know, for you, these feelings

came out of nowhere, and they're shocking. You probably feel like the world suddenly started spinning in the opposite direction."

I nodded, my eyes filling, because he understood me so well.

"It's okay, Hannah. We're going to figure this out. Maybe not tonight, maybe not tomorrow, but we'll figure it out. I promise."

"Don't make promises," I whispered. "Life makes them impossible to keep."

"Not for me," he murmured against my lips, kissing me softly. "And not that promise."

I wanted to believe him, but I couldn't. It's not that I thought he was lying to me. I knew he believed what he said, but I'd learned to be wary of absolutes.

Nothing, and nobody, was yours forever. And the moment you thought they were, the moment you let go of fear and settled into contentment, taking for granted that all your dreams would come true—that's the moment you lost it all.

———

MY SHEETS SMELLED LIKE WES, and I was slow to get out of bed the next morning. When my alarm buzzed, I turned it off and lingered for a few minutes. I wondered if he was awake yet. He said he liked to run early, but he hadn't left my house until nearly midnight last night. Maybe he'd be too tired.

Curling up on my side, I wrapped myself in the bedding a little tighter and stared at the sunlight that was just starting to filter through the blinds. It didn't seem possible that it was the same sun that had risen and set yesterday.

Everything was so different. The world was not the same place.

I still couldn't believe it—Wes had had feelings for me all these years? He'd wanted me from the start but had been too shy to say anything? He'd watched Drew and I fall in love, always wondering *what if*? That must have been so hard. I didn't regret my years with Drew, but I did feel an ache in my heart for Wes. I knew what it was like to have a silent, unrequited crush on someone. Who didn't? But how awful to be the one who introduced your crush to the person she married. To serve as best man at the wedding. To make a toast declaring them "true soul mates, a match made in heaven."

Later that night at the wedding, while Drew was drinking with some of his college buddies, I ran into Wes just outside the entrance of the venue. I'd needed some air, and he said he had, too. Big parties were never his thing. I remembered thanking him for his toast, and he told me how happy he was for us.

"So many people keep saying they can't believe Drew wants to settle down," I'd said, fanning my face. "I'm beginning to get a complex about it."

"You've got nothing to worry about." He stood with his hands in his pockets and spoke softly but confidently.

"Really?"

"Really." Then he'd said something to me I'd never forgotten, but hadn't thought about in years. His words came back to me now with startling clarity. "I knew the moment I saw you that you were the one."

It had made me feel so good. Of course, I'd assumed he was talking about Drew, but maybe there was another layer of meaning beneath the words.

And what about all the years *since* the wedding? Had

he stayed away because seeing us was painful? Because he felt guilty?

I rolled onto my back and stared at the ceiling, pulling the sheet to my chin. This was so fucked up. What were we going to do? Just because he'd had feelings for me all that time didn't make this palatable to the public.

I closed my eyes and shook my head, thinking if it was anyone but Wes, people would probably say things like *good for you, it's about time you got out there.* Plenty of people in my life wanted me to be happy, to move on, to find love again.

Just not with my dead husband's brother. Because that was absurd.

Groaning, I threw the blankets off and sat up. Wes and I might understand each other, but no one else would get why or how we made sense. I couldn't even imagine what the Grief Police would throw my way. I didn't want it. I wasn't ready for it.

But love comes without warning.

MARGOT CAME into the kitchen with a grin on her face. "Hannah. Someone's here for you."

"For me?" I paused on my way to the oven with a tray of scones. It was about eight-thirty and we were busy this morning, much busier than we'd thought since the high season was over.

"Yes." The grin widened. This morning she and Georgia had asked me how it had gone last night, and then teased me mercilessly about the way I'd blushed in response. "Go say hi."

My heart was beating fast and loose in my chest. Was it really Wes? I glanced at Georgia. "You okay for a minute?"

"Of course." She took the tray from me and stuck it in the oven. "Go on."

"Parlor table," Margot called out. "And I'm right behind you with the coffee."

With a glance at my clothing—nothing too special, I'd been totally distracted while dressing this morning—and a quick tightening of my ponytail, I pushed open the swinging door, went through the crowded dining room and into the parlor. At a table for four by the front window was Wes, Abby, Lenore, and Dr. Parks.

My stomach somersaulted as I approached. "Well, hello. This is a treat."

"Hi, Mommy." Abby beamed at me.

"Hey." Wes's voice sent a little shiver up my back. Wes and I exchanged smiles, mine nervous, his relaxed. "We decided to take a little field trip. Give Mom a break from the kitchen."

"I told them I didn't need a break," Lenore said, more than a trace of annoyance in her voice. "Hello, dear."

"Good morning, Lenore. Doc." I nodded at them both as Margot began pouring coffee for the adults. "I'm so glad you came. Welcome." Lenore had wandered in a few times to sniff around, but to my knowledge hadn't eaten a meal here.

"Morning, Hannah," Doc said cheerfully. "What's on the menu today?"

"Well, we have fresh pastries, eggs any way you like them, delicious bacon from a local farm, potatoes of course, and I'm making herb waffles with sausage, peppers, and a fried egg on top." I felt Wes's eyes on me like hot maple syrup pouring over my skin. I couldn't even look at him.

"That sounds delicious. Sign me up." Dr. Parks sat back in his chair.

"John, that doesn't sound very healthy for your heart," Lenore chided, placing a hand on his arm. "Why don't you have some plain scrambled eggs?"

This from a woman who shoveled fried chicken and smothered pork chops down everyone's throat.

"Nope." Doc stuck out his chin. "I want the waffle."

"It's divine," put in Margot.

Lenore took her hand from her husband's arm and sat back with a mini-huff.

"I'll have the waffle, too," Wes said.

"Can I have a plain waffle, Mommy?" Abby asked.

"Sure, honey."

"What would you like to drink?" Margot asked Abby.

"She'll have apple juice," I answered. "Would anyone else like juice?"

"Orange, please," said Wes.

"Do you have cranberry?" Lenore asked.

"Of course," Margot said.

Lenore seemed almost disappointed that her request was easily fulfilled. "I'll have that."

"And something to eat for you?" Margot asked.

With a sigh, Lenore looked around like she might find inspiration on someone else's plate at another table. "I'll try the fresh pastries. And maybe some fruit? Do you have grapefruit?"

"Not today, but we've got Michigan peaches, plums, and raspberries that will make your mouth water," Margot said with a smile I recognized as her Customer Smile. "I'll put together something lovely just for you."

"Thank you, dear. Bless your heart." Lenore picked up her coffee and took a tiny sip.

"I should get back to the kitchen," I said. "I'll try to come out again before you leave."

"Don't worry, dear. We know you're busy," Lenore said.

"Thanks. Okay to pick up Abby around two?"

"Of course. No rush at all."

"Uncle Wes said we can make snow cones this afternoon, Mommy. And if it's nice, we can go out in the canoe."

"But you have to dress warmly," Wes told her. "It's chilly on the water."

"Sounds like a fun day." I made eye contact with everyone for exactly the same amount of time. "See you later. Enjoy your breakfast."

Back in the kitchen, I felt like I could breathe again. I looped my apron over my head and started browning the sausage for the waffles.

"Wow. Lenore is really something," Margot said behind me, taking the juice bottles from the fridge.

"Tell me about it." What Lenore *was* was annoying. What she *would be* was another complication for Wes and me. Another obstacle.

"I've never seen her be like that, so fussy and prim. Almost like she was too good to be here."

"Pretty sure I bring out that side of her." I poked at the sausage a little harder than necessary.

"Why?"

I shrugged and admitted the truth. "She's never really liked me."

"Shut the fuck up. Who wouldn't like you?" Georgia asked, checking on the scones.

"I don't get it. What's her problem with you?" Margot placed the glasses of juice on a pretty silver tray.

"Who knows? I think she might have had a different kind of wife in mind for Drew."

"Like who?" Georgia stuck her hands on her hips.

"I don't know. Someone she knew? Someone Southern? Someone smarter, prettier, funnier? Someone with an education? Someone with two parents and a family name like Beauregard, not Randazzo?" I knew I was being childish, but Lenore always managed to bring out the worst feelings of inadequacy in me, and my emotions were running on high today.

Margot sighed heavily. "My mother is that way too about family names. She doesn't like them to have more than one or two syllables *or* end in a vowel. You should have seen her face when I told her I was marrying a Valentini! Be right back." She swung through the dining room door.

Georgia and I worked in silence for a few minutes before she spoke. "That really stinks that she treats you that way. Especially in light of what's going on with you and Wes. Do you think she'll give you a hard time?"

Of course she would, but I didn't want to think about it. "It's fine. And you know, it isn't so much that she treats me poorly, because she really doesn't. And she adores Abby. She just gets under my skin sometimes."

"All mother-in-laws do that."

We got busy in the kitchen, and I never did have time to go out and see how they liked their meals, but if the empty plates were any indication, they'd enjoyed every bite. Margot said Wes and Dr. Parks had raved about the waffles, and even Lenore had offered a few compliments on the pastries, fruit, and crème fraîche.

After work, I went over to pick up Abby, and Wes answered the door. "Hi, beautiful."

I blushed as I stepped inside. The house smelled good, like fresh-baked cookies. "Hi."

As soon as the door was shut behind me, he grabbed me and planted a huge kiss on my lips.

"Wes!" My eyes frantically skimmed the room beyond him.

"Don't worry, they're down on the beach. That was for making me breakfast. Thank you."

"You came to eat at my restaurant, silly. You paid for breakfast." My heart would not stop racing. I felt like a schoolgirl with her first crush.

"Still, you made it and I'm grateful. It was excellent."

"I'm glad you enjoyed it."

"Want to go down?"

"Sure." I followed him through the house and down the steps to the beach, where Lenore and Doc were sitting in chairs watching Abby play in the sand. "Hi, everyone," I called, giving them a wave.

"Here." Wes offered me the only other chair on the beach, which had probably been his. "You take this. I'll get another one."

I sat down, and a moment later, Wes returned, opened up a chair, and set it right beside mine.

"Wes? Daddy and I are going to take a little walk," called Lenore, dragging Doc to his feet. "Back soon."

"Okay."

"I hope Abby's been good," I said.

"She's been a riot. So much energy. We made snow cones and took the canoe out and played Barbies and we were in the middle of a very competitive game of hide and seek when she got a better offer and left me stranded in a closet."

"What?"

"Yeah. I was hiding in the front hall closet and she was looking for me, but I heard my mom say, 'Abby, want to make some cookies?' Abby shouted 'Yes!' And that was that. She abandoned me for chocolate chips."

I was laughing uncontrollably at the thought of him in that closet, ditched by his six-year-old niece. "She has a short attention span sometimes."

"*Now* you tell me." We sat in silence for a moment, each of us staring at the lake. When he spoke, his voice was much quieter. "I can't stop thinking about last night."

"Me either."

"Any regrets?"

"No. You?"

"None."

"I mean, I can't say my feelings about what we're doing aren't complicated. They are. And I'm still working through it. But I'm not sorry."

"Good. There's no pressure here, Hannah. If you need time, you've got it."

"Are you sure?"

He reached over and squeezed my hand. "I'm not going anywhere."

My insides warmed. "Thank you. Maybe if we can just keep it to ourselves for a while. I think that would help me."

"Of course. I won't say anything to anyone."

"I feel like I should tell you, though, I mentioned something to Margot and Georgia at work yesterday."

His eyebrows shot up. "You did?"

"Yeah. I needed someone to talk to and I was panicking about coming here last night. I'm sorry."

"It's okay. I'm okay with that. You trust them?"

"Totally. I also mentioned you at Wine with Widows."

"Wine with what?"

I smiled. "Wine with Widows. It's what I call my little

Wednesday night therapy group. But trust is sacred with those ladies."

"Jeez, I feel like I should have more friends or something. You're so popular."

"Haha." I swatted his arm. "I'm not really that social at all, especially since Drew died. I just tend to have the occasional meltdown in front of my small circle of trust."

"Am I in your circle of trust now?"

I smiled at him. "You're at the heart of it."

He nodded in satisfaction. "Good."

We chatted a little while longer since Abby was playing so nicely, and were still sitting there when Lenore and Doc returned from their walk.

"Don't you two look cozy," Lenore commented. Was there a note of suspicion in her voice? Behind her sunglasses, her eyes seemed to dart back and forth between us.

I straightened up in my chair, suddenly aware of the way we were leaning toward each other, our heads practically touching. "Well, I should get going." I stood up and called to Abby. "Thanks so much for having her."

"Of course." When Abby came over, Lenore tucked her beneath one arm. "We love our little Abby to pieces."

I nodded. "See you soon. Bye, Doc. Bye, Wes."

The men said goodbye, and I herded Abby up the steps and around the house to the driveway. I was backing out when I realized Lenore hadn't asked us to stay for Sunday dinner, which she always did. Was it because she sensed something going on between Wes and me? A sweat broke out on my back.

No. I was imagining things, wasn't I? It had been an intense twenty-four hours and my sensory system was on overload. Paranoia was creeping in. Probably Lenore simply forgot to ask, or maybe they were just having leftovers from yesterday, or maybe since she'd hosted us the night before, she wanted a little break from company. That had to be it. And I wouldn't have stayed anyway.

I put it out of my head.

THIRTEEN

WES

MY DAD WENT up to the house, and my mother dropped
into the chair Hannah had vacated a moment earlier.

"Any plans tonight?" she asked breezily.

"No."

"You should get out more." Her tone was reproachful.
"You're never going to meet anyone if you're always
hanging around the house with your family."

"I'm fine, Mom. I like my family. And I haven't seen
them in a while."

"Don't get me wrong, dear, family is the most important
thing in life, but aren't you thinking of starting your own?
After all, you're not getting any younger."

I gave her a wry look. "Thanks."

"Why don't you let me introduce you to someone?"

"No."

"She's so lovely." My mother went on as if I hadn't even
spoken. "Beautiful, smart, very poised and mature."

"Mom. Stop."

"She's the granddaughter of one of the ladies in my bridge group. I think she works for one of the big pharmaceutical companies, lots of traveling around to different doctors' offices, that sort of thing. She even comes to Daddy's office sometimes."

"Enough. I'm sure she's great, but I'm not interested."

"Why not?"

"Because I'm not looking for anyone."

"That's ridiculous. Of course you are."

I turned and stared at her. Was she insane?

"If you want a family, and I know that you do, then you need a wife," she said, like it made all the sense in the world. "Maybe you're not actively pursuing someone right now, but you don't want to let the perfect wife slip away just because you're not quite ready yet."

"Do you even hear yourself?"

"What?" She lifted her shoulders in a *who, me?* shrug. "I'm just pointing out the obvious, darling. Somewhere in the back of your mind, you have to be aware of the future. You're taking the steps one by one—coming home, taking over Daddy's practice, buying a house. The next logical step is a wife and family."

I frowned. "Leave it, please."

"And you're a doctor in a small town," she went on, continuing to ignore me. "People look up to you. They have to be able to trust your judgment. You can't run around with just any old Jane."

"Jesus Christ. Will you stop?" I had a long fuse, but she was nearly at the end of it.

"I'm only trying to help, Wes." She rubbed my arm. "I want to make sure you have the best of everything, darling. Choosing just the right person to share your life with is important. And sometimes people need help finding that person."

"Well, I don't. So thank you very much for your concern, but I have enough going on without adding a relationship to the mix."

"What? What do you have going on?" she pressed, throwing her hands in the air. "As far as I can see, you only have work. You never see any friends, and the only grown-up you spend any time with at all besides your parents is Hannah. And I'm not certain that's the best thing for you."

I leveled her with a look. "What the hell do you mean by that?"

She flashed her palms at me. "Don't get angry, darling. I only mean that Hannah is still getting over Drew's death. She still wears her wedding ring, bless her heart. But she's obviously very depressed and unhappy, and I don't think she's a very good influence on you. Both of you need some other friends. The only friends I know of that she has is a group of widows like herself."

Stay calm. Remain seated. It won't do Hannah any good to blow up at Mom. "Maybe she likes being around them because they understand what she's going through."

She shrank back. "But it's so morbid, don't you think? Why not cultivate a group of friends based on something healthy and happy, like gardening or cards? I invited her to my bridge club a few times, but she turned me down." Her tone and expression told me she was still peeved about it. She lowered her voice and spoke conspiratorially. "I don't think she knows how to play. Bridge is sort of an intellectual game."

Was smoke coming from my ears? Felt like it. I gripped the arms of the chair I was in. "Enough about Hannah. She's doing the best she can to recover from a sudden and unimaginable loss, to parent Abby all on her own, and I think she's doing an amazing job. You're being way too hard on her."

"Perhaps," she said with a sigh. "I don't mean to be. I guess I've simply never understood her very well. She wasn't at all who I thought Drew would choose. What did they even have in common?"

"They loved each other."

"I suppose." Another heavy sigh. "Your brother always was a fool for a pretty girl." She patted my arm. "I'm sorry if I upset you, darling. I only want you to be happy. What else do I have?"

"It's fine." At this point, I just wanted the conversation to be over. "But no match-making, okay? I'll find someone on my own when I'm ready."

"Okay, darling. I better go get dinner started." She went up to the house, but I stayed on the beach a while longer, staring at the lake and thinking about the promise I'd made to Hannah last night.

Don't make promises, she'd begged. *Life makes them impossible to keep.*

It hurt me to think life had treated her so harshly that she couldn't trust me, but I understood. Life threw some pretty bad shit at you sometimes. I'd seen plenty of it in Africa—famine, disease, war, poverty. It could wear you down, make you feel hopeless, make you feel like nothing you did mattered because we were all just pawns in a larger game being played by forces way beyond our control. It made you feel small and helpless and alone.

But you pushed forward. You kept going. Because there was beauty, too. The smile of a child you'd saved. The tearful gratitude of his parents. The people who worked beside you, sacrificing time and money and often their own health, for the greater good. And it made you appreciate things more.

The scent of cookies baking in the oven. The sound of the waves at night. The embrace of the woman you'd always loved.

Yes, life could be short and cruel. But we had each other, and we could spend whatever days we were afforded being happy together.

It was the only way to fight back.

ON MONDAY MORNING, I got a call from Brad telling me my offer on the house had been accepted. I listened to his voicemail at lunch and called him back as I drove home from work.

"Hey, Brad. Got your message. That's great news."

"Yeah, congrats. You excited?"

"Hell yes. I'm so ready to move out of my parents' house."

He laughed. "I bet."

We talked a little about securing the mortgage and setting up a meeting to sign the papers before I asked him for a favor. "Any chance I could get a key a little early so I can show my folks the house?" The owners had already moved to Florida, so the house was empty.

"That shouldn't be a problem. Want to swing by my office?"

"Now?"

"Sure. As long as you don't throw a party in there or anything, you can show it off."

I laughed. "I'm moving there to get away from people. No parties for me." *Unless it's a party of two.*

"I'll be here until seven. Come on by."

I picked up the key from Brad and sat in the parking lot of the real estate office a moment, my phone in my hand. I was dying to call Hannah and invite her to see the house, but I didn't want to invade her space. She'd asked for some time to think, and I wanted to honor my pledge to give it to her.

But a phone call would be okay, right? She could always ignore it if she didn't want to talk to me. Or maybe a text. That was better. And if she didn't answer right away, I'd just drive home and see if my parents wanted to see the house. That's what I'd told Brad I was doing, anyway.

Hey, you. My offer was accepted. Want to see the house?

I hit send and waited a moment, holding my breath. Jesus, it was like being thirteen all over again. *I like you, do you like me? Check yes or no.*

My phone vibrated in my hand. She was calling me.

"Hello?" I couldn't keep a smile off my face.

"Hey! Congratulations!"

"Thanks."

"That's such great news. I'm so happy for you."

"Now I can get out of my mother's house."

She laughed. "A very good thing. I can't wait to see it!"

"Want to? I have a key. Brad said it would be okay to go there since the owners are already gone."

"Oh my gosh, I'd love to!"

"I'll pick you up." I started my car, eager to see her.

"Can Abby come too?"

"Of course!"

"Great. I'm so excited, Wes."

"Me too. See you in a few."

I practically sped to Hannah's house. When I pulled

into the driveway, Abby came running out, a big smile on her face. I got out and opened up the back door. "Hi, Abby. How was school?"

"Good." She climbed into the back seat. "Mommy's getting me a booster seat."

"Ah." I hadn't thought about that.

"And she said maybe we can go for ice cream after we see your new house."

"That sounds good. Although I haven't eaten dinner yet. Maybe I can just have ice cream for dinner."

She giggled as the garage door opened and Hannah emerged with a purple booster seat. She gave me a smile that made my heart speed up. Her hair was down again, and I wished she could give me a hug so I could smell it.

"You look nice," she said. "I never see you in your work clothes."

"Thanks." I walked over to her and took the seat. "I got this."

"Okay." She got in the passenger seat while I secured Abby on the booster in the back.

On the drive to the house, I felt ridiculously light-hearted. Just having them in my car, the fact that we were going somewhere together for the first time, made me happy. "Want the radio on?" I asked.

"Yes! Put it on seventy-three!" said Abby.

Hannah laughed. "She likes the forties station on satellite radio."

"Perfect." I turned on the radio and found the station she wanted. Frank Sinatra's smooth baritone filled the air.

"I love this song," Hannah said wistfully. "I wish popular music was still like this."

"Me too," I said.

"And you could dress up and go to a supper club on a

Saturday night and dance with your sweetheart. No one dances like that anymore."

"You like to dance?"

"I used to. Drew hated it."

"That's probably because our mother dragged us to dance class when we were young."

"What?" she said, laughing. "I never heard that."

"It wasn't just a dance class, actually. That was just the part we hated the most. It was more like a course on manners and behavior. Social skills. Etiquette for caveman boys."

"Oh my God. That's hilarious. And you went?"

"We had to." I turned into the driveway, which sloped downhill toward the house.

"And did you learn to dance?"

"I did. And I was pretty good at it, thank you very much. The part I dreaded most was the asking. I was too shy and always scared the girl would say no."

"Of course you were."

"One time I worked up the nerve and the girl said yes. But halfway through the song, she said, 'I'm sorry. This is just too awkward.' And she left me there."

"No! The horror!" She clutched her chest. "Were you scarred for life?"

"I was. To this day, I hate that song."

"What was it?"

I shuddered. "More than Words."

"Oh my God, I love that song!"

"You and everybody else but me."

She patted my shoulder consolingly. "I promise I will always say yes if you ask me to dance, and I will finish the song every time." Then she gasped. "Look at your house! It's beautiful!"

"It needs some work, but thank you."

I let us in and gave them a tour, and Hannah's enthusiastic praise for everything from the view of the lake to the high ceilings and roomy kitchen made me feel even better. Abby liked the purple and orange sponge paint in one bedroom, and was disappointed when I told her I'd probably have it repainted.

When we finished touring the house, we walked down to the beach. Abby asked if she could take off her socks and shoes and put her feet in the water, and Hannah said it was fine, but not to get her clothes wet. We stood side by side and watched her splash around and toss stones at a giant rock sticking out of the water about fifteen feet out.

"It's a great house, Wes. I'm happy for you."

"Thanks." I glanced at her profile. My hands ached to touch her. "How are you?"

"Good." She gave me a shy smile. "You're so handsome. I keep wanting to stare at you."

"God, Hannah. You have no idea how much I want to kiss you right now."

She sighed. "I beg to differ."

But we stayed a respectable distance apart. "I missed you last night."

"I missed you, too. I kept wanting to call you, but then I'd talk myself out of it because I'm supposed to be taking time to think."

"I know. I was the same. I picked up my phone a hundred times to text you, but told myself to leave you alone."

"And I *am* thinking. But the problem is that I always wind up thinking about the sex and then I'm so distracted, I can't even remember what else it was I was supposed to be thinking about."

I laughed. "I believe it was something about making sure you're making good decisions for Abby. And for yourself."

"Oh, right." She hugged herself. "Getting a little chilly, isn't it?"

"Are you cold?" I couldn't help it. I wrapped my arm around her shoulders to warm her up.

She looked up at me in surprise. "Just a little. But that feels so nice."

It did. So I kept my arm around her, even when Abby turned and saw us. If she was surprised, she didn't show it. "Can we go get ice cream now?"

"Sure," I said.

"Sit down for a minute and let your feet dry, Abs. Then we'll brush off the sand so you can put your shoes back on."

"Okay." Abby wandered about twenty feet away and perched on a cluster of boulders at the edge of the water, singing softly to herself.

Hannah glanced up at me. "Think we're confusing her?"

"Maybe," I admitted, reluctantly taking my arm from her shoulders.

"No, put it back." She lifted my arm and snuggled into its curve. "If she asks, I'll tell her the truth. I was cold and you warmed me up."

"Okay."

"I'll leave out the part where I want more than just your arm on me and I can't stop thinking about getting you out of your nice work pants and fucking you on your new kitchen floor. Or maybe in your new shower. Or even in your backseat. My imagination isn't being too picky." She kept her eyes on Abby as she spoke, her voice low.

"Christ." I tried to adjust the crotch of my pants

without letting on what I was doing. She was speaking quietly, but my dick heard every word.

She giggled and glanced down. "Problem?"

"Just don't talk for a minute."

She laughed again. "Okay. I'll be nice. But maybe you can come over later?"

I hesitated. "What about Abby?"

"She goes to bed by eight. Come at nine."

"Are you sure?"

"Yes." She tipped her head to my shoulder, but only for a second. "I want to be with you tonight."

WE WENT FOR ICE CREAM, but when Hannah heard that I hadn't eaten dinner yet, she made me promise to come in when we got back to her house so she could feed me. My mother probably had dinner waiting for me, but I couldn't say no to Hannah. I shot my mom a quick text.

Don't hold dinner for me.

Feeling a little guilty, I added a heart emoji before getting out of the car and following Hannah and Abby inside the house. She warmed up the lemon chicken and vegetables she'd made earlier, and even poured me a glass of wine before joining me at the table with her own glass. Abby brought a little book she'd made in school to the table and read it out loud to us while I ate.

"Wow, Abby. You're such a good reader," I told her. "Did you learn all that in kindergarten already?"

"Some of it," she said, tugging on a blond curl. "But some Mommy taught me. I already know a lot of our popcorn words."

"Popcorn words?"

She giggled. "It's not really popcorn. It's words we use a lot."

"Basic sight words," Hannah explained, taking my empty plate to the sink. "Abby is getting really good at them. Okay, kiddo, up to the bath."

I finished the rest of my wine and brought the glass to the sink, where Hannah was loading the dishwasher. "Thanks for dinner. Delicious, as usual."

"You're welcome." She glanced over her shoulder at Abby, who was still at the table. "Say goodnight to Uncle Wes."

She slid off her chair and came over to me, reaching up.

Crouching down, I hugged her. "Night, princess."

"Night, Uncle Wes." Then she wandered down the hall and up the stairs, singing to herself again. "She's always singing. What about music lessons or something? Piano, maybe?"

Hannah sighed and dried her hands on a towel. "I wish we had a piano."

"So let's get you one."

She rolled her eyes. "Pianos are big items, Wes. And pricey."

"I'll buy it."

"No."

"Come on. Do you know how happy that would make me?"

She eyed me dubiously.

"I'm serious. Please let me do this for her. Studying an instrument is so good for kids."

"It is." She bit her lip, torn between accepting such a big gift and wanting Abby to have it. "We're not your responsibility."

"Hannah." I took her by the shoulders and turned her to

face me. "Let me. It's best when they start young. You can pay me back later, if you want to. In blowjobs, even."

She broke into laughter. "Deal."

I gave her a quick kiss on the forehead. "Good. Now I'm going to find the best, most expensive piano money can buy. I want it to take *forever* for you to work off."

"Ha. I better get upstairs. See you later?"

I nodded, but I didn't want to leave. "See you later."

I let myself out and drove home, feeling much better than I had yesterday about everything.

Trust my mother to ruin my mood.

"Wes? Is that you?" she called from the kitchen when I came in the front door.

"It's me." I wished I could just go to my room and avoid her interrogation, but I dutifully went into the kitchen to say hello.

"Did you eat?" she asked, closing up the dishwasher and turning it on. "I can make you a plate."

"I ate." I leaned back against the counter, hands in my pockets.

She waited expectantly, and when I didn't offer any details, she asked. "Where?"

I thought about lying and decided against it. "At Hannah's."

She blanched. "What were you doing at Hannah's?"

"I took her and Abby over to see my new house. Brad called today—the offer was accepted."

But instead of being happy about that, she focused on the part where I took Hannah to see it first. "You took them to the house already? *I* haven't even seen it!"

"Would you like to? I have to return the key to Brad tomorrow, but I'd be glad to run over there with you right now and show you around."

"I can't. I have bridge club tonight. I have to leave soon."

"Well, let me ask Brad if I can keep the key one more day. I'll take you there tomorrow after work."

She pressed her lips together. "That will be fine, I guess. But I won't say I'm not hurt that you took Hannah before you took me. Or Daddy," she added as she took a sponge from the sink and began wiping down the island.

"Come on, Mom. It was just a quick thing. I thought it would cheer her up, and I wanted to get her opinion on the kitchen remodel."

"*I* can help you with that too, you know." She scrubbed viciously at a spill on the marble.

"I know. And I'll be glad for your help. I'll need a lot of help with this new house. Your input will be needed and appreciated."

That seemed to mollify her, and her movements slowed, her voice softening. "Fine, dear. But I do wonder," she began in a way that let me know I wasn't going to like what she had to say. "I do wonder if all this time with Hannah isn't a little bit...tacky."

"Tacky?"

"Well, people talk. And if they see you two together around town, or catch you coming and going from her house, they might get the wrong idea. Of course, *I* know that nothing untoward is going on, but can you imagine the terrible gossip that would spread? The name calling? Poor Hannah. It would be devastating to her reputation. Not to mention little Abby."

"What do you mean?"

"Children can be horribly cruel. If they hear their parents saying things, they might repeat them." She took the sponge to the sink and rinsed it. "I'm not trying to tell you what to do, dear. I'm only concerned for Hannah and Abby."

She was so full of shit. "But not me?"

"Well, of course for you too, dear." She began wiping down the counters again. "But it's always the woman people focus on. Always the woman who takes the blame and the brunt of the criticism. Because men aren't expected to behave properly—no offense, dear—and it's never shocking when they let their you-know-whats make their decisions. But a woman is expected to know better and behave a certain way. If she doesn't, she's called a slut."

"Mom." My voice was sharp.

"What? I'm not saying it's *right*," she went on, as if she was above such nonsense. "But it's reality. It's human nature to gossip, and that's what they'll say. I'm just being honest."

"If anyone said that about Hannah, I'd fucking punch them in the face."

She stopped moving and looked up at me, shocked. "Wesley Davis Parks!"

"What? I'm not saying it's right," I went on, mimicking her tone, "but it's what I'd do. I'm just being honest."

Her spine went ramrod straight. "I did not raise a boy who talks to his mother that way."

"Should I go to my room?"

"Yes!" she snapped.

I would have laughed, except I was too furious. Instead of going to my room, I grabbed my keys again and went right back out the front door. It was only quarter after eight, so I couldn't go to Hannah's yet, but I had to get out of the house. I drove into town, parked, and ducked into a bar called The Anchor.

There were plenty of seats open at the bar, and I chose

one toward the back. I didn't feel like talking to anyone. When the bartender came over, I ordered a beer and then sat there brooding into it. Fucking mothers! Why did they have to be so difficult?

But I couldn't help wondering if there was any truth to what mine had said. Was I putting Hannah and Abby at risk by spending time with them? Were people so cruel and heartless that they'd talk that way? Deny them the chance to be happy? What the fuck was wrong with people? Did they have nothing else in their lives?

While I was fuming about it, a few women came in, laughing breezily about something. After every one of them eyed me up, they sat at a high-top table right behind me and proceeded to further destroy my faith in humanity.

"Oh my God, did you see what she was wearing?"

"I probably shouldn't say this, but I heard he can't get it up."

"I'm not trying to be mean, but someone needs to tell that woman she is not a size eight anymore.' "

"Who does he think he's kidding with that car? Hello! Midlife crisis!"

"Please. It's so obvious the way she throws herself at him."

"He's totally cheating on her. You can just tell."

In fifteen minutes, I heard enough gossip and trash talk to last me a lifetime. I felt sick to my stomach. Was my mother right?

And then.

"I know. I kind of freaked out when I saw him. I forgot he had a twin."

Jesus. Did they think I was deaf? It's not like they were whispering.

"I know. So hot."

"My mother goes to that practice. Maybe I should, too." Snicker, snicker. "Get a little mouth to mouth."

Gasp. "You're so bad."

"What? He's fucking gorgeous. I might pretend to choke right now."

"I used to be friends with Drew's wife. Have you seen her lately? Way too skinny."

"Totally. You're not friends with her anymore?"

"Not really. I just didn't know what to say to her after it happened."

"So tragic."

"So young."

"So hot. But I heard he had an affair, did you?"

I couldn't take any more. I paid for my beer, left without finishing it, and drove to Hannah's. But when I pulled up in front of her house on the darkened street, all I could hear were my mother's words in the shrill voices of the women at the bar.

I heard his car has been parked in front of her house for hours at night.

I've seen them getting ice cream together with her little girl.

I heard they went to his house while it was empty and had sex while the daughter played on the beach.

Ugh, it's so sleazy.

So wrong.

So tacky.

How could they?

It was enough to make me think twice about knocking on her door. What if my mother was right?

My phone vibrated. My screen showed a text from Hannah. **Are you sitting out there because you're scared to ask me to dance?**

I smiled for half a second. **Yes.**

I told you. I'll always say yes. And I'm in the mood for dancing.

Her words set my blood simmering. *Fuck my mother's warning*, I thought. Fuck those women in the bar, and fuck anyone who thought this was wrong. It had been a long time since I'd punched someone in the face. It would feel pretty damn good.

She was mine now. *Mine.*

Me too. Be right there.

FOURTEEN

HANNAH

I BIT my lip and backed away from the front window, drawing the curtain closed again. I wasn't sure where we'd end up—upstairs was out, since I didn't want to risk waking Abby, but we'd be in plain view on the couch if she heard something and wandered down the stairs. I had every window in the house covered, just in case, and every light off. Not that his car wasn't in plain sight, but he could just be visiting. *A friendly little visit after dark. Nothing to see here, neighbors. Move along.*

My heart was pounding as I hurried through the dark to the door. I heard his footsteps on the porch and opened it. The sight of him, still in his work clothes, tie a little loose, hair a little disheveled, made my insides clench.

"Knock, knock, little girl," he said, stepping across the threshold. His voice sounded deeper and more intense than usual. "Are you all alone?"

Nervous excitement shimmied up my spine, the feeling

you get with the *click click click* of a rollercoaster climbing uphill on the track. "No."

He pushed the door shut behind him and walked toward me, backing me deeper into the dark hallway, loosening the knot of his tie a little more, then pulling it off. "Then we'll have to be very, very quiet. Can you do that?"

Given the hunger in his eyes and the *don't fuck with me* in his voice, I wasn't sure I could. And I liked the slow, predatory way he moved toward me in the dark, like a lion that knows his strength far outweighs that of his prey but hopes she might put up a fight anyway. "Maybe."

"Don't worry," he said in his doctor voice, slipping the tie through his fist. "I'll help you."

I eyed that tie, my breath coming fast. Drew had never been into games or anything kinky during sex. He'd been a straightforward lover, generous and passionate, and had always made sure I had at least one orgasm. But he didn't talk during sex, never expressed any interest in toys or other bedroom props, and when I broached the idea of being tied up one time, just to introduce a little play into our routine, he'd said he couldn't imagine doing that to me and enjoying it. I was his wife; he thought of me a certain way, and it wasn't as a sexual object. He wanted to take care of me, not mistreat me. I'd been too embarrassed by the reproach to try again.

So when Wes backed me into the tiny hallway bathroom, stripped off my clothes, and turned me to face the mirror, I shivered with anticipation. What would he do to me? The little nightlight by the sink was on, lighting us from below with soft gold light.

He slipped the tie through his hands again as he met my eyes in the mirror. The possibilities enticed me. My eyes? My hands? My mouth? I was utterly seduced by being powerless, for once. *Go on*, I thought. *Do it.* For a moment I thought he might ask for permission and ruin the entire fantasy.

But he didn't.

He slipped the tie between my lips and worked it between my teeth, tying it at the back of my head. Immediately my heart rate accelerated, and I began to panic, but Wes's warm hands running down my arms and his soft voice in my ear were soothing. "Shhhh," he said. "It's just to remind you to stay quiet. I don't want to hear any sound from you, no matter what." One hand moved around my stomach and down between my legs, rubbing my clit in a steady, gentle circular motion.

I whimpered and he took his hand away. Both arms caged me tightly to his body. "Hush," his whispered in my ear, his eyes pinning mine in the mirror. "I said no sound."

I nodded and reached behind me, feeling his erection through the material of his dress pants. He stepped back and unbuckled his belt, pulling it from the loops. I thought he'd toss it to the floor and undo his pants, but instead, he caught my wrists and wound the strip of leather around them. I sucked in my breath.

Our eyes stayed locked on our reflection, which gave me the odd sense of watching two people that weren't us. This couldn't be us, this shadowy fantasy unfolding in the mirror. His eyebrows rose in question and I gave a tiny nod.

A moment later my wrists were bound.

"Now," he said, his voice quiet but burning with need, "I'm going to make you come twice, first with my fingers and then with my cock, and you're not going to make a sound. Understand?"

I nodded, but I had zero confidence in my ability to remain silent.

Turns out I was right—I gasped and moaned so much as his fingers worked their magic that he brought his other hand to my mouth, clamping it over my lips. And he kept it there as he fucked me hard from behind with deep, punishing thrusts, muffling my strangled cries.

But as he brought me to the brink that second time, as I felt my insides tighten and my knees go weak, my wrists straining at their bonds, I felt one more piece of me return to myself. The part that *enjoyed* being a sexual object when the objectification brought me to such heights. When I was *choosing* to be the instrument of someone else's pleasure. When I felt *empowered* by the strength of his desire. By the heat of his breath against my ear as he whispered to me— *Open your eyes. I want you to see this. You're so fucking beautiful when you come*—and by his cock, which thickened and throbbed achingly deep inside me, shaking me to the bone.

When it was over, he wrapped both arms around my waist and held me close. A moment later he untied his tie and I moved my jaw, licked my lips.

"You okay?"

I nodded.

He pulled out, and a second later I felt his hands working at his belt around my wrists. When it came loose, I took one wrist in the other hand and cradled it as I turned to face him. I was almost surprised to see he was still fully clothed. Somehow I'd forgotten. But it added another layer to the power play, and I liked it. It felt so good to *choose* vulnerability and helplessness, rather than to be an unwilling, unwitting victim of fate.

He reached for me. "Come here."

I let him take me in his arms, press me to his chest. I could smell the starch on his shirt collar and a lingering trace of this morning's aftershave or hair product. Masculine smells I'd missed. I wrapped my arms around his waist. "I wish you could hold me like this all the time."

He kissed my head. "Me too."

"Do you think the time will ever come when you can?"

"I want that more than anything."

It wasn't exactly the answer I'd hoped for and cast a little shadow over my post-sex glow. I released him and reached for my clothes while he removed the condom I hadn't even realized he wore. *Thank God*, I thought. We really couldn't afford to be careless in our situation.

"Want some water?"

"Sure, thanks. Should I—" He glanced at the small trash can under the sink.

"Oh. Yes, that's fine. I'll take the bag out later." I left him alone for a moment and went to the kitchen, turning on the light before filling two glasses with cool water from the tap. I was chugging mine when he came into the room, all put together again.

He picked up his glass and took a few swallows. "Thanks."

"You're welcome." I leaned back against the sink.

He set the glass down and stared at it like it hadn't tasted right. Immediately I was on high alert.

Something is off. "What's wrong?"

"Nothing."

"Wes. What is it?"

"I'm just—" He closed his eyes a second, his lips pressed together. "Frustrated."

"About us?"

"Yeah." Silence. "I had a conversation with my mother earlier."

A siren went off in the distant reaches of my mind. "Oh? What did she say?"

"I shouldn't worry you with this. It's pointless."

"Just tell me."

"She's got me worried about what people will say when they find out about us. I know I said 'fuck people' before, but I think I underestimated the degree to which people can be shitty to others."

My heart beat clumsily in my chest. "Does she know about us?"

"No. Not that I know of."

"Well, what did she say, specifically?"

"She thinks we spend too much time together, and when she heard I took you to the new house and then ate dinner here, she got weird about it."

Of course she did. But Drew and I had gotten into enough arguments about his beloved mother to last me a lifetime. That was a part of my marriage I did not want to revisit. And I was working on being more understanding of Lenore, anyway. I could be the bigger fucking person. "Maybe she was hurt you didn't take her first," I suggested.

"I think there's some of that for sure," he went on, turning to lean on the counter beside me, "but then she started in about what people will say if they notice my car here, or see me coming and going all the time, or see us out in public together. She thinks people will gossip about how tacky it is, and even though *she* knows there's nothing unsavory going on"—he did his best dramatic impression of Lenore—"the rumors and name-calling will be out of control."

I nodded, my eyes on my toes. "Right."

"She claims to be concerned for your reputation, and for Abby's well-being. She's worried that kids Abby goes to school with will hear their asshole parents talking and repeat what's being said."

My stomach turned. I looked up at him. "Do you think that's true?"

"I didn't at first. But then she went on about how people are more forgiving of the man in these situations, how they'll excuse him because we're all just Neanderthals following our dicks around and trying to stick it in whoever we can find, but that women are held to a higher standard and judged more harshly."

I started twisting my ring. "She's got a point."

"The moment I thought about someone calling you a name or saying anything that would hurt your feelings or Abby's, I wanted to fucking put my fist through the wall." Wes spoke through clenched teeth.

That almost made me smile.

"The conversation ended badly between my mother and me, so I stormed out and went to have a beer so I could cool off. But then this group of women came into the bar, sat at a table right behind me, and proceeded to talk about half the town, including me, in a way that made me feel like maybe my mother is right."

I picked up my head. "What did they say about you?"

The color in his face deepened. "Nothing much."

"Tell me."

"Just a bunch of stupid hot doctor jokes."

It wasn't the whole truth, but I let it go. "Yeah. Drew used to get that, too."

Wes watched me playing with my ring, his expression pained. Maybe he didn't like being reminded that I'd been his brother's wife, but that was our fucking reality. *I told you this would be too hard.*

"I don't know what to do," he said. "I want to protect you, but I want to be with you, too. It's so fucking unfair."

"It is." *Life. You bitch.*

He turned toward me and looped his arms around my waist. Our hips rested together, and I played with one of the buttons on his shirt, focusing on my fingers and not his face.

"Hey." He jiggled his hands on my back. "I'm not giving up on us. And I don't want you to, either. I'm just irritated with my mother."

"Okay." That wicked little ball was building at the back of my throat again.

"I mean it. Look at me."

I did, but it took me a minute.

"I will deal with her, okay? She is not your problem."

"But she is, Wes. She's affected by this. How she feels matters. And I can tell you right now, she is going to have a huge problem with us. Lots of people will."

"I'll handle her, I promise." He tightened his arms around me, lowered his forehead to mine. "Don't give up. Please."

"I don't want to, but—"

He kissed me, silencing the rest of my sentence. "Don't. We'll figure it out together, okay?"

"Okay." When he talked to me in that quiet, sweet voice, I couldn't refuse him.

But when I closed the door behind him a few minutes later, I felt a pit open up in my stomach. And as I plodded up the stairs, it began slowly filling with doubt, like sand trickling into an hourglass.

HE CAME over the next three nights in a row, and each

night we took another step forward. Tuesday he came for dinner and did the dishes while I put Abby to bed. He didn't leave and come back like he'd done the night before; instead, he'd gone up to say goodnight to Abby, come back down, and we stretched out on the couch together to watch a movie. With my cheek on his chest and his arms around my back and our legs tangled beneath a blanket, I felt some of the doubt recede. I had a brief moment of panic when Abby came down the stairs asking for a drink of water, scrambling out of Wes's arms and jumping off the couch, but she didn't say anything about him or ask any questions. We didn't have sex that night, but that was okay—I needed to be sure that our connection wasn't just sexual, and it felt good just being close to him.

Wednesday night he worked late and had dinner out, and I hosted Wine with Widows. I didn't say anything about Wes when it was my turn to talk, but Tess was the last one to leave, and when she asked if I'd seen him, I confessed that I had.

She gasped. "Spill!"

"There's not much to tell," I said. "We stayed away from each other for two weeks, but the feelings didn't go away."

"Told you." She looked smug. "So it's going well?"

"Yeah." My face got hot. "It is. I mean, it's brand new—it's only been since Saturday—but it feels really good."

"I'll bet it does. So the sex was just as good the second time?"

"And the third." I couldn't resist. "He tied my hands behind my back with his belt right there in that bathroom."

She glanced at the bathroom door and back at me, her eyes wide. "Who *are* you?"

I laughed. "I'm still me. I'm just figuring some new things out about myself."

He came over later and we snuck upstairs, locked my bedroom door and tore off each other's clothing before fucking like porn stars in a silent film. When the bed made too much noise, we moved to the floor, Wes on his back on the rug and me on top, riding him with reckless abandon. Before he left, around one in the morning, we laughed at the rug burns on his ass and my knees.

"Where's your car?" I asked him at the door.

He kissed me. "I parked around the block. I don't want people to see my car here so much, especially this late at night."

"Oh." It was thoughtful and sweet, but it was yet another reminder that what we were doing was something shameful to be hidden away in the dark.

Thursday Abby came home from school and showed me a picture she'd drawn in crayon of her family. There was me, with long brown hair and big brown eyes and suspiciously big feet. There was Abby, with yellow pigtails and a pink dress, holding a gray scribbly thing I could only imagine was her stuffed elephant. And there was a man, with green eyes and brown hair, whose hands seemed much bigger than anyone else's.

Was it Drew? Or was it Wes?

I felt terrible I didn't know. Abby didn't say one way or the other, but she was proud of her work and hung it on the fridge with a Valentini Brothers Farm magnet.

That night Wes came for dinner again and took us out for ice cream afterward. When we got back, I told him to pull his car into the garage.

"Are you sure?" he said.

"Yes. I don't want you to park around the block and have to sneak over like some criminal."

"I don't mind, if it protects you."

"Just do it. It will make me feel better."

He smiled and did as I asked, then waited downstairs while I put Abby to bed.

"Is Uncle Wes still here?" she asked as I turned out the lamp.

"Yes."

"I like when he's here."

"Me too."

"It makes me feel cozy."

I smiled. "Good."

"And safe," she added.

My smile faded a little. "You're safe no matter what, baby. I'm always here."

"I know. But sometimes you're sad at night."

My stomach clenched. She'd heard me crying. "Sometimes I do get sad at night. That's true. But it doesn't mean you're not safe. It's just Mommy trying to get better."

"You're better when Uncle Wes is here. You're not sad."

I didn't know what to say.

"Maybe he can move in with us," she suggested. "Then you would never be sad and I can always feel safe. We could be a *family*."

"Oh, Abby." I closed my eyes, wishing I could stop time and think of the best way to handle this. Why wasn't there a Single Widowed Parent Handbook for these moments? "We *are* a family. You and me."

"But a family needs a dad."

"Not necessarily. I didn't have a dad, remember?"

She thought for a second. "Were you sad about that?"

"Sometimes," I said honestly. "But I had my mom and I knew she loved me with all her heart, the way I love you."

"But can he move in?"

Apparently all my heart was not enough. "No, Abby. Uncle Wes just bought his *own* house, remember?"

"He could sell that one."

I smiled sadly. "Listen. The important thing is that you are loved and safe and sound here with me, okay? Whether Uncle Wes or anybody else is here or not."

"Okay. Can you send him up to say goodnight?"

I hesitated, but gave in. "Sure."

As I walked downstairs, I felt that pit open up in my stomach again. Abby was falling in love with Wes right along with me. Could I blame her for feeling safer and happier when he was around? Wasn't I? But I had to be careful. What if she grew so attached to him she stopped feeling safe when he wasn't around? As much as Wes and I felt for each other, there was no guarantee this would work. We couldn't even go out for dinner or hold hands in public, let alone spend a night together or share a home. How could I protect Abby from hurt when I couldn't even protect myself?

Wes was in the kitchen, leaning back against the counter, looking at his phone. For a moment, I was back in time, looking at another man in dress clothes after work, checking his messages, waiting to say goodnight to his little girl. Everything was good. We were a family.

He looked up at me, his forehead wrinkling with concern. "What's wrong, baby?"

I twisted my ring. "Abby wants you to say goodnight."

"Okay." He paused. "*Is* that okay?"

"Yes."

"You look like you've seen a ghost."

I pressed my lips together. "No ghosts. Just a little worried about Abby. Go on and say goodnight and then we can talk about it."

"Okay." He dropped a kiss on my head as he walked by, then put a hand over mine. "Stop fidgeting. Everything will be okay."

I tried to smile.

He left the room, and I saw that he had put the dinner dishes in the dishwasher while I'd been upstairs with Abby, and the pans I'd used to cook with had been scrubbed and set out to dry on dishtowels. *I'll say one thing for Lenore. She raised her sons right.*

Was I doing right by my daughter?

My throat tightened. I heard footsteps behind me and turned to see Wes in the kitchen doorway, his face etched with worry. "What?" I asked.

"She asked if I could be her dad."

The room spun. "What did you say?"

"I said I couldn't, because she already had a dad, and nobody could ever replace him."

I nodded as tears swam in my eyes. "That's a good answer."

"It's the truth."

"She asked me if you could move in."

His face went a little pale. "What?"

"Because she wants to be a family. Because she feels safe when you're here, and I'm not sad. My daughter doesn't feel safe with me, Wes. I'm not enough for her to feel safe. I'm not doing this right." I dropped my face into my hands and cried, conscious of the fact that this was exactly why Abby didn't feel taken care of with me. I wasn't a real adult in her eyes, because real adults don't cry. But it only made me sob harder.

Wes's arms came around me in an instant, and I let him hold me, my sobs muffled in his chest. He rubbed my back and spoke softly. "Hey. Listen to me. You are doing a great job raising Abby. I've spent enough time with kids her age to know that not all of them are as well-mannered or kind or happy as she is."

"How can she be happy?" I cried. "I can't give her what she needs."

"Yes, you can, and you are. You're giving her a home and healthy food and unconditional love every day. You're also showing her an example of a woman who suffered an unimaginable loss but picked herself up and carried on. You're teaching her that life is unpredictable, sometimes sad, but at the end of the day, what matters is that you have each other. And you'll always have each other."

"There's no such thing as always," I sobbed. "It's a lie. I thought I'd always have a husband. She thought she'd always have a father. You thought you'd always have a brother."

"I did, Hannah. And there isn't anything I wouldn't do to have him back again, even if it meant giving you up. I know I said the worst thing I ever did was walk away from you, but if I could trade places with him and spare you and Abby the pain you've suffered, give you back the life you wanted, I'd do it."

"Don't talk that way." Suddenly scared of losing Wes too, I wriggled my arms free and threw them around his neck. "I can't lose you."

"You won't. Hannah, you won't."

"I need you." I clung to him, desperate to get as close as I could, craving the physical reassurance of his body.

"You have me." His arms were warm and solid and strong. His voice held nothing but strength and certainty. "I'm here."

I started kissing him everywhere I could—chest and shoulder and neck and throat and jaw. He took my head in his hands and sealed his lips over mine, a kiss that promised *always* and made me feel like it was real as long as I could feel him next to me. Our hands moved frantically over each other's bodies. When our passion pushed us past the limits of resistance, and our clothing made us feel like we were trapped in two separate cages, Wes grabbed my hand and pulled me out the back door.

We ran across the lawn to the garage and slipped inside through the service door. Wes yanked open the passenger door to the backseat of his SUV, and I jumped into it. As soon as he got in and shut the door, I undid my jeans and shimmied out of them. He unbuttoned and unzipped his dress pants, shoving them down past an erection that sprang free from restraint.

"Oh, fuck." He lifted his hips off the seat and reached into his back pocket, pulling out his wallet.

"Let me." I grabbed it from him, fished out the condom, and tore the packet open.

"Oh my God, I feel eighteen again," I said as I rolled it over his thick, hard shaft.

"So do I, so you better get over here before I come just from watching you do that." He reached for me, swinging me onto his lap, groaning as I positioned his cock beneath me and slowly lowered myself onto him.

When my ass was resting on his thighs, I grabbed two fistfuls of his shirt, panting through the deep, stabbing twinge. But we had no time for comfort. And I liked the pain anyway—there was no pleasure without it.

"We have to hurry," I said as I began to move, rocking my body over his.

"No problem." He grabbed my ass and pulled me tight against his body as he flexed his hips, grinding the base of his cock against my clit.

Our eyes locked as we raced toward the peak together, our skin growing damp with sweat, the car windows fogging up. It was our own little world, a secret paradise where no one could find us, no one could hurt us, no one could tell us what we wanted was wrong. We were together as one, and nothing would ever come between us. "Yes!" I cried out as my body erupted in powerful, billowing waves. Wes groaned, his body stiffening, his hands squeezing my ass as his cock pulsed with life inside me.

"Tell me again," I said, breathing hard, tipping my forehead against his. "Tell me again I won't lose you."

"You won't lose me." His hands slid up my back. "I'm here."

I closed my eyes. "God, I wish you could stay the night. I want to sleep in your arms. I want to wake up and know you're there. I'm so tired of being alone when the sun comes up."

"I wish I could, too. But I think that would be very confusing for Abby."

Abby. My sweet girl who wanted Wes to be her daddy. I thought about the drawing on the fridge.

If only it were that easy.

"It would. And I don't want to confuse her any further." I sighed. "Come on. We better get back inside. I don't want her to wake up and think I left her."

We pulled ourselves together enough to sneak back into the house and check on Abby, who was sleeping soundly. Wes was nearly out the door when he noticed the drawing on the fridge.

"Is that new?"

I glanced at it. "Yes. She brought it home today."

He moved closer to it, and I followed.

"I'm not sure whether that's you or Drew," I confessed. "But I didn't want to ask her."

"I think it's me."

"You do?"

"Yeah. She always tells me I have big hands."

"Oh." Part of me was glad she'd drawn Wes, and part of me wasn't.

"They're nothing compared to your feet, though. What's going on there?"

I laughed, looking down at my bare feet. "I don't know. I only wear a six and a half."

"You look like a hobbit or something."

I hit him on the shoulder. "Thanks."

"I'm teasing. You know I think you're perfect." He moved toward the door again. "Hey, how about piano shopping on Saturday, and maybe dinner out Saturday night? You and me and Abby?"

"Really?" I smiled. "Do you think we can?"

"Yes."

"I'd love that. I'm sure Abby would, too. I have to work, but I can probably get off around eleven."

"Great." He gave me one more kiss and cradled my face in one hand.

I turned my cheek into his palm.

"We'll get there, Hannah."

"You think so?"

"Yes. We are not going to be sneaking around in backseats forever. I promise."

Stop promising me things, I wanted to say.

I was starting to believe in them.

FIFTEEN

WES

I'D AVOIDED my mother all week. Refused to take the lunches she packed for me to work. Ate dinner at Hannah's almost every night. Came home so late she was already in bed when I got there. The only time I saw her was in the morning before work, but I never initiated a conversation with her and gave only one-word answers if she asked me a question. I didn't enjoy the hurt expression on her face, nor did I enjoy freezing her out. And I knew I'd make up with her eventually, but dammit, she owed me an apology.

I didn't say anything to Hannah about it, because I didn't want her to be concerned. She had enough to deal with in her own mind. I was kicking myself for even mentioning the argument to her in the first place. I should have just kept my mouth shut.

By Friday the tension in my parents' house was almost unbearable, and my dad asked me if I'd grab a drink with him after work. "There's something I want to talk to you about."

"Sure," I said, although I had a pretty good feeling I knew what the something was and I wouldn't like it.

At least he waited until our drinks arrived. "I take it you had words with your mother," he said, lifting his scotch on the rocks to his lips.

"Yeah." I drank from mine too.

"She's a tough cookie."

"Yeah."

"But she's had to be."

I let that stew a little. "What do you mean? Because of Drew?"

"Even before that." He sipped again, his eyes on the TV screen above the bar.

I waited for him to elaborate. I'd never heard anything negative about my mother's past. Her father, a doctor, had died before I was born, and her mother had died of cancer when I was two. She'd been an only child.

Dad took his sweet old time, as usual, but eventually spoke. "Her father was an alcoholic philanderer who constantly abandoned his family. Her mother coped with pills that knocked her out and left her unable to take care of her daughter. From the time she was five, she had to take care of herself."

I was stunned. Sickened. "She never said anything."

"She never wanted you to know. That's how her family was. Big on appearances."

Some things clicked into place. Pieces of my mother's personality suddenly made sense. It occurred to me what mysteries our parents can be to us. We think we know them, but really, we only know what they choose to tell us.

"She loved her Daddy," my father went on, "and always blamed her mother for their troubles. Said if her mother was more devoted, her father wouldn't have left all the time."

I swallowed more scotch. All the scotch.

"I don't know what she said to you or whether she was right or wrong. But I do know that she loves you the way she wanted to be loved, and her children were her entire life. *Are* her entire life. Her validation."

"I'll have another," I said to the bartender.

I WENT HOME FOR DINNER.

My mother had made smothered pork chops, which I saw as a peace offering. I'd also had two drinks, so I was mellow, if cautious. The three of us sat at the table, my mother serving us all with a nervous smile on her face.

My parents talked easily about whatever—the weather, his retirement, friends, neighbors—but I stayed mostly silent. Even though I felt I understood her better, I still wanted an apology. A tough childhood didn't mean you got a free pass to be mean to others.

After dinner, my dad retired to his chair in the great room, and I helped my mom with the dishes.

I wanted to open a dialogue between us, but I wasn't sure how. *Drew, help me out here.*

As if my brother had heard, my mother broke the silence. "Are you still mad at me?"

"I don't know," I said, loading plates into the dishwasher.

"I upset you, and for that I'm sorry." She spooned leftovers into a plastic container.

"Just for that?"

She snapped the lid on the container and took it to the fridge. "How can I be sorry for wanting the best for my son? For wanting to protect him?"

"You can't," I agreed. "But you said some hurtful things."

She stuck the container in the fridge and shut it. "I'm sorry, Wes."

I looked toward her. She was still facing the fridge.

"I didn't mean to hurt you," she went on. "That's the last thing I ever want to do." She turned to face me, her expression terrified. "You're all I have left."

I exhaled, feeling the weight of being someone's only hope settle heavily on my shoulders. "Mom, that's not true."

"It is," she insisted, starting to cry. "All my life, I couldn't wait to get married and have my own family. I was going to do everything right, give my children every advantage, make sure they never lacked for anything."

"You did."

"But I couldn't save him." She sobbed openly, and I couldn't resist going to her, taking her in my arms. "I couldn't save him and I miss him so much."

My throat tightened as she wept. It was hard to measure a loss—which was greater, the loss of a twin, a child, a spouse? All of us had suffered so much. We had to help each other.

"It's okay, Mom. I'm not mad anymore."

"Are you sure?" She pulled back and sniffed.

"I'm sure. Look, this is rough on us all. We need to find our way in a world without Drew, and it's strange."

"It is." She shook her head. "Sometimes I think he's just going to walk through the door, like he always did, his voice booming, his eyes so bright. Always laughing."

But it's only me, I thought, wondering if she, or Hannah,

for that matter, was ever disappointed once the truth sank in.

"Oh, goodness." She scooted around me and reached for a tissue from the box on the counter. "I'm sorry, darling. This is the last thing you need."

I ran a hand through my hair, exhausted all of a sudden. "It's fine, Mom."

"You look so tired. You're working too much."

"I like the work."

"Did you even eat this week? You never came home for dinner."

"Yes, I ate."

"Where?"

"I've been hanging out with Pete a lot." I hated to lie about my time with Hannah, but it seemed wise for now. "At his house, or sometimes we just grab whatever."

"Oh. Well, that's good. You need to have some fun. And I'm looking so forward to your birthday dinner."

"Where is it?"

Her shiny blue eyes twinkled. "It's a surprise."

"Oh?"

"Yes. You don't have to do anything but show up next Saturday. I've got it all planned."

"But how will I know *where* to show up?"

"Never you mind," she said, busying herself by tossing her tissue in the trash and fussing with her hair. "I'll tell you in plenty of time."

Something cold and slithery snaked up my spine. I crossed my arms. "And who's on the guest list?"

"Never you mind about that, either," she said, patting me on the shoulder. "All I want is for you to come ready to have a nice time." She left the kitchen before I could protest.

Should I go after her? Tell her not to bother scheming, I wasn't interested? Admit to her I'd fallen for Hannah years ago and couldn't see myself with anyone else, and I was only waiting for her to accept me openly? Confess that we'd had sex in her bathroom, on her bedroom floor, and in the backseat of my car in the space of four days?

I almost laughed out loud. She'd probably pass out. And Hannah would be furious. No, the best thing to do was ease into things slowly where Hannah was concerned, and appease my mother whenever I could. The birthday dinner seemed like a small thing to give her, a little gift from our past, when she'd plan huge, fun parties for Drew and me.

I could do that much for her.

"YOU LOOK NICE. Where are you headed?" My mother eyed me as I scooped up my keys from the kitchen counter and stopped for a moment to check my messages.

"Over to get Hannah and Abby."

I didn't even look up at her, but out of the corner of my eye, I saw her stiffen. "For what?"

"I want to buy Abby a piano. We're going into Port Huron to check some out."

"Why?"

"Because there's a store there that sells them." As if I hadn't understood the question.

"No, I mean why are you buying her a piano?"

I slipped my phone into my coat pocket and met her eyes. "Because she wants lessons and she's talented and it's what Drew would have done."

"Oh." She thought about that. "Hannah never

mentioned to *me* Abby wanted lessons. We could have bought Abby a piano."

"This isn't about you, Mom. Hannah probably didn't mention it because she doesn't want to be a charity case."

"That's a good point, you know. Pianos are expensive. This is quite a gift."

"I'm quite a guy." I chose to brush off her comment with a joke rather than let her turn this into a discussion about the inappropriate nature of buying Hannah such an expensive gift. "See you later."

AT THE MUSIC CENTER, I asked for the salesperson I'd read was the most knowledgeable, and she helped us find the perfect piano for Abby. It was a used upright in great condition, the wood was polished and free of nicks and scars, and Abby loved its matching bench with a lid that opened and closed. When Hannah heard the fifteen hundred dollar price tag, she looked at me with panicked eyes, but I just squeezed her hand and told the woman we'd take it. Abby jumped up and down with excitement.

We arranged for delivery within a few days, and I took down several names of teachers in the area the woman recommended for a student Abby's age.

"Thank you," Hannah kept saying on the drive home. "This means so much to her, and to me."

"It's my pleasure." Glancing in the rearview mirror to make sure Abby wasn't watching, I took her hand and kissed the back of it.

She pulled her hand away and glanced into the back seat. "You shouldn't."

"I know."

We got back to town around dinnertime and went out for pizza. Abby chattered excitedly about school, an upcoming field trip to a cider mill, her friend Ella's new puppy, and what she wanted to be for Halloween (a zombie cheerleader). Hannah talked about her cookbook project for the inn, and I joyfully volunteered to be taste tester for any and all recipes that needed sampling. We talked about my new house, what renovations were the top priorities, and what the possibilities were for the kitchen.

"I'd love to see the space again," she said, taking another slice of pizza from the standing tray. It made me happy to see her with a good appetite. "When do you close?"

"The tenth. There was a little delay because the owners were out of the state. But things should move quickly now."

"I bet Lenore will be sad to see you go."

"Tough. I'm going." My phone buzzed in my back pocket, and I pulled it out. It was a text from my mother. "Speak of the devil. She wants to know if we're back yet and if we're coming to dinner at her house."

"Oops," Hannah said.

"I'll tell her we already ate."

"I feel bad. Maybe we should have invited your parents?" she asked.

"It's fine." I texted her back, and she replied with a sad emoji and a question. "Now she's asking if Abby wants to sleep over."

"Yes!" shouted Abby.

I looked at Hannah, who shrugged.

"It's okay with me."

Yes, she does, I told my mom. **We will bring her over after we finish up here.**

While Hannah took Abby to the bathroom, I paid the bill and was ready to go when they came back to the table.

"You weren't supposed to pay for dinner, I wanted to!" She made a face at me.

"I invited you, remember?" I ushered them toward the door, one hand on Hannah's lower back, one on Abby's shoulder. It was a small, perhaps insignificant thing, leaving a restaurant with them that way, but for some reason, it filled me with indescribable joy.

"But you bought us a piano today," she complained as we walked through the parking lot. Abby was between us, holding one of Hannah's hands and one of mine.

"Exactly. So what's one measly pizza?" I unlocked the car, and Abby hopped into the back seat, where I helped buckle her up.

"Uncle Wes, will you be my special person?"

Hannah, buckling herself into the front passenger seat, turned and looked at us over her shoulder. "I thought you wanted me to be your special person."

"Well, I did," Abby said, "but no one brings their moms. They're all bringing dads or other people like grandmas or grandpas."

"What's a special person?" I asked, looking back and forth between them.

"It's something at school," Hannah explained, tucking her hair behind her ear. "When you're the student of the week, you get to invite someone to school. The person comes in and reads a story to the class."

"And I get to introduce you and say what you do and they can ask you questions." Abby smiled at me. "So will you come?"

"Abby, Uncle Wes has work," Hannah said.

"I can arrange a morning off." I smiled at Abby. "I'd be

glad to be your special person. Thanks for asking me."

I got in and started the engine. "Do you need anything from home, Abby?"

"No, I brought my elephant with me."

"Okay, good."

"Want to drop me off?" asked Hannah after I'd turned out of the lot.

"Not unless you're tired of my company."

She laughed. "Not at all."

ONCE ABBY WAS SETTLED on the couch with my mother and a huge bowl of microwave popcorn, a Disney movie on the TV screen, I told my mom I was taking Hannah home.

"Okay, darling. And you're coming right back?" She eyed me expectantly.

"Not sure. I might meet Pete and Jack for a drink later."

Her eyebrows went up. "You've been seeing quite a bit of them."

"Not really."

"Just about every night last week."

"We're catching up, Mom. Anyway, have a good night."

"Night, darling. Night, Hannah."

"Goodnight."

I opened the front door, and Hannah went out, walking silently toward the car with her head down. She said nothing until we were halfway to her house.

"I hate that we have to lie about this."

I took her hand. "We won't always."

She sighed. "You can't keep telling her you're out with

Pete every night. It's not even plausible. He has a family. Plus you could get caught in that lie if she sees him."

"I don't care. I'm thirty-six years old, Hannah, and it's not my mother's business what I do. I only told the lie to protect you. If you want me to tell her the truth, I will."

"No," she said quickly. "No, I'm not ready for that."

"You just let me know." I kissed the back of her hand and held it in my lap. "I loved taking you and Abby out all day."

"We loved it, too. You're much too generous."

"It makes me happy, doing things for you."

"I can tell." She squeezed my hand. "Pull in my driveway. I'll go in and open the garage door for you."

"Are you sure?"

"Yes."

She went inside the house and a moment later, her garage door opened. I pulled inside and parked next to her car, a Honda Civic. Briefly looking it over, I wondered if it was in good condition and when her last oil change had been. I went into the kitchen through the back door and was about to ask her when I saw her staring at her phone and shaking her head.

"Oh my God," she said.

"What's wrong?"

"Look at this." She handed me her phone and I looked at the screen. "It's from someone I used to be friends with I don't see very often now."

HANNAH!!

OMG what is going on I'm dying!

I heard you were out to dinner with Drew's brother Wes?! Is that true?! EEEEEP! Weirdness!

Call me!!!

I gave her back her phone. "Ignore this. It's one person."

"Oh no," she said, "there's more. Here's another *friend*." She gave me the phone back.

Hey Hannah! Just wondering how you're doing! My mom said she saw you out for dinner tonight with Wes Parks?? What's going on there?! Give me the scoop! #affair

I groaned. "People are fucking terrible."

"And last but not least, the voicemail." She took her phone, swiped at the screen a few times, and turned up the volume.

"Hi Hannah, it's Faye. Listen, babe, my friend Lucy just texted me that she saw you tonight with Wes Parks at Windjammer and it looked pretty cozy. Then I remembered that my mom mentioned seeing a black car parked in front of your house a few times late at night—she lives right by you—and I was like, oh my god, would they *really*? I'm only teasing, I'm sure there's nothing going on, and that's exactly what I said to Lucy, but you know how she talks. Anyway, just give me a call when you can and let me know what's up. We *have* to get together soon! Miss you! Hope you're doing well!"

When it was over, she put her phone on the table. "I hate everyone."

"Hey. Listen to me." I took her shoulders and turned her toward me. "Those people do not matter. They are not your friends."

"Your mother matters. And I don't like being talked about." She crossed her arms.

"Come here." I pulled her to my chest and held her close for the first time today. She smelled so good. "I don't care what any of those assholes out there say or think about us. We don't need their permission to be happy. As far as I'm concerned, there is only one asshole whose permission we need, and I already asked him for it."

"Drew?" she guessed.

"Yes. Believe it or not, I actually had a conversation with him the night of Abby's birthday dinner."

"I believe you," she said softly. "What did he say?"

"He said..." My throat suddenly got tight. "He said, 'Love them enough for both of us.'"

She sniffled. "That sounds like him."

"And he told me I better not fuck it up."

Her laugh was half snort, half sob. "That sounds like him, too."

"He also told me to get the hell out of Mom and Dad's house."

"Also totally him."

I kissed the top of her head and held her tight. "And he said life is short."

"It is."

"So I didn't want to wait any longer. I felt like I'd been waiting to be with you forever, but Hannah—we can slow down, if you want. We don't have to go out in public together. I don't have to be here every night. I know, for you, it's only been a few weeks."

She twined her arms around my waist. "But I want you here every night. Everything is better when you're here."

"Then I'll be here."

"I don't want to be alone anymore, Wes."

I took her head in my hands. "You will never be alone again."

"When you say things like that, I get scared."

"Don't. There's nothing to be scared of, Hannah. I love you. We're gonna be okay."

She rose up on her toes and kissed me. "Stay with me tonight."

"Okay," I said, brushing the hair back from her face. "I'll stay."

SIXTEEN

HANNAH

I WON'T BE alone tonight.

The thought filled me with excitement, and I felt joy tingling in my toes. Rising up on them, I pressed my lips to Wes's, threw my arms around his neck, and jumped up so my legs circled his waist.

How he managed to get us up to my bedroom like that, I have no idea, but two minutes later we were kneeling on my bed, trying to shed our clothing and kiss each other at the same time.

"Wait," I said breathlessly when we were nearly naked and frantic with need. "Wait a second."

"What is it?"

I looked down at my hands and pulled off my ring, leaning over to set it on my nightstand.

"You don't have to, not for me," he said.

"It's for me," I told him, reaching for him again. "I want to be yours completely."

"You are." He turned me beneath him and pulled my underwear off before stretching out over me. "You are mine completely."

I looked up at his face in the dark, my heart bursting with everything I felt for him. "I love you," I said.

His eyes closed for a moment. "Is this real?"

"Yes," I whispered, wrapping my legs around him. Finally we were skin to skin and I couldn't get enough of the way he felt, of his weight on me, of his hands on me, of his masculine smell and his low murmured sounds and his tongue stroking into my mouth. Every kiss, every touch, every breath seemed to erase one more memory of a lonely night spent in this bed.

I won't be alone tonight.

I ran my hands all over his body, anything I could reach, neck and arms and shoulders and chest and back and ass. I slid my fingers into his hair as he worked his mouth down my body, tasting every inch of my skin, licking and sucking and tantalizing me with long, slow strokes and lush, swirling circles, and quick, hard flicks of his tongue that made me come so hard I saw stars on my bedroom ceiling. I shimmied down beneath him until his knees bracketed my chest, taking his cock in my hand and lifting my head to rub my lips over the tip.

He groaned, bracing his hands on the headboard. "Go slow," he said. "I beg you."

I went slow at first, stroking the crown with my tongue, working my hand up and down, sucking just an inch or two into my mouth. But before long, I had my hands on the back of his thighs, pulling him into me as he fucked my mouth, feeling his cock hit the back of my throat, listening as he cursed and growled and moaned.

Finally, he pulled out and opened my nightstand

drawer, where we'd stashed some condoms earlier in the week. A minute later, he was sliding into me, and the feeling was so sublime, I could have wept.

I won't be alone tonight.

"Wes," I whispered as he began to move, working his hips in a slow, steady rhythm that had him plunging inside me with long, deep strokes. "It feels so good. You feel so good."

So good that I wondered how I'd ever doubted this was right. So good that I never wanted it to end. So good that I could see a life together stretching out ahead of us—I was walking down the aisle toward him, I was nursing our child, I was putting a pie in the oven, I was sitting across the dinner table from him and we were surrounded by family, surrounded by happiness, surrounded by love.

"Yes," I murmured, holding him tighter, lifting my hips to meet his quickening thrusts. "Oh God, don't stop." My mind and body were spiraling out of control together. The closer I got to the summit, the more of the future I could see.

Forever was right there in front of me, unspooling like a ribbon.

Every wish would be granted. Every wrong would be righted. Every dream that had died would be fulfilled. As long as I had him, I could have everything.

I couldn't lose him.

But you will. Because you need him now. Because you let him in. Because you gave away your heart when you should have guarded it. Because you refused to see the truth even when it has been right in front of your face the whole time—love isn't enough to protect you.

And forever is only a lie.

"Don't leave me," I begged, my body on the verge of climax, my mind on the brink of hysteria.

"Never," he said between rasping breaths. "I'll never leave you." We reached the apex and hurtled over the edge together, clutching and cursing and straining to get closer as our bodies released the tension in perfect harmony.

"I love you," he said as we caught our breath.

"I love you, too."

I was staring at the ceiling in the dark, wondering where all the stars had gone.

A LITTLE LATER, Wes curled himself around me just like Drew used to do. Knees tucked under mine. An arm around my waist. His chest pressed against my back. It was exactly what I'd wanted. It felt warm and cozy and familiar. I'd missed it desperately.

It terrified me.

I wouldn't be alone tonight, but tomorrow night was a different story. After that, it could be weeks. I'd lie here missing him and wishing we could be together, having no idea when that might actually happen, if it happened at all. I'd be sad. Worried. Lonely.

Because I'd let myself need him. After everything I'd been through, after everything life had thrown at me, after all I'd done to recover my strength. After all the time I'd spent and tears I'd cried putting the pieces of my broken heart back together again, I'd set it on the edge of the highest shelf.

Was I insane?

I chewed on the tip of my thumb, eyes wide open. Behind me, Wes's breathing was deep and even, as if he were already asleep.

I'll never leave you, he'd said, and I wanted to believe

him. With every bone in my body, I wanted to. But Drew had said the same thing. Drew had made promises he meant but couldn't keep. Drew had believed he was invincible, and maybe he'd been punished for it.

Maybe I'd be punished for falling in love with his brother.

I slammed my eyes shut.

Stop it, Hannah. Just stop, before you have a panic attack. You're being paranoid and crazy and ridiculous. Nothing bad is going to happen.

But it took me a long time to fall asleep.

THE NEXT MORNING, I woke up to the sound of rain on the roof even before my alarm went off. Immediately I glanced to my right. Wes had rolled onto his back during the night, and he was sleeping with one arm thrown over his head, the covers down around his waist. I felt a tug of arousal deep inside me as I took in his handsome face and bare chest, the hand resting on the pillow, the scruffy jaw. There was plenty of time. I didn't have to be at work for two more hours. I could snuggle up to him, slip my hand between his legs, press my lips to his chest while I stroked him beneath the covers. I liked thinking about the surprised smile that would curve his lips, the way he'd look at me when he'd open those gorgeous green eyes. *Well, good morning*, I bet he'd say, his low voice a little gravelly. I wanted that. I wanted all of that.

But instead of touching him, I carefully got out of bed without waking him, made sure my alarm wouldn't go off, and snuck into the shower.

I probably didn't have that much time, anyway, I

thought as I rinsed out my shampoo. *I'd probably have been late for work.* And what was the sense in enjoying a rainy morning in bed together when I didn't know when we'd ever get another one? An addict knows she can't just take one hit. Why torture myself with the memory?

But I was torturing myself with the fantasy when I heard a knock on the bathroom door.

"Come in," I said.

A moment later, Wes peeked around the curtain. "Hi."

I had to smile at his hair. "Hi."

"Is this a private party?"

"Not at all."

He stepped into the tub, and I looked his perfect body over, head to foot. It felt strange to be naked in bright light with him. I was immediately conscious of all my flaws—the breasts that were no longer perky and full, the stretch marks on my stomach, the mummy tummy. I tried to hide behind my arms somehow, but he knew what I was doing.

"Stop it. You're beautiful."

"No, I'm not. I'm old and my body isn't like what it used to be."

"Well, guess what? I never knew your body then, so I'm not comparing, and I think it's perfect. I'm older than you are, anyway."

"That's different." I stepped aside so he could get wet. "Men aren't judged as harshly as women are. You don't have to deal with pregnancy and childbirth and all that." I thought about the images I'd seen behind closed eyes last night, and my heart beat faster.

"Good thing there are no judges here." He grabbed me and pulled me close, so the hot water streamed over both our bodies.

I rested my cheek on his chest as his arms came around

me, wishing that pit in my stomach would just go away. This felt so good.

"Mmmm." He sniffed my wet hair. "I love that smell."

"You can use my shampoo if you want."

"I don't think it will have the same effect on me."

I smiled. "You never know. Want me to wash your hair?"

"Definitely."

I washed his hair, laughing when he kept grabbing my sudsy hands to smell them, and soaped him up with my body wash. He inhaled deeply. "Oh my God, I'm going to smell like one of your desserts. What is this stuff?" He grabbed the tube from my hand. "Marshmallow Pumpkin Latte? Are you kidding me?"

"I thought you liked it." I smiled as I lathered up his pecs and abs and—

"Hold on a minute." He circled my wrists with his fingers. "I'm not sure my dick is supposed to smell like a marshmallow. Marshmallows are soft and small."

"But *you're* not," I said, wriggling free and taking his cock in my hands. Forgetting all about why I didn't want to have sex this morning, I let his hardening flesh slip through my fist.

He groaned. "Don't you have anything more manly? Like Hot Steely Wood or something?"

I burst out laughing. "No, I'm sorry, I don't."

He squirted some body wash into his hands. "I get to do you now."

"But I'm not done," I said coquettishly, batting my lashes at him as I worked my hands up and down his thickening shaft.

"Take a break." He switched places with me. "Or

there's going to be a marshmallow pumpkin explosion in here."

"I don't mind." But I let him lather me up, enjoying the sensual, slippery feel of his hands on my skin and the scent of the steam clouding around us as we rinsed off. *Another little world all to ourselves. If only we never had to leave.*

Maybe I could lose this anxious feeling by distracting myself from it. "So I have a few minutes before I have to get dressed."

"Oh yeah?" His eyes darkened a little as he watched me rinse off.

Five minutes later, I was braced against the wall as Wes drove into me from behind, my legs still weak from the orgasm he'd just given me with his fingertips, my gasps echoing off the tiles. His hands gripped my hips, his fingers digging into my skin. He was rougher with me than Drew, and I liked it. It made me feel strong and sexy that I could take it. *Yes, yes, this is what I needed.*

He pulled out before he came, and I turned around to watch him finish himself off. It was so fucking hot, watching him come all over his hand, his abs flexing, the muscles in his arms taut. I could barely breathe.

But as the glow faded, the unease crept back in. I tried to brush it off. *It's the weather. It's the worry that Lenore will catch him coming in. It's the decision we made to leave separately.* But as I watched him run out to the garage through the rain, I could not shake the feeling that something bad was going to happen. That I'd made a mistake somewhere along the way. That we were on borrowed time.

What I really needed was a sign, I decided on the way to work. I needed some indication from the universe that I was doing things right. That I wasn't fucking up my life, or more importantly, the life of my daughter. If I could just see a sign or two, I'd feel better. Nothing big, nothing drastic, just something to let me know everything was going to be okay.

Or that it wasn't, and I needed to retreat before I got hurt.

Suddenly the rain started pounding my windshield, coming down so hard and fast I couldn't see. "I said nothing drastic," I complained, turning up my wiper speed.

But I ended up pulling over and waiting it out, worrying about everything and playing with the fourth finger of my left hand, where my ring used to be.

SEVENTEEN

WES

IT HAD BEEN a long time since I'd tried to sneak into my parents' house. Back in the day, Drew and I used to climb this one tree to get onto the roof, and from there we'd just go through his bedroom window. As I pulled up, I so dreaded the inquisition I was sure to get from my mother that I actually considered giving it a try.

But I didn't. I wasn't that nervous teenager anymore. I was a full-grown man, and I had the right to come and go as I pleased. If she wanted me in her house for the time being, she'd have to deal with that.

Still, I sort of hoped no one would be in the kitchen to witness my walk of shame.

No such luck.

"Well, my goodness!" said my mother, seated at the kitchen table with Abby and my dad. "Look what the cat dragged in."

I probably did look like something the cat dragged in,

wearing yesterday's clothes, wrinkled from a night on Hannah's floor and rained-drenched from this morning. I ran a hand through my damp hair. "Morning."

"Morning," said my dad.

"We're having waffles," Abby announced. "I made some, just like Mommy makes."

"But even better," added my mom, "because they're Nana's secret recipe."

I rolled my eyes and headed for the stairs.

"And where were you?"

None of your business, I wanted to say. But I'd promised my dad I'd tolerate her better, and I didn't want to be an asshole in front of Abby. "I slept at Pete's."

"At Pete's?"

"Yeah, fell asleep on his couch. I'm gonna change real quick."

Upstairs in my room, I traded my wet clothes for dry ones, and sent a quick text to Pete. **Hey. Give me a call later.**

On the off chance that my mother ran into him somewhere, I didn't want him to be blindsided by her questions about how we'd been spending so much time together recently.

I'd have liked to hide out in my room for a while, but those waffles had smelled pretty good, and my stomach was growling. I went back to the kitchen, poured a cup of coffee and brought a plate to the table, where a big platter held waffles, scrambled eggs, and bacon. My dad had taken his coffee cup into the great room, where he always spent a couple hours in his chair, reading the Sunday paper. I took his seat and piled my plate with food.

"This looks delicious." Always good to open with a compliment.

I could feel my mother's eyes on me as I ate.

"Any plans today?" she asked.

"Not really."

"How about this week?"

"Not sure."

"Uncle Wes is going to be my special person at school," said Abby, smiling proudly. "He said he would."

"Oh?" My mom looked from Abby to me. "What's a special person?"

"It's someone in the family who visits their classroom, reads a story, that kind of thing," I said. "Right, Abs?"

"Right. It's for when I'm student of the week. A lot of kids bring their dads, but I asked if I could bring an uncle, and my teacher said it was fine."

"How nice." My mother sipped her coffee.

"Because I asked Uncle Wes the night before if he could be my dad, and he said he couldn't."

My mother's cup clattered onto the table. "What?"

"Mom. Don't worry about it."

"He said I already had a dad," Abby went on, "and no one can take his place."

"That's right." My mother reached out and touched Abby's arm. "Your daddy was Drew, remember? We looked at all the pictures together?"

"Yes, but that daddy isn't here anymore, and my mom and I are sad about it. And it's okay to be sad," she said, probably echoing Hannah or maybe her therapist, "but it's better when you're happy. Mommy is happy when uncle Wes comes over."

"Is she?" My mother pinned me with a stare.

"Yes. She doesn't cry as much during the night anymore. That's why I thought he could move in with us.

But Mommy said he can't, because he just bought his own house."

"That's right, I did." Maybe I could get the train back on the tracks before it completely derailed. "Remember that orange and purple bedroom?"

"I said he could sell that house." Abby looked at me pleadingly. "So can you? Sell that house?"

"Oh, Abby." My mother looked like she was about to cry. "Even if Uncle Wes sold his house, he can't be your daddy."

"Why not? My friend Kenzie got a new daddy after her parents got a divorce. She got to be a flower girl in the wedding."

My stomach was tightening up, and I set my fork down, trying to think of some way to get off this topic before the conversation took a horrible turn. But I was too late.

"Because he's your uncle, and your uncle cannot be your daddy, ever." My mother's tone was final.

"But he could get married to Mommy," Abby said.

"No, darling, because your mommy was his brother's wife, and he'd never do that to his brother." She looked right at me as she said it. "A man can't marry his brother's wife. It's wrong. Terribly, despicably wrong."

"It is?" Abby looked at me. Her eyes were full of tears.

"Yes," my mother snapped.

"But they love each other. They hold hands and kiss."

My mother gasped. The look she gave me singed my skin. "No. I'm sure you're mistaken, Abby. You couldn't possibly have seen something so vile."

"What's vile?"

"Okay." I cleared my throat. "I think we've talked about that enough. Abby, what story should I read to your class? Do you have a favorite?"

She didn't answer. After poking at her breakfast for a moment, she put down her fork. "Nana, my tummy hurts. Can I be done?"

My mother pursed her lips. "Yes."

Abby slid off her booster seat and slowly walked out of the kitchen, her mouth turned down, her eyes on the floor. I felt horrible—my stomach hurt too.

Fuck. Fuck. Fuck. This was a mess. And Abby was sure to go home and tell Hannah about it.

"Wesley Davis Parks, is there anything you want to tell me?" my mother asked coldly.

"No." That was the truth, at least. I didn't want to tell her a damn thing.

"Don't be smart with me. What is going on with you and Hannah?"

"It's none of your business, Mom."

"Have you lost your mind?"

"Keep your voice down." I sat back in my chair and crossed my arms. "We're friends. We enjoy spending time together."

She cocked her head, her eyes narrowing. "Were you really at Pete's house last night?"

I didn't answer. She got up from the table and started doing the dishes, handling them so roughly I was shocked one didn't break.

God, I was so angry with her! Why did she have to say those things? Why did she have to believe those things? Did that mean she wasn't ever going to accept me and Hannah together? Was she going to make me choose between them? I'd choose Hannah, because my mother was the one who was terribly, despicably wrong here, but I hadn't been able to stand up for myself because I didn't want to out Hannah and me without her permission or in front of her daughter.

My mother couldn't remain silent for long. She faced me, hands on her hips. "Don't you care what people will think?"

"Nope."

"And what about that little girl?" She pointed in the direction Abby had just gone. "Can you see what you two are doing to her? Confusing her? Leading her to believe you could be her daddy? Letting her mind wander to all kinds of terrible places? No wonder her tummy hurts! It's emotional abuse!"

"That's enough." My tone was sharp. "Drop it."

"I can't. I'm sorry, but if you two don't have enough sense to see the damage you're inflicting on Abby, someone needs to show you. Do you really think she isn't affected by this? Do you think it's normal for a child to think her uncle can become her daddy? Do you think it's okay that she feels physical pain because of what you're doing?"

"Stop yelling! She'll hear you. What we're doing isn't wrong."

She came closer to the table. "I cannot believe," she fumed quietly, "that you would do such a thing to your brother."

"This isn't about Drew!" Now it was me being loud. I didn't like raising my voice to my mother, but I was fed up with her.

"Oh, yes it is! It's about all of us. It's about loyalty to your family, Wesley Parks. That's what matters above all. Loyalty to your family. And if you think for one second that what you're doing isn't wrong, or that it affects only you, or that people won't judge you for doing something so immoral and...and *sleazy*, then I didn't raise my son right. How do you think people will feel about coming to a doctor who displays such poor judgment? Did you ever think about that?"

"It's not immoral to love someone."

She blinked, a shocked expression on her face. "You want to talk about morals? Where is your conscience? Where is your sense of right and wrong? Your brother is turning in his grave. He never would have done this to you." She burst into tears.

My father came into the kitchen. "What's going on? What's all the yelling?"

I said nothing, and my mother continued to cry. He went to her, and she turned into his arms, crying on his shoulder while he patted her back. I sat there with my head down, feeling guilty even though I hadn't done anything wrong.

I hadn't, had I? Why did it seem unclear, all of a sudden? Why was she making me feel like maybe Hannah and I hadn't thought this all the way through? Were we crazy to think that we could be together without negative consequences? Was she right about patients not trusting me? And the comment about Drew cut deep. Was she right about that too? Would he be against us? Was my conversation with Drew on the beach simply a convenient delusion, a subconscious ploy to excuse my behavior? Wishful thinking, so I could have what I want?

"Wes?" My dad was looking at me. He was probably thinking about our conversation, the one where I'd promised to give my mother a break. The one where I'd learned how disloyal her father had been and what it had done to her mother and her childhood. It was no wonder she identified with Abby.

I exhaled and rubbed the back of my neck. "I'm sorry."

"What exactly are you sorry for?" My mother turned to

me. "Carrying on with your brother's wife? Betraying his memory? Confusing his child? Disgracing your professional reputation?"

"Lenore," my father said. "That's enough."

She grabbed a tissue and turned on him. "You can't tell me you don't see what's going on around here."

"I see it."

Both of us stared at him. He knew?

"And it doesn't bother you?" she asked, incredulous.

"Wes and Hannah are adults. They can make their own decisions."

"Oh, that's fine. Just fine!" my mother yelled. "Take his side."

My father held up his hands. "I'm not taking sides."

"Yes, you are!" She shook her head. "I guess I'm the only person in this family who cares about Abby's well-being and our good name." Pulling another tissue from the box, she marched out of the kitchen. A moment later, I heard her feet on the stairs.

My dad came to the table and sat down. "You okay?"

"Yeah." I closed my eyes. "But I just made a really big mess."

"Life's full of messes. They can be cleaned up."

"I don't know. This one is pretty big, Dad." I rubbed a hand over my jaw and dropped it into my lap. "You knew about me and Hannah?"

"You didn't hide it very well, if that's what you were trying to do. I could see it happening pretty easily."

"Do you think it's wrong?" I held my breath.

He sighed. "I don't think it's wrong, Wes. But I can't take a side. My marriage hasn't lasted nearly forty years for nothing."

"I get it," I said grimly.

"You and your mother are going to have to work this out."

I leaned on the table. "Why is she so against this? Why doesn't she want us to be happy?"

"Oh, I think she does. In the long run, Wes, that's all any parent wants for their child. But it's hard not to think we know what's best for them, even when they're grown."

"I love her. How can that be wrong?"

"Some people will see it that way. Others won't."

"So what should I do?"

"Give your mother some time. That's my advice. Let her get used to the idea."

"You think she could?"

He shrugged. "Who knows? But I do think the two of you could both take a little time to see things from each other's perspective."

"Yeah." I slumped back again. "Maybe. But what if she doesn't come around? What happens then?"

"I guess you'll have to decide what it's worth to be with Hannah. And Wes..." He waited until I looked him in the eye. "It could be worth everything."

I nodded. "Thanks."

He got up from the table and went back to his Sunday paper in the other room, and I sat there feeling miserable and guilty. I knew he'd essentially just told me that he wouldn't blame me if I chose Hannah over my mother, even if it tore my family apart, but I still felt like shit. It would be like my mother had lost both sons. Depending on how Hannah felt, it might mean they couldn't see Abby anymore. And speaking of Hannah, I needed to break the news to her that my parents knew about us, and my mother, as expected, wasn't happy about it, to say the least.

Fuck. I rubbed my face with both hands.

How had this day, which had started so brilliantly, gone so horribly wrong?

I WENT up to my room, shut the door, and lay back on my bed. With my hands behind my head, I stared at the ceiling and tried to do what my father had said—consider things from my mother's perspective. But I couldn't. No matter how hard I tried, it all came down to one thing—we made each other happy. Why should we have to care what anyone else thought?

How could love be wrong?

After a while, I heard my phone buzzing on my dresser, so I got up and grabbed it. It was Pete.

"Hey," I said. "Thanks for getting back to me."

"No problem. What's up?"

"I need to talk to you about something."

"Whoa. Sounds serious."

"It kinda is."

"You okay?"

"Yeah. At least physically."

He laughed. "You need some mental help?"

"I think I might."

"Well, you're in luck. Because I'm making chili today, and I'm offering a free counseling session with every bowl. Want to come over this afternoon? About four?"

I looked at my watch. It was almost eleven now. I needed to talk to Hannah after she was done working, preferably before she showed up here to get Abby. But I could get to Pete's by four. "Sounds good. See you then. And thanks."

We hung up and I called Hannah.

"Hello?"

My insides warmed at the sound of her voice. "Hey."

"How are you? Everything okay there?"

"Yes and no." Damn, this was going to suck.

"What's wrong? Is Abby okay?"

Great, now I was making her panic. "Abby is fine," I said, which actually wasn't true. I knew her stomachache wasn't stemming from a physical issue, but that didn't mean it wasn't real. "Mostly."

"Mostly? You're scaring me, Wes."

I pinched the bridge of my nose. I was fucking this up already. "She's fine. When do you think you'll be done with work?"

"I'm about done. I can leave now and come get her. Can I talk to her?"

"Wait—don't come here yet. I want to talk to you first."

"No. I want to talk to Abby. Put her on."

"Hannah, please."

"Put. Her. On."

"Okay, okay. One second." Groaning inwardly, I left my room and went into the hall. "Abby?" I called out.

"I'm in my room," she called back.

I went down the hall to the guest room that my mother had furnished for Abby. The door was open halfway, and I could see her lying on her bed. "Your mom wants to talk to you."

She sat up, and I could see that she'd been crying. My chest felt painfully tight as I handed her the phone and listened to her end of the conversation.

"Hello? Yes. Just lying in my bed. I had a tummy ache so Nana said to lie down. It's still there. Can you come get me? Okay." She handed the phone back to me.

"Hello?" I said.

"I'm coming to get her."

I squeezed my eyes shut for a second. "Okay."

"I don't know what's going on, but she doesn't sound right. She said she has a stomachache. Can you take a look at her?"

"Of course."

"Thank you. I'll be there in twenty minutes." She sounded stressed, and I didn't blame her. It wasn't going to get any better when she got here, either.

Suddenly I had an idea—I'd go to the inn and talk to her before she left. Explain to her what had happened and tell her not to panic. Things would be okay. I'd fix them.

Somehow.

"How's that tummy?" I asked Abby, whose lower lip was sticking out. *She has Hannah's mouth.*

"It hurts." She cradled her belly.

"Where?"

She shrugged. "Everywhere."

"Hmmm. What do you think would make it better?"

"I don't know." She looked up at me. "I heard Nana yelling at you. It made me sad."

Just when I thought I couldn't feel worse. "I'm sorry, honey."

"Why is she mad at you?"

I sighed. "It's complicated."

"Is it because of me?"

"Oh, Abby, no." I sat down next to her and took her hand. "You didn't do anything wrong, okay? No one is upset with you."

"Abby?" My mother entered her room. When she saw me in there, her shoulders snapped back. "What's going on?"

"Nothing," I said, feeling guilty about her puffy eyes

and red nose despite being angry with her. "I was just checking on her. Hannah will be here soon to pick her up."

At the mention of Hannah, my mother's mouth became a thin line. "Fine. Abby, darling, would you like Nana to read you a story?"

"Okay."

I stood up. "I have to run out for a while."

"Fine." She didn't even look at me.

Moving quickly, I took the stairs down two at a time, grabbed my keys, and hustled out the back door. On the drive to the inn, I tried to think of a bright side in all this that I could present to Hannah. Something hopeful to offer. Something that would make her feel like I could deliver on all the promises I'd made.

But I came up with nothing.

And by the time I pulled into the lot next to the inn, Hannah was already coming out the door, rushing through the rain toward her car.

"Fuck," I muttered. Rolling down the passenger window, I pulled up alongside her. "Hannah!"

She stopped running and squinted at me. "Wes?"

"Get in!" I leaned over and pushed the door open, and she jumped in.

"What are you doing here?" she asked as I rolled up the window. I could hear the panic in her voice.

I parked next to her. "I needed to talk to you."

"About what? What's going on?"

Shifting in my seat, I faced her and spoke calmly, even though I didn't feel calm inside at all. "First, I don't want you to panic. Everything is fine."

"Then what are you doing here? And why does Abby have a stomachache?"

"My parents know about us." Rain hammered the roof and windshield.

"What? How?"

"A combination of things. My dad said he could see it happening. My mom probably suspected, but Abby sort of confirmed it."

Her jaw dropped. "*Abby?*"

"She said we hold hands and kiss."

She gasped. "She's seen us?"

"Apparently. I guess we're not as careful as we think."

"Oh my God." She clutched her stomach, just like Abby had done. Her eyes closed. "I knew it. I knew something bad was going to happen. I could feel it. What did they say?"

I exhaled. There was no use in sugarcoating this. "My mother is very upset."

"Of course she is. And your dad?"

"Privately, my dad told me he doesn't think it's wrong. But he also said he can't side with me against my mother. He's sort of staying neutral, I guess."

She nodded and took a deep breath. "Tell me everything that happened."

I filled her in on the entire breakfast table conversation, watching her grow more and more dismayed, her eyes filling with tears.

"Oh, God," she whispered when I told her that Abby had heard my mother yelling at me. "The poor thing is probably totally traumatized."

"It was pretty rough for her," I admitted, rubbing the back of my neck.

She shook her head, tears dripping down her cheeks. "I'm a terrible mother. This is all my fault."

"Hannah, stop." I reached over and took her hand. "I'm

the one who stayed silent while my mother poisoned Abby's mind. I should have spoken up."

"And said what?" She pulled her hand away. "What could you have said that would make your mother see this any other way?"

"I don't know," I said miserably. "Something."

"The truth is, your mother has always had something against me, and she was never going to be okay with us. She was barely okay with me and Drew!"

"Don't say that."

"It's true! And now my daughter is hurting because she feels like she wanted something *bad*, or because she thinks she'll never have a family, or because she thinks she's not loved enough." She sobbed openly. "And she thinks you and I can never love each other because it's *wrong*, so if we do stay together, she'll be even more confused, and your mother will continue to fill her head with garbage, and there isn't anything we can do about it."

She said if.

I took her hand again and held on tighter. "Hannah, things will be okay. We'll get through this."

She looked at me like I was nuts. "How? What can either of us do? The circumstances are totally beyond our control, Wes. We can't go back and do things differently. We can't change the past or who we are. And we can't change her mind."

Everything she said was true, but I refused to give up. "We can't just unlove each other, either."

"We might have to."

My chest ached. "No. I'll figure it out, Hannah. I promise."

"Don't." She snatched her hand from me. "Don't say that anymore. Don't make promises you can't keep."

"Goddammit, I don't want to lose you." I could have put my fist through the windshield. This was so fucking unfair.

"I don't want to lose you, either," she said, fresh tears welling. "But I have to put my daughter first. Obviously, she feels like something is wrong or missing in her life since she doesn't have a father, and that means I'm not doing a good enough job."

"Yes, you *are*. Maybe she just wants to see you happy. Maybe it's not so much about filling the role of her father but about wanting her mom to smile more."

"Maybe." She reached into her purse for a tissue and wiped her eyes and nose. "But I need a few days, okay? To think things through? Maybe we're moving too fast. I feel like things are spinning out of control, and I need to get a handle on them, or I'm going to end up in a bad place."

I didn't want to be apart from her, not even for a few days, but I understood. "Of course."

"Thanks." She looked over at me with huge, sad eyes. "I do love you."

"I love you, too."

"You probably wish you didn't."

I reached out and took her face in my hands. "I will never wish I didn't love you."

"But you could have anybody. Somebody your mother would approve of."

"But I love *you*." I kissed her softly. "Remember that."

She nodded and took a deep breath. "I should go pick up Abby now."

"Do you want me to be there?"

"No. It's okay. I have to be willing to look your mother in the eye, or else she'll make the case that deep down, I don't think this is right, either."

I nodded. Sometimes she surprised me with her strength. "Call me later?"

"Okay."

"I'm sorry, Hannah. For whatever pain my feelings for you have caused you and Abby."

"I'm sorry, too. I never meant to drive a wedge between you and your mother."

"It's her driving the wedge, not you."

"Still. I'm a mother, too. And yours has gone through something I can't even imagine. I try to remember that when she gets to me."

"I'll try as well."

She got out of my car and quickly jumped into hers. The rain still hadn't let up. I watched her drive off and prayed my mother would go easy on her, or better yet, say nothing at all.

She had such a big heart, and it had been broken so badly. I didn't want to see it broken again.

EIGHTEEN

HANNAH

MY STOMACH WAS IN KNOTS.

It had been that way ever since Wes's phone call, but now my head was pounding too. And this fucking rain—I felt like I was drowning in it, drowning in everything.

I knew it. I knew this was too good to be true. How could we have been so careless? How could we have thought that everything would just go our way because we wanted it to? How had I ever believed Wes when he said things would be okay?

But I hadn't really, had I? Deep down, something in me had always refused to believe the universe would let us be happy together. Life just didn't work that way.

But what now? What, now that I loved him and wanted him and needed him? What was I going to do? There were no clear answers, no easy way out of these woods, and no one was coming to rescue me. It didn't compare to the agony of losing Drew, but it reminded me of that time in my life, when I felt like I couldn't see my way forward.

And it scared me. I never wanted to feel that lost again, that pummeled by life, that powerless to help myself. Yet I'd put myself in this position. I'd tempted fate. I'd allowed myself to love again.

You should have known better.

When I made it to Lenore's house, I turned off my car and ran for the door. Any other day I might have sat there for a minute and waited to see if the rain would slow down, but all I wanted was to get Abby, take her home, and hug her all day long. And who knew what Lenore was saying to her?

I knocked on the door, and she answered it.

"Hello, Lenore."

"Hannah." Her eyes were bloodshot, her expression cool. "Come on in."

I stepped into the foyer. "I hear Abby isn't feeling well."

"Well, of course not. She's crushed."

"Where is she?" I asked, ignoring the comment.

"She's upstairs. But before you get her, could I speak to you in the kitchen please?"

I wanted to say no, but I stood tall. "Okay." Following her into the kitchen, I rubbed the space on my finger where my ring used to be.

"Have a seat." She gestured toward the chairs at the island.

"No, thanks. I'll stand."

She sighed. "Hannah, I don't want to argue about this. I tried to talk some sense into Wes, but he won't listen."

"Say what you want to say, Lenore."

"You loved Drew. I know you did. And I know that it must be confusing for you to see Wes again."

"Of course I loved Drew. I'll always love him. But I'm not confused." Scared, yes. But not confused.

She tried again. "I don't blame you for wanting to be close to him. It must feel like you have your husband back."

"No, it doesn't."

"You don't love Wes," she said, as if the idea was preposterous. "You just think you do. You're lonely and depressed. And he's a caretaker. He can't see anyone hurting and not want to heal them. He's always been that way. Same as his brother."

She was implying that Wes—and possibly even Drew—didn't really love me, and even though it made me sick to my stomach, I refused to take that bait. "I know how I feel."

She crossed her arms. "Well then, if you love him, you should realize that this tawdry affair you're having could ruin his career. Who's going to trust his judgment after word of this gets out? The whole practice could go under. And what about Abby?" she went on, without giving me a chance to get a word in. "I cannot believe that any mother would think it was okay to expose her child to the shame of such a thing. Not to mention the fact that she honestly harbored the illusion Wes could suddenly replace her father."

"Wes told her he cannot replace Drew," I said firmly. "She knows who her father is."

"She's going to forget him." Lenore's eyes filled with tears. "I'm worried she's going to forget him. Like you have. Like Wes has. I feel like I'm the only one remembering him."

Her tears tugged at me a little, because I could tell that this was a legitimate fear she had—that her son would be forgotten. "We haven't forgotten him. We talk about him all the time. He'd want us to be happy."

"That's an easy thing to tell yourselves, isn't it?"

"This wasn't easy for me at all. I fought it. Wes fought it. But it happened."

"Love doesn't just *happen*," she said irritably. "It happened because you two let it happen. Because you jumped into bed together without a single thought to the consequences, and they are many, including a little girl who hears her mother crying at night, probably because she feels so guilty about what she's doing with her brother-in-law."

"Okay, that's enough. Please go get Abby so I can take her home."

When I tried to walk away, she grabbed my arm. "Hannah, wait. Just think about what you're doing. That's all I ask. Think about what you're doing and what's best for Abby. Think about what people will say and how embarrassing it will be for everybody. I don't want to have to explain to people why my son is dating his brother's wife."

I yanked my arm free. "This isn't about you."

"Yes, it is," she said. "It's about family and loyalty, and I don't understand why neither you nor Wes seems to get it."

But I was already striding out of the kitchen, heading for the stairs. Abby happened to be coming down them, her elephant tucked under her arm. "Mommy!" She hurried down the steps and ran over to me.

I reached out and scooped her up, hugging her close. "Hi, pumpkin. Ready to go?"

"Yes."

I set her down. "Say thank you to Nana." Mad as I was, I would not let it be said of me that I didn't have manners.

"Thank you, Nana." She went over and gave Lenore a hug.

"You're welcome, darling." Lenore's eyes closed and she sniffed as she held Abby close. I wondered if she was scared

I'd try to keep Abby from her. *After what she just said to me, she should be.*

Doc came around the corner from his office, a newspaper in hand. "Hello there, Hannah. Thought I heard your voice."

"Hi, Doc."

"Come give Papa a hug, Abby," he said, opening his arms.

She walked into them, and he squeezed her tight. My throat lumped up. They really did love her. And they probably felt like she was all they had left of Drew. I didn't want to prevent Abby from spending time with them. But I didn't want her hearing me badmouthed all the time either. God, this was such a mess! How had we ever thought we could make this work?

On the way home, we stopped at the store and bought some groceries. I let Abby choose what we'd have for dinner, and she chose hot dogs wrapped in crescent rolls, something she and Lenore had cooked up one time. I gritted my teeth but stuck the hot dogs and dough in the cart.

"How about a vegetable?" I asked. "We need something healthy with that."

She thought for a second. "Green beans."

"Works for me." I scooped some into a plastic bag.

"What about dessert? Can we bake a pie?"

"We sure can. What kind?"

She tapped her chin with one finger. "Apple. Because apples are good for you."

I laughed. "Right."

At home, I made lunch and we ate together at the table. Then we put on our matching aprons, rolled out the pie crust, prepared the filling, assembled the pie, and put it in the oven. Abby was cheerful and talkative, and some of the worry in me eased. Maybe she was okay.

"How's that tummy ache?" I asked her as we cleaned up.

"Better," she said.

While the pie was in the oven, Abby got out her crayons and colored at the kitchen table. I made a cup of tea and sat across from her.

"What are you coloring?"

She looked up at me like I was crazy. "It's a heart."

"Ah." I looked at the picture. "So it is."

"Nana said any time I feel sad about my daddy or miss him, I can just touch my heart, because that's where he is now."

My throat threatened to close, and I steadied myself with a deep breath. "That's a nice idea." Another deep breath. "Uncle Wes told me about this morning."

She kept coloring.

"Do you want to talk about it?"

"He said he can't sell his house. And Nana said it would be wrong for him to be my dad. And that you can't marry him."

"How did you feel about that?"

"It made me sad."

"Do you still feel sad?"

"Yes," she said. She touched her chest. "I love the daddy in my heart, but I would like a daddy in real life too."

I didn't know what to say to that. While I was thinking about it, she asked another question.

"Is it true that you can't marry Uncle Wes?"

I thought carefully before I answered with the truth. "No. It isn't."

Abby looked up at me with wide eyes. "But Nana said."

"Nana thinks it would be wrong. I don't."

"I don't understand. How can it be right and wrong at the same time?" She tilted her head. "Is *she* lying, or are *you* lying?"

"No one is lying, Abby. Sometimes people just disagree. This is one of those times. But that doesn't mean it will happen. Right now Uncle Wes and I are just good friends."

She appeared to think about that for a moment and then went back to coloring.

Later, we ate hot dogs and green beans, followed by slices of apple pie. We did Abby's homework, read a story and filled out her reading log, and got ready for bed. Then we cuddled on the couch in our pajamas, watching America's Funniest Home Videos. Her little giggle made me feel good, like maybe I hadn't done irreparable damage.

Maybe things would be okay.

AFTER PUTTING ABBY TO BED, I dug my phone out of my purse and sat on the couch again. Grimacing at the text messages that had upset me last night, I deleted them without replying. Same with the voicemail.

Then I dialed Wes, but it went to voicemail. I left a message.

"Hey, it's me. Just wanted to let you know Abby is doing okay. We talked about it, and I think she understands better now. Anyway, hope you're having a good night. I love you."

I turned off all the lights, locked up the house, and went upstairs. It was only eight o'clock, but I was exhausted—physically, mentally, emotionally. I felt better about Abby, but that still didn't change the fact that Wes and I had huge problems. As I slid between the sheets I'd shared with Wes last night, I tried to think it through.

Mad as I was at Lenore, I had to admit, some of the things she said were true. For example, she was right about people talking—if my text messages were any indication, the gossip was already spreading. And even if we had skin thick enough to endure it, *she* would remain a problem. What if she didn't come around? What if she refused to accept us? What if she made Wes choose?

What if he didn't choose me?

The knots in my stomach that had unraveled somewhat over the course of the afternoon raveled right back up. If it came down to it and Wes had to make a choice, there was no guarantee he'd pick me. Why should he? I was a fucking mess.

And what about the thing Lenore said about Wes being a caretaker, implying that he didn't love me so much as he wanted to heal me? Was there any truth in that? *Same as his brother*, she'd said. But Drew had truly loved me, hadn't he?

Maybe. But he's not here anymore.

Because love wasn't enough to save anyone.

Why did I keep forgetting that?

NINETEEN

WES

AFTER HANNAH LEFT to pick up Abby, I drove around for a while, cursing the rain, cursing my mother, cursing myself for not handling this situation better. But what could I have done differently?

Hannah was right. We couldn't go back and change the past. She'd been my brother's wife. There was no getting around it. But if *we* weren't bothered by that, what the fuck did anyone else care?

And it was inevitable that people were going to find out, but it would have been nice to break the news to my parents on our own terms. To be there together presenting a united front. If my mother could see how much we loved each other, and that we weren't doing this just for the forbidden kick of it, maybe she'd change her mind. I didn't give a fuck about anyone else, but this would be hard if I couldn't get her to come around. And Hannah was panicking.

I had to try again.

But I'd be more tactful this time. Less angry. I'd play the long game. I'd concede that this was unusual and agree that many people were going to find it distasteful, but I'd assure her that the only opinions that mattered to me were hers and my father's. I'd assure her that my professional reputation would not suffer. I'd appeal to her romantic side, remind her that real love was rare—I'd never felt it for anyone else. And now that I'd found it, I couldn't let it go. I'd tell her how inspired I was by her forty-year marriage, and how I wanted that for myself. I'd convince her that Abby and Hannah and I were meant to be a family, just like Abby wanted. I'd take care of them, just like Drew would want me to.

Once I had her listening to me with a more open mind, I could offer more hope to Hannah that everything would be okay. We would be happy together.

I would keep my promise.

Determined to sway my mother gently this time, I headed for home.

I FOUND her sitting on the couch with an old photo album in her lap.

"Hey," I said. "Where's Dad?"

"Taking a nap."

I sat down next to her. "What are you looking at?"

She angled the album so I could see. It was open to a page of pictures showing Drew and I around age eight, dressed in our Halloween costumes. I was Batman and Drew was the Joker.

I laughed. "Oh my God, I remember that year."

She flipped the page and there we were at the Thanksgiving table, wearing neckties that were probably clip-on, our haircuts painfully short. Then Christmas, with photos of us opening gifts, playing in the snow, sitting on the hearth dressed in matching red sweaters. She kept turning pages, without saying anything, without laughing or smiling. Easter. A trip to Florida. Last day of school. Riding jet skis on the lake. The final page was the two of us standing on the beach in our bathing suits, Drew's arm around my shoulder, both of us tan and damp-haired and grinning.

I felt a deep tug of longing for him, grief hitting me all over again, hollowing me out. I swallowed hard.

My mother sniffed as she closed the album. "Your father is displeased with me."

"Is he?"

"Yes. He thinks I'm being unfair."

So he did take a side. I was surprised and yet not. My father has always had a big heart.

"But I just can't stomach it, Wes. I'm sorry, but I can't. Why does it have to be her?"

"Because I love her."

She stared at her hands on the album.

"Mom. Look at me." When she met my eyes, I repeated myself. "I love her."

"But why?" Her chin jutted. "I don't understand. You can have anybody. Why do you have to love the girl your brother chose?"

"I don't know, Mom. It wasn't a choice for me."

"But you've never even tried to find anyone else."

"I wasn't a monk before I came home. I've known plenty of women and never fell in love before."

"You didn't give yourself a chance! You took up with Hannah the minute you got back in town!"

"When you know, you know." I was determined to

stay calm.

"I just don't understand how she can be in love with one brother for so long, and then suddenly decide she loves the other," she sniffed.

"It wasn't like that, Mom. Hannah didn't just *decide* to love me. Our feelings grew as we spent more time together."

"How do you even know she loves you? How do you know she's not just substituting you for Drew?"

That cut a little close to the bone, but I kept my temper in check. "The same way I know you love me. I can feel it."

She sighed. "I do love you, Wes. I want you to be happy, but I can't accept this. It feels wrong to me."

"What about giving it some time?"

"What do you mean?"

"I mean taking some time to reflect on it, try to see things from our point of view. See if you can find it in your heart to accept that we love each other and want to be together."

"And what if things go wrong?" she said. "Have you stopped to think about that? What's that going to do to Abby? What's that going to do to our family?"

"Things aren't going to go wrong." I said it firmly and looked her right in the eye. "This is it for me. This is what I want. I know people are going to talk, and I don't care about them. But I do care about you. I want you to be happy for us. Do you think you can?"

"I don't know." She looked down at her hands.

"Please, Mom. Hannah and I want your blessing."

"Are you sure she even cares what I think? I don't think she does."

"Of course she does. She's so upset right now, she asked me for a few days to think things over. She thinks she's driving a wedge between us."

"She is," my mother said petulantly.

I ignored that. "I'd like to be able to tell her that you and I talked calmly and there's hope for accord. Otherwise, I'm afraid she's going to decide to end it. And that will break my heart." I could have told her that I was going to be with Hannah whether I had her blessing or not, but I didn't think that would get me closer to my goal. It would hurt and anger her, and that did nothing but make this worse.

She continued to study her hands for a moment, and then she spoke. "I suppose I could give it some time."

I inhaled and exhaled, relief swelling in me. "Thank you."

"Don't thank me yet. I still might not be able to give my blessing."

"All I ask right now is that you try."

"Okay." She looked at me again, a little hopeful this time. "Can I still plan a birthday dinner for you?"

"Sure. Can you please include Hannah and Abby?"

Her face fell. "Oh, Wes couldn't I have you to myself for one night? I just want to make dinner for you here, nothing fancy. I want to make your favorite meal and talk about old times and remember Drew without feeling any awkward tension. You said I could have some time," she said when she saw my expression. "Couldn't I at least have one night? One little night? You said she wanted time apart anyway."

I considered it. On one hand, I didn't want to do anything without Hannah, and I wanted my mother to see us together. The sooner she got used to us, the better. On the other, I *had* promised to give them both time, and in the grand scheme of things, what was one night? If I gave her that, maybe she'd be more favorably inclined toward me and Hannah moving forward. I'd be doing us a favor. "Okay."

Her face lit up. "What should I make?"

"Surprise me," I said.

———

AROUND THREE THAT AFTERNOON, I got a text from Pete telling me to go to Jack's house instead of his. Jack lived in their parents' old farmhouse, which was right across the road from the inn. As I hurried through the rain up to the front porch, a brown paper bag under my arm, I glanced at the lot where I'd said goodbye to Hannah this morning and wondered how she was doing. I hadn't heard from her, and I hadn't texted or called her after my conversation with my mother because I was trying to give her the time and space she'd asked for. She'd been so despondent, and she was so hard on herself.

But I couldn't help feeling more hopeful than I had earlier in the day. My mother was stubborn, but she would come around. I was sure of it.

I knocked twice on Jack and Margot's front door, and Pete answered it. "Hey, come on in. We decided to eat here so they didn't have to drag all the baby shit over to our house. It's easier just to drag Cooper across the street."

"Thanks for inviting me." I followed him to the back of the house, where the kitchen was. It was much bigger and fancier than I remembered. "Wow. This place has changed a lot. Hey, Jack."

He nodded at me from where he sat at the kitchen table, feeding a baby a bottle. "Hey."

I set the bag I'd brought on the island. "I picked up some beer, but I promise not to drink so much I need a ride home."

Pete laughed, going over to a pot on the range and lifting

the lid. "I'd make you walk in the rain. Cooper, get out from underfoot. You're in my way."

A little brown-haired boy scurried out from behind the island, a toy truck in his hand.

"Say hi," Pete instructed.

"Hi," the little boy said before running out of the room.

I shook my head. "The kitchen isn't the only thing that's changed around here. Look at you guys with *kids*. Anyone want a beer?"

"Me," they both said at once.

I pulled three bottles from one of the six-packs I'd brought, and put the rest in the fridge. Pete handed me a bottle opener, and after prying off the caps, I set Pete's beer near the stove and Jack's on the table. He had the baby over his shoulder now, but he picked up the beer and took a long swallow.

I grinned as I took the seat across from him. "Father of the year."

"You know it."

"Looks good on you."

He smiled. "Thanks."

"The girls working?"

"Yep." Pete grabbed his beer and tipped it up. "Somebody's gotta bring home the bacon. So what's going on with you?"

I took another pull on my beer and dove in. Earlier I'd decided to confide in the two brothers, mostly because I fucking needed someone in my camp after my mother's reaction and seeing those texts on Hannah's phone last night, but also because I could use their support to cheer up Hannah. If she heard there were more friends on our side, she'd feel better. "Well, originally I needed to talk to you because I'd been lying to my mother about where I've been at night, using you as my excuse."

"Huh?" Pete looked confused.

"I've been telling my mother I'm hanging out with you at night, but as you well know, I haven't," I clarified.

He cocked his head. "I don't get it. Where have you been?"

"With Hannah."

His head snapped upright when it sank in. His mouth fell open.

"*With* her, with her?" he asked.

"Yeah."

"That's...interesting." He rolled his shoulders. "How'd that happen?"

I shrugged. "When I came home, we started spending time together and it just sort of happened. At first we tried to fight it, but it was impossible. So we hid it because of what people would say."

"Fuck people." Jack's tone was firm. "It's not their business."

I had to smile, because it was kind of hilarious to see this big, muscular guy with an angry expression say *fuck people* while cuddling a tiny baby. "That's what I said too, but Hannah is sensitive."

"She is," agreed Pete. "She's been quiet and kind of tense at work the last few weeks. No wonder. I was worried she didn't like the job anymore, but Georgia told me she was just going through a rough time."

"She loves the job," I assured him.

"It's hard to feel okay about moving on after your spouse dies," Jack said.

"I know, and the fact that it's *me* adds a whole other

layer of challenge." I drank from my beer bottle again. "And then my mother found out."

"Oh, shit." Pete's eyes went wide. "What did she say?"

"She freaked. Said it was wrong and disgraceful and that Drew was turning in his grave."

"It's not true," Jack said. "Don't believe it."

I shook my head. "I don't. I have to believe Drew would have wanted us to be happy."

"I agree." Pete nodded. "I knew Drew a lot of fucking years, and he could be crazy and loud and obnoxious, but he was never selfish or mean. In fact, I think he would want it to be you, because he'd trust you."

Gooseflesh broke out on my back. "Thanks, you guys. I needed to hear that."

I HUNG out with Jack and Pete until around seven, when they had to get bedtime routines going for the kids. Back at home, I put away some laundry my mother had left on my bed, tackled some paperwork I'd been putting off, checked my email, and stretched out on my bed with a book. But after the three beers and three bowls of chili I'd had at Jack's, I was drowsy and couldn't keep my eyes open. I dozed off, and when I woke up, it was after nine. I picked up my phone and saw that I'd missed a call from Hannah. After listening to her voicemail, I called her back.

"Hello?" she said softly.

"Hey. Did I wake you?"

"No. I'm in bed but I can't sleep."

"I wish I was there."

"Me too."

A few beats of silence went by. "How's Abby? You said

she was okay today?"

"Yes. We spent the day together and I think she's okay." She sighed. "I mean, who knows what's going on in her mind, but I tried my best to answer her questions and make sure she isn't confused."

"Good."

"It's hard when she wants things I can't give her, like a dad. It makes me feel helpless and sad."

"I know, baby. Hang in there. You're doing things right."

"Thanks."

"How did it go when you picked her up?"

"It wasn't pleasant. But I handled it."

"What did my mother say?"

"Probably the same things she said to you. She thinks we don't really love each other, she thinks we're being disloyal to Drew, she can't believe I exposed my daughter to such shame, and she's embarrassed of us."

"I'm sorry."

"She also wondered if we've given any thought to how awkward it's going to be for everyone in the family after we break up."

"Ignore her."

"I'm trying, but it's hard."

She sounded so sad, I was desperate to give her some good news. "Hey, I hope you don't mind, but I told Pete and Jack about us."

"What did they say?"

"They were one hundred percent supportive."

"That's nice. And I don't mind. Their wives know, so they might as well know." She didn't sound any better, so I tried again.

"And I talked to my mom."

"You did?"

"Yes. She agreed to give herself some time to get used to the idea of us."

"Really?" Her voice rose.

"Really. No guarantee, of course, but I have hope."

"How'd you convince her?"

"I told her she could cook me dinner for my birthday."

"That's it?"

"That's it." I couldn't bring myself to tell her that I'd promised not to invite her. But it wasn't that big of a deal, was it?

"On Saturday? Your actual birthday?"

"Yes."

There was an awkward pause. Should I tell her?

"I take it I'm not welcome on the occasion."

It was like a punch in the gut. "Hannah."

"She wants you to herself."

"You know her well. That's exactly what she said when I asked."

She was silent at first. "Of course it is."

"I only said yes because I figured in the grand scheme of things, this was only one night. We'll have a lifetime together."

"Maybe."

"Don't say that. Don't give up hope."

"It's just...been a hard day."

I wished more than anything I could take her in my arms and show her that she meant more to me than anything in the world. Words weren't helping me. "You need a good night's sleep. Call me tomorrow?"

"Okay."

"I love you."

"I love you, too."

But she said it like she wished she didn't.

TWENTY

HANNAH

HE CHOSE HER.

It was all I could think.

He'd had to choose, and he chose her.

All night long, that thought pummeled my brain like a heavyweight champion, keeping me awake. While I was glad Wes had friends who were supportive, Lenore had forced him to choose between us, and *he chose her*.

Just like that, my fears were magnified. Multiplied. Intensified.

Maybe she really was going to re-examine her feelings about Wes and me—I had my doubts—but she'd scored a massive victory over me in the process. And Wes had delivered it. It felt like a crushing blow.

How could I have trusted him with my heart? What was I going to do now that he had it? Could I get it back somehow?

I must have fallen asleep eventually, because I woke

from a terrible nightmare around five a.m. It was one from the nightmare grab bag I'd suffered in the months immediately following Drew's heart attack, the one where I'm trapped in a closet being suffocated by someone or something I can't see, or by darkness itself.

When I opened my eyes, I was shaking and panting, drenched in sweat. My pulse thundered in my ears. I couldn't catch my breath.

I got out of bed and checked on Abby, who was sleeping peacefully. I was tempted to crawl into bed with her, but didn't want to disturb her slumber. Back in my room, I changed the sheets, put on new pajamas, and attempted sleep again, but I only managed another forty-five minutes before my alarm went off.

I dragged myself out of bed and skipped the shower, throwing on jeans and an old sweatshirt before waking up Abby for school. Now that it was October, the inn didn't need me during the week. After half a pot of coffee I felt a little better, and I spent the morning putting together recipes for the inn cookbook and trying to come up with blog post ideas. When it was clear creativity had abandoned me in the wake of a near-sleepless night, I went back to bed and buried myself in the covers.

It felt all too familiar, and it terrified me further.

Around two, I forced myself to get out of bed and go downstairs. When I checked my phone, I noticed I'd missed a call from Abby's school and had voicemail. Immediately, my sense of dread deepened.

"Hello Mrs. Parks, this is Abby's teacher, Kim Lowry. I'm a little concerned about Abby and wanted to touch base with you about something that happened today. I wondered if you might be available after school for a brief meeting?

Give me a call back, please." She recited her number and thanked me before hanging up.

My stomach roiled as I imagined what could have happened at school to concern her teacher. My hands shook as I called her back. My voice trembled as I left a message saying yes, I would be there after school and thank you for calling.

I ended the call and set my phone down, lowering myself onto a kitchen chair. For several minutes I sat there staring into space, feeling as if I were getting smaller and smaller and everything around me was getting bigger. The kitchen was cavernous. My house was enormous. The world was monstrously huge and spinning out of control. I couldn't hold on.

I shut my eyes and flattened my palms on the table. *Stay calm. You can handle this. Whatever it is, you can handle it.*

After a few deep breaths, I went upstairs and took a shower.

"MRS. PARKS. THANK YOU FOR COMING." Mrs. Lowry smiled at me, but it was the kind of smile you gave someone you felt sorry for, the kind where your eyes say *you poor thing*.

I didn't want her sympathy. "Of course."

"Please sit." She gestured to one of five big round tables in the room, which were surrounded by chairs sized for kindergarteners. I chose a seat, and she took one across from me, smoothing her skirt behind her legs before she sat down. She was older than me, maybe in her fifties, with chin-length blond hair she kept off her face with a headband and tortoise shell glasses. "I wanted to talk to you about something Abby did today."

I glanced at the classroom door, which was closed. Abby was sitting right outside of it at a little table in the hall, coloring a picture of a butterfly Mrs. Lowry had given her. "What did she do?"

"She tried to kiss a male classmate. On the lips."

"She did?"

"Yes. The classmate was less than pleased, shall we say."

I pictured a six-year-old boy spitting and wiping his mouth on his sleeve to get the cooties off. "Right. Um, I'm sorry about that. Abby is an affectionate person."

"Yes, well, it goes a little deeper than that, I'm afraid." Mrs. Lowry adjusted her glasses. "Afterward, when I was explaining to Abby why we don't kiss our friends at school, she told me that it's okay to kiss your good friends."

"Oh, no." All at once, I saw where this was going.

Mrs. Lowry went on. "She said that her mom and her uncle are good friends and sometimes kiss. She also told the class today that your uncle can be your dad if he marries your mom."

I closed my eyes. "Did she?"

"Yes. And that she hoped her uncle would marry her mom so he could be her dad. As you can imagine, the children were quite confused by all this, and there was some arguing."

"I can imagine."

She paused. "Mrs. Parks, I know only a little about your family, and I'm still getting to know Abby, of course, but is there anything you'd like to share with me that might help me understand her a little better?"

I fortified myself with a deep breath and sat up taller in

the little chair. "Abby's father died when she was three. Recently her father's identical twin brother returned to town after years away. He'd been in Africa with Doctors Without Borders," I explained. "Anyway, his return has caused some confusion for Abby."

Mrs. Lowry nodded. "I'm sure."

"Uh, in addition," I went on, wishing I could crawl under the table, "Abby evidently witnessed some...displays of affection between her uncle and me."

"I see." And I judge, her tone said.

I shifted in the little chair. "Without going into anything too personal, I'll simply say that Abby's uncle and I are very close, and Abby harbors hope that we might someday get married."

"Is this a possibility?"

"I'm—I'm not sure." *Don't cry, don't cry, don't cry.* I steadied myself with another deep breath. "We've sort of placed things on hold for now. As you might imagine, certain family members are not supportive of our relationship."

"Indeed." She clasped her hands primly on the table.

"Yesterday, her grandmother told her it was wrong, using words like *vile* and *shameful*. And even though she likely doesn't understand those words, she does understand that her grandmother was saying that something Abby wants is bad and can't happen, and that the...the affection she senses between her uncle and me is wrong."

"That must have been very difficult for her."

"Yes. She was very upset. So later, when she asked me if what her Nana said was true, I said it wasn't. I wanted her to know the truth. But I also didn't want to give her false hope, so I told her that even though it wouldn't be wrong for her uncle and I to get married, as of now we are just good friends."

"Ah." Mrs. Lowry nodded. "Good friends. Now I understand."

"I'm very sorry about what happened today, and I will of course speak to her about it and...try to further clarify things."

"I think that would be a good idea."

"I'll also ask her not to talk about this at school anymore, but of course, she's six. I can't promise she won't."

"I understand." Her eyes dropped to her clasped hands. "Mrs. Parks, I appreciate your candor in this situation. I know it can't be easy for you."

I shook my head, praying I could at least get to the car before I broke down. "It isn't."

"Abby is a very sweet girl."

"Thank you." I sniffed. "I never wanted to be a single parent. I'm doing the best I can."

"That's all anyone can ask," she said. "Thank you for coming in today."

I nodded and stood up. "Please let me know if you have any further concerns."

"Will do."

I collected Abby in the hall, and we walked to the car. It had finally stopped raining, but the air was damp and chilly, and I shivered as we crossed the parking lot. "Brrr. Cold today, isn't it?"

"Yeah." She swung her lunch bag back and forth. "Did Mrs. Lowry tell you about the kiss?"

So much for opening with the weather. "Yes. She did."

"It was Robert. He didn't like it very much."

"That doesn't mean he doesn't like you, Abby. But six-year-old boys don't really want to be kissed by girls." We reached the car, and I unlocked it. "And kissing isn't allowed at school."

"Okay." She climbed in and I buckled her seatbelt.

"So you know not to do that again, right?" I asked.

"Yeah." She was silent on the ride home, but as soon as I pulled into the garage, she said, "Kids at my school say your uncle can't marry your mom. You said it was okay."

"I did," I said carefully, "but only in certain situations. And even then, it's very, very unusual."

"Oh."

"And it's not really something you should talk about at school, okay? It's a grownup thing."

"Okay."

We went inside and I got her a snack, which she ate at the kitchen table. I made a cup of tea and sat with her, asking her about her day and what she'd learned. She seemed unscathed by the incident at school, which was more than I could say for myself. I couldn't help seeing it as part of a larger pattern indicating my life was off track somehow, another sign that I was making bad choices, fucking things up.

While Abby was at gymnastics class, I called Tess, but it went to voicemail. I thought about calling Margot or Georgia, but I didn't want to bother them. I wanted to call Wes, but I couldn't bring myself to do it. I didn't want to be dependent on him, and besides, he'd only tell me everything was going to be fine, when really, he didn't know that at all. No one did.

But when he called me later that night, I answered. It was almost ten, and I'd just gotten in bed.

"Hello?"

"Hey, you."

I hadn't heard his voice all day, and I'd missed it. I didn't want to miss it. "Hi."

"How was your day?"

"It was okay." I told him about the incident with Abby at school.

He found it much more amusing than I did, chuckling a little. "She actually tried to kiss the kid?"

"Yes. It's not funny, Wes. She's still confused. And she's talking about us at school."

"So what? What do we care what a bunch of kinder-garteners think?"

He's dismissing my feelings. "What about her teacher?"

"What about her? Sounds like she just wanted some background on Abby so she could better understand the situation."

"You weren't there. She was judging me," I snapped.

"What did she say that was judgmental?"

I couldn't think of anything, and it made me angry. "It was the way she was looking at me."

"Hannah, are you sure this isn't all in your head?"

"What's that supposed to mean?"

"I mean that you're so hard on yourself. You think people are judging you, but no one judges you more harshly than you do, whether it's your body or your feelings for me or your parenting."

Was he right? Was I overreacting? Making more out of everything than I needed to? Somehow the notion only made me feel more insecure.

"Don't do that," I said. "Don't make me feel like I can't tell what's real. I know what I feel."

"I'm sorry. I don't mean to discount your feelings. I'm only trying to look at the bright side. Abby tried to *kiss* someone, not punch him. She did it to show him she likes him, not to be mean. I can think of a lot worse things a kid could do."

"But what about arguing with her classmates about uncles and moms getting married?" I wouldn't be talked out of this. Everything was terrible, and I couldn't fix any of it. "Don't you think that means she's still confused?"

"No. I think it means she listened to what you said yesterday, and she trusts you. Frankly, I'd be more worried if she went around telling kids what *my* mom said."

I squeezed my eyes shut. What he was saying made sense, but this *thing* in me, this ever-present pit of fear and doubt, refused to let up.

"Hannah? You there?" Wes asked.

"Yes. I'm here. I'm just—frustrated."

"With what?"

"With my feelings. I get what you're saying, but it's not enough to convince me I'm not doomed to fail at everything."

"You're not."

"Or fucking up my kid."

"You're not."

"Or being punished for the way I feel about you."

"You're not. Hannah, what is this about? I feel like this is more than just concern over Abby."

It's about the promises you can't keep, the lies we told ourselves, the choices you made.

It's about being scared you'll break me, when I've been broken before.

It's about the fear of loving you too much, of being unable to live without you. I'm powerless, don't you see?

"It's nothing." My throat was thick. "I guess I just had a bad day."

"I wish I was there so badly."

I nodded, tears burning my eyes. "Me too." But part of me was glad he wasn't. *I can't let him fool me anymore.*

"Can I see you tomorrow?"

"I don't know, Wes."

"Please. I need to see you."

I wanted to say yes, but what was the point? "Not tomorrow. I need more time."

He sighed. "Okay. If that's what you want."

It wasn't. Of course it wasn't. I wanted him to get in his fucking car and drive over here and make me believe that love could win. But he couldn't. No one could.

"It is." My heart ached horribly in my chest, and I wanted to cry so damn badly.

He was silent a moment. "Okay. I love you, Hannah. So much it hurts."

I nodded, the tears finally spilling over. "Me too."

TUESDAY WAS MISERABLE. Wednesday was worse. Without work I had nothing to distract me. I spent both days lying in bed feeling sorry for myself and wondering if I'd made the biggest mistake of my life by falling for Wes, or if I'd make it by walking away. I thought the days to myself would help me see the answer, but they didn't. And I missed him terribly. He was at once the only person who could make me feel better and the cause of my anguish.

Wednesday night I got myself together enough to go to Wine with Widows at Tess's house, but I was almost sorry I did, because all of us were having a bad week. Tess's sister had been diagnosed with breast cancer, Grace was struggling with the anniversary of her boyfriend's death, Anne's cat had had to be put down—the one her husband had gotten her for her last birthday before he died. When it was my turn to speak, I admitted to what had been going on with Wes, but said I was struggling with it because his mother disapproved so strongly. We tried to comfort each other, but it was hard not to leave the meeting wondering at the frailty of life and the futility of love.

I thought about calling my therapist, whom I hadn't seen since August, but I was embarrassed by the setback and knew she'd only tell me this was all in my head, just like Wes had.

But it wasn't. It wasn't.

On Thursday morning the piano was delivered, and I sat there staring at it for an hour, marveling that it had only been five days ago that we'd shopped for it. I'd been so hopeful that day.

I was so desperate for some distraction, I called Georgia to see if they needed me at the inn, by any chance.

"We don't, but are you okay? You don't sound too good."

I didn't want to worry her, but suddenly the truth came out. "No. I'm not. I kind of feel like I'm losing my mind."

"Whoa. Is it Wes? Or something else?"

"It's everything, but I think it's stemming from what's going on with Wes."

"Want to talk about it?"

I bit my lip. "You can't talk. You're at work."

"True, but why don't we meet up later for a drink or something?"

"I'd have to see if I can get a sitter."

"Do it. I'll check with Pete and make sure he can watch Cooper. Should I invite Margot?"

"Sure. I'm open to all advice."

I called my sitter and she said she could do it, so I texted

Georgia I could make it work. About twenty minutes later, she replied.

Great. I'm in, and Margot is too. Let's try the new martini bar downtown. With a Twist. About 5?

Sure, I texted back. **See you there.**

"SO WHAT HAPPENED?" Georgia asked. We were sitting in a small, round booth at the back of the bar, which was small, dimly lit, and not very busy. Truthfully, I wasn't sure how well a martini bar was going to do around here, but it was a nice place, cozy and romantic. Even the music was perfect, the old standards I loved. *If Wes and I could ever be seen on a date together, it would be the perfect spot.*

"A lot." I picked up my Lemon Drop and took a sip. "And none of it good."

"But it was going so well, I thought," Margot despaired. She looked right at home in this kind of bar with her elegant blond blowout and perfect red lips. She was drinking a martini that looked ominously clear, and pretty simple, considering the amount of instructions she'd given the server on how the bartender should make it.

"It was. But then it all went to hell." I told them what had happened, starting with the gossipy texts I'd gotten Saturday night.

Margot rolled her eyes. "So tacky. Do not pay those people any mind."

"I could probably tune them out, but Lenore is a little louder." I explained what had happened with Abby and Wes at the breakfast table, and their eyes grew wide.

"Wow," said Georgia. "We should have asked for a double shot in your drink."

"I totally panicked I was the world's worst mother, and then Lenore basically made me feel that way when I went over there to get Abby. And she suggested that I don't really love Wes, that I was just substituting him for Drew. And that he doesn't really love me, he just likes to take care of people with wounds."

Margot raised one sculpted eyebrow. "There's a word I'd like to call her, but I won't."

"But wait, there's more." I took a drink before continuing with the birthday dinner, the kissing episode at school, and the conversation with Wes Monday night. "And that was the last time I spoke to him."

"Holy shit." Georgia sat back. "That is a *lot* to deal with. No wonder you're not okay."

Propping my elbows on the table, I rested my forehead on my hands. "I don't know what to do, you guys. I'm in love with him, but it's hopeless."

"Why are you so convinced it can't work?" Margot was looking at me curiously. "I totally get that it won't be easy, and you're definitely having a really bad week, but why is it hopeless?"

I dropped my eyes to the napkin under my drink. "I don't know. It's just how I feel."

"Is it his mother?"

"Mostly," I admitted. "She's *never* going to accept us. I know her."

"So what?" Georgia shrugged. "That will be her loss, won't it? If Wes loves you, he'll choose you."

"But he *didn't*," I said, tears filling my eyes. "He *didn't* choose me, remember? He told Lenore she could have him to herself on his birthday, even though he said he wants me to be there. And I know it's just one night, but it's an important night in all our lives, because it was Drew's birthday too. She's doing this on purpose to hurt me, and he's letting her."

Margot sighed. "Men can be so clueless. Did you tell him how you felt?"

"Not exactly."

"Well, maybe you should. Maybe he doesn't realize how much it hurt your feelings."

"But I'm afraid." I didn't want to ruin my eye makeup, but tears began to fall. "What if he still sides with her? What if he doesn't love me enough? What if I jinxed myself the moment I fell for him?"

Georgia looked confused. "Jinxed yourself?"

"Yes. After I lost Drew, I swore that I'd never love anyone like that again. Because it tricks you. It makes you feel like you can do anything, but secretly it makes you weak." The tears were really flowing now, and I dug in my purse for a tissue.

"Love makes you *vulnerable*," Margot said. "There's a difference. Here." She handed me a handkerchief with a little monogrammed M on it.

"Thanks." I cleaned up my face the best I could, soiling the white cotton with snot and tears and mascara. "Can I keep this and give it back after I wash it?"

"Of course. I have tons."

I dabbed at my eyes again. "I hate to be so fatalistic about love. But I can't help it. After what I've been through, I don't know any other way to be. And I feel like all the bad things happening to me are giant signposts saying, *Warning! Danger ahead! Turn back now! Point of no return!*"

Margot sighed. "Have I ever told you how hard Jack fought me when we first met?"

"No."

"Oh boy," said Georgia, picking up her drink.

"What happened?" I asked.

"Well, I'm sure you've heard that Jack was married before me. Her name was Stephanie, and she was killed by a drunk driver shortly after they were married."

"I'd heard that," I said quietly.

"After losing Steph, Jack was miserable and determined to stay miserable. When I came along three years later, he was flat-out rude to me. I mean Grade A dickhead. Category five asshole. But he felt like he had to be. It was his defense mechanism. Underneath all that broody bluster, he was scared to let me in." She leaned forward. "I think your giant signposts are exactly that—a defense mechanism. Jack wasn't really an asshole, and you're not really doomed to heartbreak. But you tell yourself that you are to lessen the chances of life pulling the rug out from under you again. You stay off the rug altogether."

I frowned. It felt like Margot was saying the same thing Wes had—I was imagining things. "But I feel it in my gut," I insisted. "Wes and I will never be happy."

"Your gut is telling you that?" Georgia asked. "I don't think it's your gut."

"I don't either." Margot shook her head. "I think it's your head."

I thought about it and agreed my head was definitely a problem. "You could be right. There is a lot of doubt swimming around in there."

"When you look at Wes, or think of him, is your *first* reaction love or fear?" Margot asked.

I pictured him. "Love."

Georgia pointed at me. "*There's* your gut."

"And your heart," Margot added. "You just have to

figure out a way to overrule your head. Stop looking at everything as a sign of doom."

"But I could get hurt." My chest grew tight at the thought of it.

"Yes, you could. And you might." Margot grabbed my hand and squeezed it. "Love is a risk, Hannah. But it's always a risk worth taking."

Deep down, I wanted to believe her. Because I ached for Wes. He had my heart and I wanted his. And I wanted to be the kind of person who lived life fully and didn't let fear hold her back. But could I be that brave? "I just don't know if I have it in me."

"You do," they said together, then laughed.

I smiled too, despite the tears, and made my decision. "Thanks, you guys. I'm going to call him when I get home."

"Good girl," said Margot.

"Cheers," said Georgia, holding up her glass. "To love."

"To love," echoed Margot and I as we clinked glasses.

One more chance, I told myself. I'd give love one more chance to prove it could overcome all the odds stacked against us.

Ten minutes later, that chance went up in smoke.

TWENTY-ONE

WES

THAT WEEK, I'd looked at my phone more than any human being should look at an electronic device. I willed it to ring. I begged it to buzz with a text. I checked it obsessively, to the point where I was starting to go nuts.

But I didn't call her. I didn't want to be the guy who smothered the woman he loved. I didn't want her to think I couldn't give her space when she needed it or make her feel like what she'd asked for was wrong. Only the biggest asshole in the world would be like *you don't need space, babe, you need my big hard dick*, although deep down I felt like going caveman on her. Driving to her house, carrying her up the stairs, throwing her down on the bed and worshipping her body until she was convinced that I loved her enough that I'd never let anything keep us apart. But I didn't do that, either.

Although I thought about it a lot.

My mother was in a particularly good mood all week,

which shouldn't have bothered me, but it did. I couldn't help thinking how miserable Hannah and I were in comparison. Maybe because I was home for dinner every night. Maybe she was truly that excited about my birthday dinner. Maybe she was secretly glad Hannah and I weren't spending any time together this week. I wasn't sure what it was, but by Thursday morning, her cheerfulness was borderline grating.

Don't be an asshole. She's your mother, and she's happy you're home.

That afternoon, she called me as I was leaving work. "Hello, darling," she trilled. "How was your day?"

"Fine. Yours?" I unlocked my car and got in.

"Oh, fine. Listen, I'm downtown at that cute little martini place, the new one, and I wondered if you wanted to meet me for a drink."

A drink sounded pretty damn good. "I guess I could."

"Fabulous," she cooed. "It's called With a Twist. I'm right up front at the bar. You can't miss me."

"Okay, see you in a few." I hung up and drove downtown, thinking it was a little curious, since I'd never known her to frequent bars on her own before, but then again, I'd been gone for the better part of ten years. She might have developed all kinds of new habits I hadn't seen in the last month because I'd been so preoccupied with Hannah.

Still. I was slightly wary as I walked into With a Twist, which was located in an old storefront. It was dark inside, but I spotted her right away—and the pretty, well-dressed blond in the chair beside her.

Fuck me. She didn't.

She saw me before I could escape. "Wes, darling!" My mother motioned me over and I grudgingly obeyed. When I got close enough, she grabbed my arm, like she was afraid I might try to make a run for it. "Wes, this is Becca, my friend Mary's granddaughter, the one I've been telling you about. Becca, this is my son, Wes."

Becca smiled beguilingly and held out her hand. She was young, probably mid-twenties, and wore lots of makeup. "Hi, Wes."

"Hello." I shook her hand and gave my mother a murderous look that she ignored.

"This is such a delightful coincidence, because I've been wanting to introduce y'all."

A coincidence. Right.

"Sit down, darling. Here, take my seat." She vacated the barstool next to Becca. "I actually have to run, but you two should stay and chat."

I was fuming. I did not want to have a drink with Becca, but I didn't see a way out of it without being rude. When I got home I was going to throttle my mother.

"Stay," Becca coaxed, giving me a flirty look. "I'll buy you a drink. You look like you could use one."

"You have no idea." Feeling outmanned and outmaneuvered and *really* fucking thirsty for some whiskey, I dropped onto the barstool next to her.

My mother beamed. "No rush to get home, Wes."

"What time is dinner?" I asked her.

"Oh, don't worry about that. I can make you a plate any time. Y'all enjoy yourselves."

"Bye, Lenore," said Becca. "Thanks for the drink."

I ordered some whiskey on the rocks, Becca ordered another Cosmo, and while we waited for them, I stewed about my mother. I couldn't believe how she'd tricked me into this. However, it suddenly occurred to me that maybe this would help my case. My mother thought I was hung up on Hannah because I didn't give anyone else a chance. If I played along with her little matchmaking game for twenty minutes or so, I could go home and report there was absolutely zero chemistry with Becca, I was madly in love with Hannah and always would be. Maybe then she'd believe me. At least she wouldn't be able to say that I hadn't looked at anyone else.

"Bad day?" Becca angled her body toward me and tilted her head. Her legs were crossed in my direction, her hands clasped over one knee. She had very good posture, or else she was trying to put her breasts on display, because her back was ramrod straight, almost arched. She was big-chested, and her breasts strained at the buttons of her blouse, which was already low-cut.

Okay, yes, I noticed them, but after that, I kept my eyes above her neck. And they didn't do anything for me.

"Not really. Just tired."

"Me too. I've been working a lot of hours. It's so nice to relax and unwind." She put one elbow on the bar and propped her head in her hand.

"Yeah." What did she do again? I tried to recall what my mom had said. "You're in sales?"

She nodded. "Pharmaceuticals. I used to come to your office a lot, but then my territory got switched. I knew your brother."

"Oh."

"I was really sorry to hear what happened. He was such a great guy."

"Thanks."

Our drinks arrived, and I took a healthy swallow.

"So you just bought a house, I hear?"

"Yeah." I felt like a dick with my one-word answers and my obvious lack of interest, but this was not my strong suit—small talk with strange women.

"Where is it?"

"On the lake, north of town."

"Nice."

There was an awkward pause, and we both drank. At this point, I couldn't even make eye contact.

"Wes." She put a hand on my knee. "You don't have to be nervous. I don't bite."

"I'm not nervous." I looked at her hand on me and wished she'd remove it.

"Your mom said you were shy." She leaned toward me a little, her blouse falling open. "Don't worry, I think it's cute."

Oh, Jesus.

I was trying to think of what to come back with, how to nicely request that she take her hand off my leg, when I heard a voice say, "Wes?"

I turned, and there was Hannah. Slack-jawed, stormy-eyed, and trembling as she looked back and forth from Becca to me. "I knew it," she said. "I fucking knew it."

Then she was gone.

TWENTY-TWO

HANNAH

I HEARD him calling my name as I speed-walked down the street, flanked by Margot and Georgia, each of whom had an arm around me. "Don't stop. I don't want to talk to him."

"But maybe there's an explanation," said Georgia.

We turned the corner onto the quiet side street where I'd parked. Rage and regret coursed through me. "No. There might be an excuse, but I don't want to hear it."

"Maybe she's a work friend," Margot suggested.

"Oh, she's a work friend all right. The same work friend who fucked my husband while I was home with a newborn baby."

"What?" Margot screeched. Georgia made a similar noise of disbelief.

"Yes." The sight of her sitting there with him, so smug, her hand on his knee, her full breasts practically on his lap, had sickened me. Brought back all the horrible, wretched feelings of betrayal and self-doubt I'd suffered back then. I wanted to vomit.

"Hannah!" Wes was getting closer, so I sped up, moving ahead of my friends. But my heel caught on a crack in the pavement and I went down on my hands and knees.

Margot and Georgia reached for me, but I stayed there and burst into tears.

Next thing I knew, Wes was helping me to my feet. "Are you okay, baby?"

I wrangled my arms from his grasp. "Let me go. I'm not your baby."

"Hannah, please. Let me explain."

"No." I tried to start walking again and he grabbed my arm. "Let me go, Wes."

"I can't," he yelled. "I tried for *years* to let you go, Hannah. Years! I never could!"

Margot gasped and clutched Georgia by the elbow.

"I don't believe you!" I cried. "If that were true, you wouldn't have hurt me like this!"

"It was just a drink!"

"With the woman Drew fucked while he was married to me? No, that wasn't just a drink. It was the final sign that this"—I gestured back and forth between us—"can never be. And I was an idiot to think it could."

"Oh my God." His face conveyed his shock. "Hannah, I had no idea. You know I didn't!"

"I don't know anything except that I need to stay away from you!"

"Please. Just listen to me." Now both his hands gripped my upper arms, and I was no match for his strength. "My mother set that up. She tricked me into coming to the bar and then left."

"Why didn't you leave?"

"I was just trying to be nice! I didn't know she was the one! I swear to *God* I'd have left if I had." He shook his head. "I should have left anyway. I'm sorry."

"Too late now."

"I thought I was doing us a favor," he went on.

"What?" I shrieked. "How was that doing us a favor?"

"My mother thinks I only fell for you because I never gave myself a chance to fall for anyone else. I thought if I met the damn girl she wanted me to meet, I could go home and say, 'Guess what, Mom? I met the girl and I'm still in love with Hannah.' I thought it would help convince her to accept us."

"It doesn't matter," I said, sobbing uncontrollably now. "It doesn't even matter because she'll try something else next. She was never going to accept us, Wes. And you were always going to choose her."

He shook his head. "What are you talking about?"

"I mean the birthday dinner! Do you know how much it hurt me to learn she didn't want me there and you said okay?"

"No! Because you didn't tell me! I was just trying to do anything to make things easier on us. I thought I was helping! I love you, Hannah, but I can't read your mind."

"I didn't expect you to read my mind. I expected you to fight for us like you said you would!"

"I'm sorry, I should have considered how it would make you feel. I should have fought back. If it matters to you that much, you can come. Or I won't go. Whatever it takes," he pleaded. "I'll make this right, Hannah. I promise."

"No more promises." I closed my eyes, tears dripping off my lashes. "It's too late."

"But I *love* you."

"It's not enough, Wes. Love isn't enough to save us. Face it—we were never meant to be."

His grip relaxed slightly on my arms, but he didn't let go. "Do you remember," he said quietly, "what I said to you the night you married my brother?"

My eyes flew open. Of course I did.

He said the words again, his voice strong and sure. "I knew the moment I saw you that you were the one." But this time he went on. "The one I'd always love. The one I'd always dream about. The one I'd always wish was mine."

One of my friends gasped. From the corner of my eye I saw them clutching at each other.

Wes stared me down hard. "It was snowing the day we met. February twenty-fifth. A Tuesday. You were wearing a black shirt with a picture of a pineapple on it. You smiled at me, and I thought, 'My God, the most beautiful girl in the world just smiled at me.'"

"Wes," I wept. "Stop. We just weren't meant to be. It's too hard. It's too much."

"I knew the moment I saw you that you were the one, Hannah. I walked away then because I was too scared to tell you how I felt, and I'll walk away now because it's what you want, but you listen to me." He pulled me closer. "I don't care what anyone says. I've loved you since the day I met you, and I'll love you until the day I die. And I will never, ever believe it was supposed to be any other way."

And then he kissed me. Like he should have done then. Like he'd never kiss me again.

And he walked away.

"Oh. My. God." It was either Margot or Georgia who said it, but I was covering my face with my hands so I wouldn't have to watch the second love of my life leave me.

You made him leave. You chose this.

Maybe I had. But at least I hadn't been blindsided this time.

"Are you okay?" My friends came to me, stroking my arms, patting my back, hugging me as I cried.

"No," I sobbed. "I'll never be okay again."

"Oh, Hannah." Georgia looked like she was about to cry too. "I'm so sorry."

"Me too. That was..." Margot paused. "I don't even know what that was."

"Intense," Georgia supplied.

Margot nodded. "And sad. Heartbreaking. He's loved you all along?"

"He says he did." But it only made me feel worse.

"That's some heavy baggage," said Georgia. "He was in love with his brother's wife?"

"He met me first," I explained, trying to get control of my breath. "But was too shy to ask me out."

"Oh my God." Margot clutched her heart.

"And then I met Drew, and he swept me off my feet."

"You're killing me." Margot fanned her face with both hands, like she was trying not to cry. "This entire thing is killing me."

"It killed me too, when he told me. I'd had no idea." I sniffed, looking around for my purse with Margot's handkerchief in it. Spying it on the ground about three feet away, where it must have landed when I fell, I scooped it up and dug through it.

"And that woman at the bar..." Georgia faltered.

"Oh, God." I took out the handkerchief and wiped my nose. "It makes me sick that he was with her."

"Drew actually cheated on you with her?" Margot asked. "You're sure?"

I nodded. "He confessed."

"No wonder you got so upset." Georgia rubbed my back again. "But maybe it was like Wes said, just a drink set up by his mom."

"Doesn't matter." I steeled myself against any inclination to believe him.

"I so wanted you to give love another chance," Margot said softly, brushing my hair off my face.

"I almost did." I shook my head as the tears came again. "God, you guys. I'm a mess."

"You're not," insisted Georgia. Then she paused. "I mean, right now you kind of are, but you'll get through this, Hannah. I know you will."

"But I love him," I sobbed. "What am I going to do about that? I love him. And he walked away."

"He walked away because he thought it was what you wanted," Georgia reminded me gently. "Not because he doesn't love you. He does."

"Is there any chance you can work this out?" Margot asked. "I can't stop feeling like this isn't over."

"No. It's over," I said, squeezing my eyes shut. "It never should have started."

TWENTY-THREE

WES

I WAS SEETHING.

I drove home, blood boiling in my veins. How could I have been so stupid? How could I have hurt her like that? How could I have lost my chance with her, the only woman I'd ever love?

You fucked up.

But I hadn't meant to! I didn't know she would be so upset about the stupid dinner! And I had no fucking idea about goddamn Becca, whom I'd left sitting at the bar after throwing a twenty dollar bill at the bartender and storming out. How could Hannah think I'd betray her like that?

Because she'd been betrayed like that before, asshole.

I frowned and pounded the heel of my hand on the steering wheel. I was furious with Drew for cheating on her. Furious with myself for leading Hannah to believe I wouldn't choose her over anybody. And furious *as fuck* with my mother, who was about to bear the brunt of my rage.

I barged into the house and strode into the kitchen, where she was making dinner. "How could you do that to me?"

She feigned innocence as she set a pot of water on the stove. "What?"

"How could you set me up like that?"

"Wes, don't be so dramatic, darling. It was just a drink. I thought it would be nice for you to get out of the house. Meet some new people. You've been so down this week."

"I was down this week because Hannah asked for time apart. Because *you* made her feel bad."

"*I* didn't do anything to her." She continued moving about the kitchen like everything was fine.

"Yes, you did. You said cruel things when she came to get Abby on Sunday. You shamed her, and you scared her."

"I didn't say anything she didn't deserve to hear." Taking a peeler from the drawer, she started peeling potatoes in the sink. "If she felt bad, it was because she heard the truth from me."

"What do you have against her?"

"I don't know what you mean."

"Yes, you do. Look at me." I crossed my arms and waited. When she finally met my eyes, I could see she knew perfectly well what I meant. "Even before you knew about us, even when Drew was alive, you had something against her. Why?"

"I told you. She just wasn't who I'd have chosen. I never understood it. And he was different after he married her. He wasn't my same Drew."

"He wasn't your Drew at all, you mean."

"She turned up her nose every time I tried to tell her how Drew liked anything!"

"No woman wants unsolicited advice from her mother-in-law."

"But I'd been taking care of him for thirty years! Who was she to come along and think she could do it better? But all of a sudden he preferred *her* chicken and *her* apple pie and the way *she* ironed his shirts."

"Mom! Are you hearing yourself?"

"He took her side in everything!" Color was rising in her face, and she gestured wildly with the peeler. "Any time there was a disagreement, he always took her side. After Abby was born, I tried again to be helpful. After I had raised two perfect boys—she should have listened to my advice. But did she? No! She nursed Abby so constantly that she wouldn't take a bottle. No one else could feed her! I told them not to let the baby sleep in their bed, but they ignored me and they had all kinds of problems getting her to sleep. When I saw how tired and miserable Drew was after the baby was born, I reminded Hannah that she couldn't neglect her husband just because there was a baby in the house. I didn't neglect your father, and I had *two* babies to take care of! Everything she had to do, I had to do double!"

"Which I'm sure you reminded her of plenty of times." I shook my head. "You made her feel small and inadequate."

"You're missing the point."

It was almost laughable. "No, you're missing the point. You picked on her because Drew loved her so much. You were *jealous*."

She lifted her chin and went back to peeling. "She didn't know how to take care of him and look what happened."

"Jesus Christ. Hannah is not responsible for Drew's death! How could you even think such a thing?"

She started to cry, but she kept peeling the damn potatoes. "It's just how I feel. I lost him to her. Then I lost him forever."

"He loved her. And you resented her for it. You want to punish her for being loved by him. And now by me."

"Maybe I was hard on her. But she took him away from me," she wept, "and she'll take you, too."

"It's not like that, Mom. She's not your rival. Or she wasn't until you made her one." I didn't like seeing my mother in tears, but I had to get this off my chest. "You hurt her with your petty, jealous behavior. You made her daughter cry. You deceived me and embarrassed me. And you ruined my chance to be happy. You're the one who should be ashamed of yourself."

"Wes, please."

"But you got what you wanted."

She looked at me. "What do you mean?"

"Hannah and I are done. She broke it off."

"Are you going to blame me for that?"

"Partly. But it's partly my fault, too. If I could go back, I'd do a lot of things differently." With that, I left her standing there in the kitchen and went up to my room to pack my things. I couldn't stay there in that house any longer.

An hour later, I came down with my bags and headed straight for the front door. She spotted me from the kitchen and came hurrying into the foyer. "Wes? Where are you going?"

"I don't know. Tell Dad I'll see him tomorrow at work."

"Don't leave," she said, tearing up again. "Please. I'm sorry."

"Too late, Mom. You had the chance to support me, but you chose to judge me instead." Two seconds later I was out the front door, heading for my car. Once it was loaded, I drove away from the house and never looked back.

Only problem was I didn't really have anywhere to go. I wouldn't take possession of my house for another week. There were a lot of vacation rentals in the area, but at seven p.m., it was too late to contact anyone about those. As I was driving through town, I remembered the inn. Maybe Pete and Georgia would rent me a room for a week? But Georgia had been there tonight—I cringed with embarrassment. It would put her in a really awkward position to host me, wouldn't it? I didn't want to cause tension between her and Hannah, or between her and Pete.

There was another bed and breakfast in town called Inn the Garden, so I went there and booked a room for a week. The owners were gracious, the house was beautiful and quiet, and it was a short walk into town for dinner.

But I was miserable.

Somehow I'd lost the one thing I'd spent all those years dreaming about. I'd been offered a second chance to make her mine, and I'd fucked it up again. I didn't blame Hannah for being mad or scared. I'd known all along how fragile she was, how disillusioned about love. I blamed myself, because I should have fought harder, like she said. I'd tried to placate my mother when I should have stood up to her. I'd done it from a place of love, and because I'd been so sure that things would turn out fine in the end. I'd thought love would prevail.

But maybe Hannah was right. Maybe love wasn't enough.

PETE TEXTED me the next day and I saw the message during lunch. **I heard. You okay?**

Not right now, I replied. **Maybe someday.**

Ouch. Want to grab a beer later? Lexington Brewery at 7?

What I wanted was another chance with Hannah, but it wasn't going to happen. **OK.**

After work I took a run, even though I hadn't slept well the night before and felt rundown and exhausted. I did it because I was hoping to maybe spot her around town, but it didn't happen. I went back to my room and cleaned up, feeling frustrated and sad.

"You look like shit," Pete said when I took the chair next to him at the bar later on. Jack was there too.

"I feel like it."

"Georgia and Margot told us what happened." He shook his head. "Man. What a fucked-up situation."

"Yeah." I stared at the menu without reading it. "Do they hate me?"

"Not at all," Pete said.

"Margot feels sorry for you," Jack said.

"So does Georgia," added Pete. "Trust me. She's been talking about it all. Day. Long."

I grimaced. "Sorry."

We ordered some food and a couple beers. "What are you gonna do?" he asked.

"What can I do? She doesn't want me."

His expression was puzzled, and he paused with his beer bottle halfway to his mouth. "That's not how I heard it."

"How did you hear it?"

"I heard she wants you, but she's scared of your mom and a bunch of other shit in her head."

"My mom." I had to take a few long swallows from my beer before I could even think about her. "I'm so mad at her. I moved out."

"You did? Where?" Pete asked.

I hesitated, feeling guilty. "To that inn on Huron. The bed and breakfast."

"What? Why didn't you just come to my house?"

"Or mine?" said Jack.

"Because I didn't want to get in your way and I wasn't sure how your wives felt. The scene was pretty ugly."

Pete punched my arm. "Fuck you. We've been friends for thirty years. You should have come to us."

I held up my hands. "Sorry, sorry. I'm fucking things up left and right."

"Did you really not know about the girl?" Jack asked.

I shook my head. "I had no idea. That was all my mother. But it was stupid of me to even sit there with her. Hannah was right, I should have just walked out."

"Georgia thinks the thing with the birthday dinner was the bigger deal," said Pete. "Like it confirmed in her mind that you wouldn't choose her if it came to that."

"But I *would*. That's the thing, I *would*. I don't know how she doesn't see that."

"Because she's blinded by fear." Jack spoke firmly. "She associates love with loss, and she thinks she's protecting herself. The human mind can be a scary place."

"I know," I said miserably. "And I promised her everything would be okay. I promised her I'd find a way for us. And I failed."

"No, you didn't." Jack sat up taller. "I mean, you might

have made some mistakes, but you're human. Don't give up on her. If she's anything like me, she needs time."

"But I gave her time. I said she could have as long as she wanted."

He shook his head. "No. She needs to think you really walked away. She needs to own the fact that she chose that, and then realize she was wrong. But it takes time."

"Really?"

He picked up his beer. "Trust me on this."

Pete exhaled. "I feel for you, man. *I* don't have any advice, but I feel for you. And you're always welcome at our place."

"Thanks. I appreciate that." It didn't make up for losing Hannah, but it was good to know. "I should be able to move into my own house end of next week, although I need to buy some furniture. I don't even have a bed."

"At least you'll be busy."

"Right."

But I didn't want to be busy.

I wanted to be with Hannah. I wanted her to be there when I chose my new bed. I wanted her naked in it. I wanted it to be *our* bed, not mine, where I'd lose myself in her body and know she was mine.

I wanted to love her, and dammit, she'd said she would let me.

How had it all gone so wrong?

TWENTY-FOUR

HANNAH

TEN DAYS WENT BY. Ten joyless, colorless days during which I only dragged myself out of bed for Abby's sake. She was all I had, and even though every morning was worse than the one before, I forced myself to get up, get dressed, and put on a smile.

But she was no fool. The first Sunday night after we broke up, she asked why we hadn't seen him all weekend. I said it was because he was busy.

"Are you still good friends?" She looked at me expectantly across the dinner table.

"We are, in a way. We're just not able to spend as much time together as before." I pushed some food around on my plate, but had no desire to eat it. In fact, I was vaguely nauseated by the sight of it.

"Can he still be my special person at school?"

"I don't know, Abby."

"But my day is coming up."

"I'm aware of that." I'd seen the note from Mrs. Lowry in her backpack on Friday when she got home, and instead of dealing with it then, I'd stuck it on the fridge with a magnet right next to the picture Hannah had colored of her family. Then I'd ignored it for two days. "I'm just not sure he can be there."

"But he *said*."

"I know. But he's—he's busy."

"He promised!"

"Sometimes promises get broken!" I got up from the table and angrily scraped my dinner into the garbage as she wept, feeling sick and tired and guilty and overwhelmed with everything. Closing my eyes, I exhaled. "I'm sorry, Abby. I'll ask him about it, okay?"

She didn't answer, just continued to blubber into her spaghetti, making me feel more than ever like I wasn't enough. I cried myself to sleep that night, making sure to do it silently so Abby wouldn't hear me.

I cried for the girl he'd fallen in love with back then, when I'd worn a shirt with a pineapple on it and smiled with my whole heart and wanted to fall in love. For Abby, who deserved a better mom than me, who deserved two parents and a happy home, who deserved a life of promises kept. And for myself, for the pain of missing Wes, for the life the two of us could have shared, and for the crushing doubt that continued to smother me. I was choking on it.

But *why*? Why couldn't I be sure I'd done the right thing? Where was the relief I thought I'd find in certainty, in *knowing* I'd protected myself and my child from heartbreak? How was I going to get through the pain of losing him if I didn't have that conviction?

Wednesday night I went to Wine with Widows and couldn't even talk when it was my turn. Tess asked how I was, and all I could do was shake my head, squeezing my eyes shut. They didn't push me, but each of them let me know she was there for me if I needed someone to talk to.

The next night, Margot called. She and Georgia had taken to checking in with me every couple days. "How are you doing?"

"Okay. Or trying to be."

"I'm sorry." She paused. "Has he reached out to you or anything?"

"No. I'm sure he's trying to get over me, just like I'm trying to get over him. It's the only thing we can do."

"Are you sure?"

"Yes."

But it was a lie. I wasn't sure of anything but how miserable I was without him. A thousand times I'd picked up my phone to call him, like I'd promised Abby I would, but *every time,* I remembered how much it hurt seeing him sitting next to that woman at the bar, and I'd set it down again.

Maybe it had all been a ploy orchestrated by Lenore, but Wes had played a role, hadn't he? He'd stayed when he should have gone. That proved something.

What, that he's a nice guy?

No! My stubborn side refused to give in. *He should have said no to Lenore about the birthday dinner and no to a drink with that bitch who couldn't even look me in the eye.*

I wouldn't call him. If I heard his voice, I might crumble.

Saturday at work, Georgia asked the same thing. "Have you heard from Wes?"

Just the sound of his name being spoken made my chest hurt. I wanted to say it out loud, wanted to whisper it in the dark. "No."

"Pete says he's miserable. Did you know he moved out of his mom's house the night you broke up?"

I stopped what I was doing and stared at her. "No. Where did he go?"

"He stayed at a bed and breakfast for a few days, but now he's in his new house."

"He is?" I remembered walking through those empty rooms with him, how hopeful we'd been then. He'd asked for my help with the kitchen and I wouldn't be around to give it.

Let Lenore help him. He deserves her hovering.

Even so, it didn't make me feel any better.

I hadn't heard from Lenore, either. No invitations to dinner, no requests for Abby to spend the night, and certainly no apology. I wasn't planning on forbidding her to spend time with Abby, but hell if I'd go out of my way to arrange it. If she wanted to see her granddaughter, she could damn well put aside her pride and call me.

After work that day, I got in the car and drove past his new house very slowly, so slowly the car behind me honked, and I sped up.

Stop it. You're being ridiculous, acting like a teenager spying on her ex-boyfriend. This is beneath you.

Abby asked again that night at bedtime if I'd heard back from him.

"Not yet," I said, feeling guilty that I hadn't even asked him yet.

"But this is my week. He has to come on Friday." She looked up at me despairingly. "Can I try to call him?"

"No. I'll—I'll do it."

But I put it off another day.

On Sunday night, after I put Abby to bed, I sat down on my bed and worked up the courage to text him.

**Are you available Friday morning? That's
Abby's day to have her special person at school.
I understand if you don't want to or if you're
unavailable.**

Then I sat there holding my breath while those three
little dots tortured me. *He's reading it. He's writing back.*

Was he at his house? Was he working on it? Was he
looking at the lake? Was he standing in the kitchen? Did he
miss me like I missed him? Like a piece of his heart was
gone? Was he lonely at night? Did he wish he could
hold me?

Those three fucking dots went blurry, and I sniffed.
God, I was sick of crying. I'd always been emotional, but
the last couple weeks had been insane. I felt like I was
fighting off tears at every little thing, whether it merited
them or not. A baby picture of Abby on the mantle. My
wedding ring tucked in its velvet box. A dead bird on the
sidewalk out front. A silly Sandra Bullock movie on cable
one night. (Although, in my defense, it was the one where
she fell in love with the guy's brother while he was in
a coma.)

His reply appeared. I still couldn't breathe.

Of course I am. I promised her I'd be there.

That's it? That's all he had to say to me?

*What did you expect him to say? He pretty much laid
everything out for you ten days ago on the street, didn't he?*

I exhaled in a huff. And since when did he decide he
kept his promises?

Another message appeared.

**Just let me know the time and location. Tell
Abby I can't wait to see her. I miss her.**

What about me? I was dying to ask him. *Don't you miss*

me? It was petty and unfair to be jealous of his words about my daughter, but I was.

As if he could hear me, a third message popped up.

I miss you too. I think of you every day. And I still love you.

My stomach fluttered. My breath caught. A chill swept up my spine. I touched the reply box as a war raged between my head and my heart. I wanted to say it back. I wanted him to know he wasn't alone. I wanted him to drop everything and rush over here and make everything better.

But I wanted to punish him, too. For loving me. For making me love him. For showing me that I could be happy again, if only I wasn't so terrified.

11 AM on Friday morning. She is in Mrs. Lowry's room. You have to sign in at the office.

He wrote back, asking, **Will you be there?**

Of course, I started to cry. With tears rolling down my cheeks, I replied, **I think it's better if I'm not.**

Then, before I completely broke down and begged him to take me back, I went over to my dresser, shoved my phone into a drawer, and slammed it shut.

I stood there sobbing for a moment before I crawled into bed without even bothering to undress.

How was I going to get through this?

THE NEXT MORNING, I rolled over in bed to shut off my alarm and winced. My breasts were sore. Had they been that sore yesterday? What was the date? When my foggy head cleared enough to remember what day it was, it made sense. I was due for a period today or tomorrow.

I sat up, and the room spun a little. *Jesus. I need to get more sleep.*

When the dizziness passed, I got out of bed and went into Abby's room to wake her. My body felt foreign and heavy, like my bones were made of iron. I was exhausted beyond belief.

Abby was thrilled to hear that Wes would be there Friday morning, and went to school with a smile on her face. At home, I tried to work up the energy to shower or eat something or even turn on the television, but I couldn't. Instead, I went back to bed and napped for three hours.

The next few days were more of the same. Crying jags. Overwhelming exhaustion. Occasional dizziness. Sore breasts. And I didn't get my period.

I made up all kinds of reasons.

My body was rebelling against too little sleep. (Except all I was doing these days was napping.)

I was wrong about the dates. (Except I wasn't—I remembered the first day of my last period with sterling clarity because it was the day after the hallway sex.)

I was just having an abnormally long cycle this month. (Except it would be the first time in years that it was longer than thirty days.)

All the emotional upheaval had disrupted my cycle.

This seemed like the most likely explanation, and I let it give me peace of mind for exactly five minutes Friday morning before I panicked and went to the drugstore for a test.

I drove into Port Huron because I didn't want to risk seeing someone I knew. Back at home an hour later, I stood in the bathroom with the box in my hand, staring at myself in the mirror.

What was I going to do if I was pregnant?

But I couldn't be. We'd been careful, hadn't we? At least mostly? What were the chances?

My heart was pounding. Taking a deep breath, I opened the box and took the test.

Two minutes. Two minutes that would potentially change my life forever. I closed my eyes and began slowly counting off the seconds, concentrating on each number rather than on what the result might be. At one hundred twenty, I opened my eyes.

Positive.

Incredibly, my first reaction was pure, unadulterated joy.

Oh my God! I'm having a baby!

Five seconds later was a different story.

Oh. My. God. I'm having a baby.

I stared at myself in the mirror almost like my reflection was someone else. I brought a hand to my stomach. What the hell was I going to do?

Immediately, I sensed another presence in the room. I saw nothing, heard nothing, smelled nothing. But somehow I knew I wasn't alone.

"Drew," I whispered. "Help me. What do I do?"

You know what to do, sweetheart.

"I don't. I've made such a mess of everything."

You'll be okay. You'll be more than okay. You'll be happy.

"How can you be sure?"

Because I can see it from here. Life goes on for you, Hannah. Life goes on with Wes.

I closed my eyes, and they filled with tears. I wanted to believe him. I wanted to feel like everything would be okay. I wanted love to win. But I just didn't know how to get there. All the same problems still existed for us. All the same obstacles were still in the way. "Help us," I whispered. "Help us get this right."

I didn't hear anything, and when I opened my eyes, I knew he was gone. I was alone again. Immediately, I took the second test in the box to make sure the first one hadn't been a fluke, but the result was the same.

I was pregnant. With Wes's child.

The first thing I had to do was tell him.

I checked the time—it was nearly eleven. He'd be at Abby's school. Without even thinking about what I was going to say, I got in the car and drove there.

TWENTY-FIVE

WES

"THANK YOU SO MUCH FOR COMING," said Abby's teacher, offering her hand.

I shook it. "It was my pleasure. The kids were great."

"It was very nice of you to let them all try your stethoscope, too."

"Of course." I turned to Abby, an ache in my chest. "Bye, sweetheart."

She'd worn a huge smile for the last hour, but now she looked troubled and sad. "When will I see you again?"

"How about I take you out for ice cream this weekend?"

"Okay." But she still didn't look happy.

I bent down and gave her a hug. "I'll see you soon, promise."

"Okay, Abby. Time to get to work." Mrs. Lowry took Abby by the shoulders and steered her toward a table where three other kids sat working on a math activity. "Thanks again, Dr. Parks."

I gave Abby one final wave before leaving the classroom, shutting the door behind me. As I walked down to the office and signed out, I wondered what to do with the rest of my day. I'd told my dad I wouldn't be in at all, but I was almost tempted to go to the office anyway, just to have the distraction. There was plenty of work to be done at my house—rooms to be painted, carpet to be ripped out, furniture to buy—but I didn't feel like doing that, either. What I wanted to do was drive over to Hannah's house and tell her to stop being so stubborn. Convince her that I'd always, *always* choose her. Let her know that I hadn't spoken to my mother in two weeks, I'd refused her calls, and I'd repeatedly told my father to tell her I wasn't ready to talk.

But Jack had said she needed time to get over her fears. Was he right? Or was I an idiot, stepping aside again when I should have been going after what I wanted?

Angrily, I pushed open the heavy metal door that led to the parking lot and headed toward my car. Then I stopped dead in my tracks, because there she was.

I almost thought I was imagining her, standing by my car, brown hair loose around her shoulders, arms wrapped around herself like she was chilly in the brisk October air.

As for me, I'd started to sweat.

I resumed walking toward her as my heart galloped in my chest. *I'm not walking away this time*, I vowed. *No matter what, I am not fucking walking away.*

"Hi," she said when I got close enough to hear her.

"Hey." Her eyes were red, as if she'd been crying. I wanted to hug her, but I wasn't sure I should. "How are you?"

"I'm okay. You?"

"Okay." Then I frowned. "No. You know what? I'm not okay. I've spent every minute of the last two weeks being miserable without you and regretting all the mistakes I made that led to that point. I'm so sorry, Hannah. I'm sorry about what my mother said to you, I'm sorry I didn't fight harder for us, and I'm sorry I didn't have the right words to make you understand that I would die before ever letting anyone come between us." I gripped her upper arms. "Say you still love me. Say we still have a chance. Say you could be happy with me, and I'll spend every damn day of my life making sure it happens."

"Wes," she whispered, tears in her eyes. "I'm pregnant."

Nothing she said could have stunned me more.

"What?"

"I'm pregnant." She sniffed. "I'm sorry. I know it wasn't—"

I crushed my lips to hers as adrenaline rushed through me. *She's pregnant. I'm going to be a father. We're going to be a family.*

Suddenly it made sense—my feelings for her all these years. We were always headed for this moment. I lifted my head and looked down at her in disbelief. "This is incredible. Oh, my God."

She didn't look as if she thought it was incredible. Her expression was worried, her arms still tightly wrapped around herself. "But this doesn't solve anything. All our problems aren't going to magically disappear because of a baby."

I took her face in my hands. "We don't need magic. Do you love me?"

"Yes."

"Do you trust me?"

"Yes."

"Then listen to me. No matter what, we are going to be a family. You and me and Abby and this baby. We are going to make a life together. I don't care if we leave this town and never come back. I don't care what anyone thinks. I don't care about anything but you. *Us.*"

She'd started to weep. "But your parents. And your house. And your practice."

"I don't give a fuck about any of it. Do you hear me? I'm going to take care of you, Hannah. For the rest of our lives." I knew it was true. As surely as I knew my own name, I knew it was true.

"But—"

"Shh." I put my finger on her lips. "You just made me the happiest man alive, Hannah. I don't want to argue with you. You know what I want to do?"

"What?" She wiped her eyes.

"Dance."

"Huh?"

"You heard me." I moved her aside, opened the car door, and leaned in to start the engine. My radio was still tuned to the forties station she and Abby liked, and I turned up the volume. The song playing was a ballad, an instrumental big band tune I recognized but didn't know the name of. I rolled down the windows and shut the door. "Will you dance with me?"

"Wes." She looked around, her cheeks coloring.

I took her hand. "You once said that you'd always say yes if I asked you to dance."

"Did I?"

"Yes." I pulled her into my arms. "And I intend to hold you to that promise. Forever."

"But kids could be watching."

"I don't care who's watching. In fact, I wish everybody in the entire world could see us right now."

She laughed as I swayed her to the music. "You're crazy."

"Nope. I'm just in love."

"Me too," she said softly.

I pulled her closer and whispered in her ear. "I'm never going to let you go."

She laid her cheek on my chest. "Good."

I TOOK her to my house. "I only have one piece of furniture," I said as we walked in the front door, "but it's the only one I care about right now anyway." Taking her by the hand, I led her up the stairs to my bedroom, where we undressed each other and slipped between the sheets. I didn't even have curtains on the windows yet, so the room was bright and I could admire her naked body all I wanted.

"You're so fucking beautiful," I told her, running my hands all over her golden skin. "The most beautiful girl in the world."

"Oh, stop."

"I mean it. I thought so then, and I think so now."

Her voice softened. "Thank you. You make me feel that way."

I pressed my lips to her bare stomach. "Hi, baby."

She laughed gently and played with my hair.

"I love you," I said to the life inside her. "You surprised us, but I love you. And I'm so grateful." I kissed her belly again and laid my cheek on it, looking up at her. My heart was fuller than it had ever been.

"What are you thinking?" she asked.

"How lucky I am. How crazy this is."

She smiled.

"How fun it will be to watch your belly get enormous."

"Hey!" Laughing, she slapped my shoulder.

Grinning, I sat up and stretched out next to her, placing a hand on her stomach. "I can't stop touching you."

"No complaints."

I kissed her, pulling her closer to me. She reached between us and stroked my cock, which was already hard and aching for her. The hand that had been on her stomach slid lower. She moaned and moved her hips against my hand.

"Wes," she whispered against my lips. "I want you so badly."

I turned her beneath me, and knelt between her thighs. My fingers slid inside her with ease.

"Please," she begged, reaching for me. "It feels like it's been forever."

We don't have to use any protection, I realized, and the thought made my dick even harder. It had to be some kind of ridiculous Cro-Magnon instinct that had survived the evolution of man, the possessive pride I felt as I pushed inside her, knowing that I'd gotten her pregnant. I felt all-powerful as I began to move, rocking my body into hers, reminding her who she belonged to.

Mine, mine, mine, I thought with every thrust of my hips, every stroke of my cock, every strangled grunt that tore from my throat. Her body, her heart, her soul, her life—all of it was forever and inextricably intertwined with mine. And when she whispered my name and told me not to stop and begged me to come with her, my body obeyed, because she owned me just as fully as I owned her.

"I love you," I said, over and over as I throbbed inside her.

She clung to me, her body pulsing in tandem with mine, her heart beating hard against my chest.

"Hannah," I said, looking down at her. I hadn't even caught my breath, and my heart was racing madly. "Marry me. Be my wife."

She put her hands on either side of my face. "Yes," she said, tears dripping from her eyes. "Yes."

I brushed her hair back from her face. "No more tears, okay? From this moment on, we're going to be happy."

She nodded and smiled. "Love wins."

I smiled too. "Love wins."

LATER WE TOOK Abby out for dinner, and I couldn't get enough of her smile as she ate her cheeseburger and fries and told Hannah about my visit at her school.

"Hey Abby," I said as she dug into her ice cream sundae. "Did you know it's my birthday tomorrow?"

"It is?" Her eyes were wide as she licked chocolate sauce from her spoon. "How old are you?"

"Thirty-*seven*."

"Oh my gosh," she said. "You're even older than Mommy."

"I am." I grinned at her. "Know what I want for my birthday?"

"What?"

"I want to go shopping with you."

"You do?"

"Yes. While Mommy is at work tomorrow, will you hang out with me?"

She looked at her mom for confirmation, and Hannah nodded, but she looked a little concerned. "It's okay with me, but the sitter is coming. I have to leave for work pretty early."

"Cancel the sitter," I told her. "I'll come early and take her out for breakfast."

"Yay!" Abby smiled, her mouth decorated with chocolate sauce.

When Hannah excused herself to go to the bathroom a few minutes later, I motioned Abby closer. "Guess what I want to buy for your mommy?" I whispered loudly.

"What?" she whispered back.

"A ring. Do you think you can help me pick one out?"

Her eyes danced with excitement. "Yes!"

"Okay but it's our secret for now. Don't tell her until we give it to her."

"But when will that be?"

"Soon," I told her. "Maybe even tomorrow night." I spied Hannah coming back to the table, and put a finger to my lips. "Shh."

She nodded.

"And what has you two looking so mischievous?" Hannah asked as she sat down again.

"Oh, nothing." I gave Abby a wink, and she put her hands over her mouth, giggling girlishly.

We'd agreed to hold off telling her about the baby for now, just until Hannah was a few more weeks along and we'd decided on a plan—when we'd get married, where we'd live, how we'd break the news to our families.

Hannah was sure her mom would be happy for us. My mom was a different story.

"We'll tell her together and give her one chance to be happy for us," I said quietly on the drive home. "If she chooses to be otherwise, that's her loss."

She nodded. "When should we do it?"

But I didn't answer her, because I'd just turned onto Hannah's street and noticed a car in her driveway—a beige Mercedes that looked a lot like the one my mother drove.

Sure enough, as we got closer, I saw her get out of the car.

Hannah saw too. "Oh my God. What do we do?"

"Relax." I took her hand. "We're okay. Let's find out what she wants."

I parked in the street, and we got out of my car. When Abby saw her grandmother, she immediately ran to her. "Nana!"

"Abby!" My mother scooped her up and hugged her. "I have missed you and missed you and missed you! My goodness, I think you got taller."

Abby laughed. "We were out for dinner."

My mother looked at Hannah and I on the sidewalk where we stood holding hands. "Were you?"

She seemed nervous to me, but it was getting dark and I couldn't read her expression that well. "What are you doing here, Mom?"

"Actually, I came to talk to Hannah."

"Whatever you have to say to Hannah, you can say to me."

My mother nodded, but Hannah squeezed my hand. "Wes, maybe you should take Abby inside."

We exchanged a look, and I understood—she didn't want Abby to overhear anything negative. "Okay. I'll be right inside if you need me."

She handed me her keys, and I reached for Abby's hand. "Come on, princess. Let's go in."

With one final look at my mother—a warning—I led Abby up the front walk and took her inside.

TWENTY-SIX

HANNAH

I FOLDED my arms in front of my chest. "What do you want?"

She opened her mouth, closed it, then opened it again. "This isn't easy."

"What isn't?"

Her hands were fidgety. "Coming here to admit I was wrong."

"About what?"

"Lots of things."

"I'm listening."

She glanced at the house. "My son hasn't spoken to me in two weeks."

"I heard."

"And I guess I deserved it for what I tried to do."

I agreed, but I let that one go by.

"I miss him. I feel like I've lost both sons." Her voice

caught, and I felt a pang of sorrow for her. "We had terrible words, he and I. Before he left."

"Oh?"

"Didn't he tell you?"

"No."

She nodded, then she stood up straighter. "Hannah, I owe you an apology. I've treated you unfairly. Not only in the last few weeks, but for years."

I couldn't believe what I was hearing. "Go on."

"It was hard for me," she said, pausing to pull a handkerchief from her purse, "to see Drew so taken with you. He no longer seemed to care what I had to say about anything. He loved you more than he loved anyone else. I resented you for that, and it was unfair."

"Yes, it was."

"And later, when Abby was born, I thought you'd turn to me a little bit more. I thought you both would need my help."

"We could have used it, Lenore. But you always made me feel like I was doing things wrong. I was nervous enough being a first-time mother. I didn't need the criticism."

"I know. I know. And I'm sorry. I let my jealousy get the better of me, and it was wrong." She took a breath. "Then when Drew died, I—it was so unfair, so unthinkable that he was gone, I needed someone to blame."

"So you chose me."

She nodded and dabbed at her eyes. "I chose you. Because he'd loved you more. And I'm sorry."

I felt my anger dissolve a little. "It wasn't a competition, Lenore. Love isn't a zero sum game."

"You're right," she said, crying openly now. "But when I saw it happening with Wes, I felt all those terrible things all over again. I saw you taking away my son, the only one I have left. I saw him choosing you over me, and I panicked. I'm sorry."

How ironic, I thought.

"Please forgive me, Hannah. Let me try again."

At the sound of the front door opening, we both turned. Wes came out and walked toward us, his hands in his pockets.

"She's on the couch watching a movie," he said. "I hope that's okay."

"It's fine." I nodded toward Lenore. "Your mother apologized to me."

"Oh yeah?" He looked at her.

"Yes," she said. "And I owe you an apology too, Wes. I'm sorry I acted the way I did. It was wrong. Can you forgive me?" She looked back and forth between us.

"Can you accept that Hannah and I are going to be together?"

"Yes. If you truly love each other, I'll give my blessing."

"We do." Wes put his arm around me.

"I just want you to be happy, Wes. And I want to be part of your life. And part of Abby's life. When I think of having to live without you—" She broke down, weeping into her handkerchief.

"I forgive you, Lenore." I reached out and touched her arm. "You don't have to live without anybody."

"Thank you, dear." She sniffed.

"I forgive you, too," said Wes. "Let's move forward, okay?"

"Okay." She took a deep breath as she looked at us. "Will you both come to dinner tomorrow night, please?"

Wes and I exchanged a glance, and he raised his eyebrows, leaving it up to me.

"Of course," I said. "We'd be happy to."

"Oh, good." Lenore looked relieved. "I was worried you wouldn't."

"Family is important to us," said Wes. "You're important to us, Mom."

She smiled. "Thank you. I guess I raised you right, after all."

"You certainly did," I said, watching as Wes gave his mom a hug.

She turned to me, and I embraced her as well, telling myself this would be a fresh start for everyone.

"We'll see you tomorrow night," Wes said. "We've got a lot to celebrate."

"WANT TO STAY OVER?" I asked him. We were lying naked in my bed, my head on his chest, my body tucked alongside his.

"Of course I do. But what about Abby?"

"I think she'll be happy to find you here in the morning. You were going to come early, anyway. She might not even realize where you slept."

"Who says I'm going to sleep?"

I laughed and snuggled in closer, and he kissed the top of my head.

"This is everything I've ever wanted, Hannah. Better than any birthday gift I could have asked for."

"Good. I love you."

"I love you, too."

I drifted off to sleep wrapped in his arms, surrounded by his love, swept away by my hopes and dreams.

Eternity was real, and it belonged to us.

EPILOGUE

HANNAH

ABBY and I stood next to each other, looking in the mirror.

Margot beamed as she came into the room. "You both look *gorgeous*."

"Thank you," I said. There were a few times I'd actually felt gorgeous in my life. This was one of them.

"I think you made the perfect choice with the dress."

"Me too." I'd chosen an ivory dress of beaded lace and a deep V neckline in front and back. It wasn't overly fussy or fancy, and it had a slight Victorian feel to it, which suited our wedding venue—the Valentini Farms Bed and Breakfast.

Pete and Georgia had closed the inn for the entire weekend for us as a wedding present. They claimed it wasn't a big deal, since mid-November wasn't busy season up here, but it meant a lot to us. So that they wouldn't have to work during the affair, we'd hired a catering crew to prepare and serve.

"I have something for you." Margot handed me a handkerchief of white cotton edged with eyelet. "Unfold it."

I did as she asked and saw that she'd had it embroidered with an H in one corner. "Oh, Margot. I love it. I'm going to cry."

"That's exactly why I had it made for you." She grinned. "But don't cry yet. Your makeup is perfect."

"Knock, knock." Georgia came in, a huge smile on her face. "Everything is ready down there. Wow, Hannah. You're stunning."

"Thank you."

"And look at you!" Georgia gestured at Abby, who wore a long dress of ivory satin with a tulle skirt. "Give me a twirl, let me see!"

Abby happily spun in a circle, the dress floating around her like a cloud.

"So pretty." Georgia clasped her hands together. "This is such a great day."

"It is." Margot fussed with a few pieces of my hair, which she'd curled and styled for me. The top was loosely twisted and pinned at the back of my head, and the rest hung in soft waves down my back. Rather than wear a veil, I'd asked her to tuck ivory and blush-colored roses into the twist. "So do you have everything? Something old?"

I touched my earlobes. "Yes. Lenore lent me her pearl earrings. She said she's had them for twenty years."

"They're beautiful," said Margot. "I love pearls. So classic."

They were beautiful—white pearl and diamond drop earrings that sparkled and shone. I'd been touched when she'd offered them.

"Something new?" asked Georgia.

"The handkerchief." I smiled and held it up.

"Perfect," agreed Margot. "You can wrap it around the stem of your bouquet. I even have a little pin to keep it in place."

"Something borrowed?"

"The earrings were borrowed," I suggested.

"No, it has to be something different." Georgia frowned, then her face lit up. "Oh! Oh! Hold on!" she exclaimed before dashing out the door.

"What on earth? Where is she going?" I asked.

Margot shrugged. "To get something from her room? While she's doing that, let's make sure you have something blue."

I grinned and lifted up the hem of my dress to show off the blue satin heels I wore. My toes were painted blue too. "Got it."

She laughed with delight. "You certainly do."

A moment later, Georgia raced back into the room. "Here," she said breathlessly. She held up a penny and a roll of Scotch tape. "In my family, brides always put a penny in their shoe for luck. This is the penny I had in my shoe when I married Pete. I'll tape it into yours."

I laughed and slipped off one of my shoes. She scooped it up and taped the penny onto the arch.

"There." She nodded. "Put it back on and make sure it won't bother you."

I put my foot back into the shoe. "Can't feel a thing."

"Yay!" Georgia clapped.

Margot handed Abby's flowers to her. "Here, sweetie. Hannah, give me the handkerchief and I'll pin it to your bouquet."

I handed it over and flattened a palm on my stomach. "I have a million butterflies in here."

"That's not all." Margot winked at me. She and Georgia

were among the handful of people who knew I was pregnant. We were planning to tell everyone else, including Abby, after the wedding.

Georgia's eyes went misty. "Oh Hannah, I'm so happy for you."

"Thank you."

"Okay, done." Margot held out the bouquet, and I took it in my hands. "I'm ready." I looked down at Abby, who grinned up at me. "Let's do this."

The four of us walked to the top of the stairs. "I'll go down and tell everyone we're about to start," Margot said. "Georgia, you'll stay at the bottom of the stairs and signal Abby and Hannah when it's time to start?"

"Yes," Georgia confirmed.

"Okay." Margot gave me one last smile and touched my arm. "Here we go."

I watched her descend the steps and disappear around the corner into the parlor, where dining tables had been removed and rows of chairs had been set up. It was a small wedding, just sixteen guests, including my mother and aunt, who'd driven up from Detroit two days earlier. She'd been a little stunned by the news of my relationship with Wes, but fully supportive. We'd found that was the reaction of pretty much everybody—once the initial shock wore off, people seemed genuinely happy for us. Even Lenore had come around, hosting a beautiful engagement dinner for us at her house.

Although he'd already asked me to be his wife, Wes officially popped the question on his birthday, slipping on my finger the ring he and Abby had chosen for me earlier that day. He did it on the beach at his house before we left for dinner at his parents' that evening. Abby had stood right next to me, jumping up and down with excitement. We let her announce our engagement to Doc and Lenore, which she did the moment we walked into their house. There were some tears, but they were more sentimental than sad, and Lenore, to her credit, behaved beautifully. "I'm happy for you," she'd told me.

She was beside herself with excitement about the baby, and promised to be a big help without being overbearing this time around. So far, that was proving true. She'd pitched in a ton the day Abby and I moved into Wes's house, and had shopped with me for furniture and kitchen cabinets, at my invitation. My house had sold quickly, and even though I'd cried in Wes's arms before leaving it for the last time, I had no regrets.

From the bottom of the stairs, Georgia looked up at me and smiled. I noticed the hum of conversation coming from the parlor had quieted, and a moment later, the music began. It made me smile—we'd considered a string quartet for the occasion, but ended up going with a recording of Glenn Miller's "Moonlight Serenade," which was the song we'd danced to in the elementary school parking lot.

"Okay, you two," Georgia whispered. "Come on." Abby and I held hands as we carefully went down the steps, and then I stood at the bottom while Abby slowly walked into the parlor and turned to her left to face the guests. She glanced over at me and smiled before starting to walk to the back of the room, where I knew Wes was waiting for me. My stomach fluttered wildly.

"Your turn," whispered Georgia, who would sneak into the room once the ceremony began.

"Thank you." I took one deep breath to steady my nerves, and walked into the parlor. As I turned to face the back, the guests stood. I saw Jack and Margot, my mom and aunt, Doc and Lenore, Tess, Grace, Anne. All the people who'd gotten me through the worst phase of my life and would be with me through the next, which promised to be infinitely better.

And Wes. He looked good in everything—and he looked spectacular in nothing—but standing there in his gorgeous black suit, my God...he took my breath away.

We locked eyes as I moved toward him, and his were shiny with tears. On his face was all the love he showed me every single day, which he'd kept hidden inside for so long. My heart beat wildly in my chest. How had I gotten so lucky? What had I ever done to deserve him?

He took my hand when I reached him, and I laughed a little at the tear that slipped from the corner of one eye. "For once it's you, not me," I teased.

He laughed too, brushing it away. "Can't help it."

The music finished, the guests sat down, and we faced the officiant, ready to start our life together.

"CAN I HAVE EVERYONE'S ATTENTION?" Champagne glass in hand, Wes stood at the table where he and I were seated, along with Abby, Pete and Georgia, Margot and Jack. The rest of our guests were all seated at round tables for four placed around the room, which we normally used as a restaurant dining room. He offered me his hand and helped me to my feet.

"Hannah and I want to thank you for being here with us today. It means everything to us. You'll notice the guest list for this occasion was small, but in this room are the most important people in our lives. People without whom we would not be standing here today."

I met Tess's eyes across the room, and she smiled.

"But there is someone important to us who is not here today." Wes squeezed my hand, and I squeezed back, fighting the lump in my throat. "And that person is my brother Drew."

He looked down at me—even in my heels, I was much shorter—and I could see his eyes were wet. Mine were too.

"Not a day goes by where we don't think of him, and we will miss him forever." He paused, closing his eyes briefly. "But rather than mourn him any longer, we asked ourselves what he would have wanted for us—and without a doubt, we know he'd have wanted us to be happy. To celebrate every day as a gift. To appreciate all the beauty around us. To remember that no matter how great the loss, life and love go on." He raised a glass.

"To the bride and groom!" called Pete.

I picked up my water and touched it to Wes's champagne as the room erupted in a chorus of cheers and clinking glasses. We took a sip, and before we could even sit down again, the room resounded with silverware clanking on glasses.

Wes looked down at me and smiled. "I think they want me to kiss the bride."

"Good. Because that's me."

He smiled. "I always knew you were the one."

As his lips touched mine, I closed my eyes and saw our life unfolding in front of us, long and full and happy. But this time, it didn't scare me at all. This time, I embraced it.

I knew in my heart it was meant to be.

Love wins every time.

THE END

ACKNOWLEDGMENTS

I am so grateful to the following people, who agonized and celebrated with me while I wrote this book.

My husband and daughters. You're the best. Thanks for understanding. I adore you!

Danielle, for being the FTM book fairy and my bestie for life.

Kayti, Laurelin, and Sierra—Camp Snatch, plot walks, and good gin forever (but without pain next time...or accidentally blackened salmon).

To Jenn Watson, a true pro and awesomely classy woman. I feel so lucky to have you as my publicist and friend.

To Melissa Gaston, the gold standard of PA's.

To Chanpreet, Nina, Sarah, and the entire Social Butterfly team, you're amazing. Thanks for all you do!

To Nancy, for fast, thoughtful edits.

To Michele Ficht, Laura Foster Franks and Amanda Maria for your eagle eyes.

To Rebecca Friedman, for being a lovely human being.

To Flavia and Meire, for taking Melanie Harlow on her first world tour. Merci bien, mes amies!

To my PQs, cheers to two years of inspiration!

To my Harlots, for being the best fans around. I adore you!

To my ARC team—you have no idea how much I appreciate you. When people ask why I give out more than 200 ARCs to you every time, I just smile. You're worth it.

To the bloggers and event organizers who work so tirelessly, all for the love of books. I appreciate every single one of you.

To my readers, you're always on my mind. I hope I made you smile today.

ALSO BY MELANIE HARLOW

The Speak Easy Duet

Frenched

Yanked

Forked

Floored

Some Sort of Happy

Some Sort of Crazy

Some Sort of Love

Man Candy

After We Fall

If You Were Mine

Strong Enough

The Tango Lesson (A Standalone Novella)

ARE YOU A HARLOT YET?

To stay up to date on all things Harlow, get exclusive access to ARCs and giveaways, and be part of a fun, positive, sexy and drama-free zone, become a Harlot!

https://www.facebook.com/groups/351191341756563/

NEVER MISS A MELANIE HARLOT THING!

Sign up here to be included on Melanie Harlow's mailing list! You'll receive new release alerts, get access to bonus materials and exclusive giveaways, and hear about sales and freebies first!

http://subscribe.melanieharlow.com/g5d6y6

ABOUT THE AUTHOR

Melanie Harlow likes her heels high, her martini dry, and her history with the naughty bits left in. In addition to FROM THIS MOMENT, she's the author of MAN CANDY, AFTER WE FALL, IF YOU WERE MINE, the HAPPY CRAZY LOVE series, the FRENCHED series, STRONG ENOUGH (a M/M romance co-authored with David A. Romanov), and the SPEAK EASY duet (historical romance). She writes from her home outside of Detroit, where she lives with her husband and two daughters. When she's not writing, she's probably got a cocktail in hand. And sometimes when she is.

www.melanieharlow.com
melanieharlowwrites@gmail.com